The

A.L. Nelson

ISBN: 1519157487
ISBN-13:9781519157485

ACKNOWLEDGMENTS

This book might never have happened if not for my husband, Mick. He has been unwavering in his support and encouragement of my attempt at writing, even though it has meant he received less of my attention. He lets me bounce ideas off him, reads my books before anyone else, and gives me good insights. He is the one responsible for the second and third books in this trilogy. When I expressed to him how much I felt I would miss writing about these characters and exploring them further, he suggested I write more books and extend their lives.

I would also like to thank some other family members. My daughter Kalen read this first book to let me know if I got those eighth-grade girls right, since she was that age at the time. My young son, KC, gave me wonderful shoulder massages when I needed them. My mother, Betty Avers, is my dedicated proofreader and has always provided me with praise. My adopted mother-in-law, Treva Henley, made me feel like the greatest author in the whole world.

My good friend Mike Hughey, who I have known for many years, checked the book's camping survival sequences, since that is one of his multiple areas of expertise. Another friend in particular that I would like to thank is Theresa (Teri) Monroe. She helped with formatting both my cover and the book itself –I am fortunate to have access to her talent.

CHAPTER 1

Full-sized Hummers, along with a couple of large ATVs, are retreating into the distance until nothing remains except a thin dust cloud, which floats slowly skyward from the dirt path. There is little wind today. The sky is a deep, cloudless blue. I catch myself sighing deeply with regret as I turn away. I can't help it; that's how I feel. Besides, nobody's close enough to hear me, so it doesn't matter. Ahead of me, the reluctant group of young campers isn't waiting, so I shift my heavy burden and start out after them.

I'm just barely on the low side of average in both height and weight. Yet I still have to carry a bit more than what I otherwise would in my backpack in order to help out with the load for the kids. I agreed to it, though. All of the adults did. Most of the girls are shorter and more petite than me, yet they are carrying their fair share. This is supposed to be a long trip with lots of food, water and other supplies to hike in and the remains brought back out again. Leave nothing but footprints, as the saying goes. I hope we're carrying enough food to get us through, because where we're going civilization is too far away for anyone to be able to run down to a store for more provisions, should we get low on something vital… like food, for instance. Or if we need a doctor, God forbid.

Fourteen days of my life are being devoted to watching over my niece and ten other middle school girls in my assigned "pod". Fourteen days. That equates to two weeks' worth of my vacation. That's all I had remaining of my accumulated total from working at the City of Raleigh for the past soon-to-be four years. I had intended to save it for a long trip to Hawaii come next winter. I hate being cold. Ever. Now I'm walking across a meadow burgeoning with wildflowers toward mountains still retaining visible snow on them. The sight makes me shiver. I tug my old Georgia Bulldogs baseball cap further down on my head, making sure my blonde curls still cover my ears. The morning sun is already shining brightly with the promise of continuing the hot, dry, early spring into an even earlier, hotter summer. It has to be climate change. The distant mountaintop snow will no doubt entirely melt away soon.

Midmorning… we are supposed to hike along this trail for three or four hours before stopping for our prepared lunch. The excursion operators have packed enough food for us to cover our meals until we reach our destination, a campsite in the adjacent newly-created National Forest, a projected three days' journey from here on foot. We're supposed to hike until we find a place we all like for camping, totally unplanned. I find it strange, but guests apparently clamor for the mystery and for the independence from civilization. I, on the other hand, don't have anything against civilization.

I guess the hike isn't really all that far to go, considering how rough the terrain is and how slowly we're moving, not to mention all the rest stops we have to make along the way. Plus time to break down the camp the morning after setting it up the previous evening… that's the thing that will take the longest – set up. We have to find a suitable spot, lay out our gear, including tents if we have them – and quite a few people do – gather firewood, build a fire the old fashioned way, gather roots, plants and anything else edible around us, as well as catch fish if they are available and in a mood to be caught, clean and cook them, and finally clean up our mess before bedtime. That makes the late afternoons through evenings the real daily time consumer on this trip.

After the majority of our pre-packaged foods run out, we are to forage for ourselves for the most part, but we'll still have other food items to supplement the fish that is intended to sustain us in large part for the five days to be spent at the campsite. The streams in this area have been heavily stocked with trout for the tourist and fishing expedition industries for years, so there should be plenty to go around. Breakfasts are going to consist of granola bars and pop tarts. We're carrying enough of these to get us through every morning of the trip, and then some. I imagine the Meals Ready-to-Eat, or MREs, will be interesting... I've never had those before. We also carry bottled water, filters, canteens and a first aid kit, plus other assorted supplies.

This warm morning has the impression one might have in May in Atlanta, only minus all the humidity. I inhale the mountain air deeply. No smog, either. It's definitely peaceful. All in all, not too bad, I guess.

My strides are not particularly long, but from habit they come quick, so it doesn't take long for me to catch up to the group from the all-girl school and their other adult chaperones, who have gotten quite a good lead on me. My niece has buried herself in the crowd of teens where I can't see her dark blond head, but I know Elise doesn't particularly want me nearby anyway, at least not right now. It would be even worse if her mother was here instead of me. No teenager wants to be seen hanging out with her mother when her other teenaged friends are around. It would definitely not be cool. I'm content to bring up the rear and give the kid some space. With the added bonus of letting somebody else flush out the bugs and snakes. You just know there *have* to be snakes somewhere in this high grass. Sometimes, I think the great outdoors is greater when it's on television.

We stop for lunch in a small clearing which overlooks the long, flower-strewn meadow we have just crossed. I sit near my assigned "pod" of girls, but since it includes my niece, I stare out at the meadow while eating my sandwich and pretzels. That gives them privacy to discuss just how cute our young male guide, Jason, really is. He's the sole man in the entire group of seventy three. I kind of feel sorry for him. He's way outnumbered.

Jason Walker is an employee of the tour business the school contracted with, the Wilderness Expeditions Company. He is in his early twenties, but appears even younger than that; and, according to the paperwork, he's been with the company since he was sixteen. He is of average height, has neatly trimmed blond hair, unbelievably blue eyes and a lean but muscular build; definitely handsome but not really my type. Plus, I'm several years older than he is, so that alone rules him out in my book. The day before, he told us chaperones how much he loved being a wilderness tour guide. He said he'd never had a group of all females before, though. I'm sure it must be a little disconcerting for him, to say the least.

And now my mind wanders away, again. Staying focused on the present has always been one of my biggest problems. I think sometimes maybe I have ADHD or something. A commercial airliner off in the distance has caught my eye. I wonder where all the people onboard are going, what they will do when they get there. I love flying, even though I have only flown once before the flight for this trip, for a vacation with my girlfriends to Hawaii, after I had a particularly bad break up with my long-term boyfriend. He had decided he needed some adventure in his life and moved to Las Vegas... right. That break up had been terribly painful, for me anyway, and made me realize that I needed to be independent and the one in control of my life... I'm determined to make that happen.

The sound of hushed giggles brings me back to the moment. A glance over at the girls tells me all I need to know. Anastasia's light brown cheeks are showing a noticeable blush, and her deep brown eyes sparkle as she peers over the back of one of her friends in the direction of Jason. Anastasia has been Elise's best friend since childhood, the two girls having grown up on the same street in a community in the northern suburbs outside of Atlanta.

This is the kindergarten through eighth grade institution's first attempt at a major multi-curricular outdoor learning activity, coupled with an extended graduating class field trip. It's a great school, but I'm concerned this trip is too long for the young girls to cope with, not to mention the adults. The trip caused some consternation amongst the girls since they were banned from makeup, cell phones and other electronic devices. The trip is a requirement, though, and all the parents liked the idea. The kids – well, not so much. My sister Noel is a teacher at the school and is expecting an unplanned baby brother for Elise, so not only was she unable to come along on the trip, she had to put up with a depressed daughter, too. I guess that's the main reason why I agreed to come in my sister's place... I felt bad for her.

By the time we stop to make camp for the night and eat dinner, I can easily hear my stomach growling. The girls are chattering away. You would think they would have run out of things to talk about by now. I was young like that once; it seems like ages ago. I don't remember being so talkative, but I'm sure I was. I have a vague memory of getting into trouble for it in school at least once.

The sun is sliding behind the distant trees as we unpack sleeping bags and tents. Some of those who have elected not to sleep in tents move out in small groups to collect firewood, but I volunteer to build a fire pit with Jason. I didn't volunteer in order to spend time with him; I just want to learn how to build a fire for myself and to make sure that this one is nice and big to stay warm by. And especially to see that it is good enough for keeping away unwelcome wildlife in the night.

"Jason, I know we're not supposed to ask anything about this, but are we in the remote vicinity of that Fountain of Youth plant that's been in the news lately? The one that they say might be able to reverse the aging process…," I can't help myself; I'm curious.

He hesitates before answering. "We can't talk about that. I'm sorry, Miss Gerringer… I mean, Nicole. It's a sensitive situation. The government is involved, and there are all the concerns about poaching."

"Oh, you can call me Cole, Jason. That's what all my friends call me. And I understand about the plant. I just think it's cool how we haven't discovered everything that's out there in the world yet. It gives people reasons to protect what wilderness we still have," I say.

"I wish more people felt that way. Everyone wants to get their hands on it. The government is supposed to be sending in some kind of federal agents to protect the plant. It can't be detected until it comes up in the spring. They'd better hurry up and get some people in here pretty quick, before the poaching starts. We've already spotted the first plants coming up," he says with a concerned face.

Nearly all the time, Jason has a ready smile and friendly demeanor, on top of his good looks. Most of the adult females on the trip seem to be drawn to him like moths to a flame. I just smirk and shake my head when a couple of the girls and all of the teachers gather by the fire pit near him. They end up spending the majority of their time just chatting with Jason, hanging on his every word, laughing at all the appropriate moments. How annoying.

I'm unable to work around the small but growing crowd occupying the space, so I simply abandon the task and instead help girls who are unloading well-insulated supplies that have been pre-positioned in a small, secure, solar powered storage facility. It is owned by the Wilderness Expeditions Company and is the only outpost they have beyond the main buildings, called Camp Correll. The storage shed sits at the edge of the new National Forest. The company had said they use the facility for their longer outings, as a special surprise for both the beginning and the end of the camping trips. They had found it to be a nice treat, particularly for preparing the groups for the extended time foraging for sustenance out in the wilderness. The solar facility is supposed to be restocked before our group returns this way for a welcome home evening meal, if our timing works out as planned.

As the last rays of sunlight slip away behind the trees, the smell of hot dogs and baked beans fills the air around the campsite. We're going to follow them up later with s'mores. The groups of teenagers continue to chatter away excitedly as they eat their dinner.

Following the meal, I volunteer to assist Regina Whittaker, the long-serving science teacher, DeShondra Whittaker, Regina's daughter and young math teacher, and Elizabeth Curry, the seasoned art teacher, in helping the girls with the first official lesson of the trip. They are to find a constellation and map it out. They are also supposed to create their own constellation myth to accompany the real legends behind the star groupings. After completing their evening assignments, the young teenagers snuggle into tents and their sleeping bags, tired from nearly a full day of hiking. The chaperones soon follow suit, including me. I am asleep on my feet.

I think even Jason is tired. The girls had kept him busy answering a multitude of questions since we'd stopped to camp for the night, overcoming their initial shyness pretty quickly. His voice has been dwindling to a raspy whisper throughout the evening. I watch drowsily as he stacks more wood near the fire so he can stoke it during the night as necessary. We didn't expect temperatures to dip much below fifty-five degrees; the moon is at last quarter and long since set, unable to provide us with any light. The fire will provide the comfort that comes with the illumination of a dark night. It is far better than a flashlight, in my estimation.

The morning dawns and the sky is a bright, clear, sapphire blue, just like yesterday. The early risers amongst the campers are busying themselves packing while satisfying their hunger with granola bars and the one and only piece of fresh fruit each of us brought, an apple.

When we head out, I am grateful I had purchased the lightest-weight sleeping bag I could find. I know sore legs and aching backs will become a problem for many of us in a day or two, if not sooner. I have a strong back, but a couple of the teachers are already groaning when they put on their packs. Most all of us are in rather poor shape when it comes to long-distance hiking, especially with gear. Jason, on the other hand, is having no trouble at all. He's laughing good-naturedly and jogging in circles around the lead pod of girls. I suppose he's trying to encourage them or something.

We encounter our first snake this morning. It's a young green snake, sunning itself on the end of a broad-leafed weed. Most of the girls are reluctant to approach it. Jason steps forward and takes a photo, then helps the girls who want a snapshot of the tiny snake.

"This is likely to be the only snake we come across on the entire trip," Jason says loudly enough for all of us to hear. "Snakes tend to slither away and hide when we're coming. They can detect us through vibrations we make on the ground when we're walking; at least, most of the time. Just remember they are more afraid of us than we are of them, okay ladies?"

"Not likely," Elizabeth says under her breath, rolling her eyes toward the sky.

"Tell me about it," DeShondra adds softly.

We are snake-free the rest of the morning, at least as far as we know. We all follow along in the path Jason's feet make through the weeds, just in case. When we stop for lunch, I polish off my peanut butter sandwich quickly, giving me free time. I decide to show my disinterested niece and her friends how to make a simple pinhole viewer to look at the sun. I carefully poke the end of my pen through a small notecard, then, holding it at the proper angle, cast a pinpoint of light onto a second notecard, the size of the solar image changing as I increase or decrease the distance.

"Hey, that's a pretty neat trick," Jason says from just over my shoulder. "You other girls should take a look at this, too."

I hadn't noticed him there, and I'm surprised he is interested. Suddenly, nearly every camper is crowding in for a look. I smile at the attention, but I know it is all thanks to our handsome young guide.

"As long as you are all here, I'm going to give you a warning," I say. "Some of you have binoculars and cameras. Never look at the sun through them without a special filter or you will damage your eyes and you can even go blind. Watch this and I'll show you how to do it a different way that's safe." I borrow Elise's small binoculars and hold them up to project twin images of the sun onto a notecard. The group watches as I bring the bright discs into focus.

"You can't do that for very long on flammable material, though, I'll warn you now. It would be very easy to start a wildfire that way, since all the vegetation around here is so dry." Jason reminds all of us about the instructions we had received before leaving Camp Correll on this hike. Be careful not to start a forest fire, whatever you do.

I respond, "That's true, so we have to look fast and be very careful. You can even see a really huge cluster of sunspots right in the middle of the sun there. You know, we might even be able to see the Northern Lights while we're on this trip, since the sun is so active right now, showing us such a big cluster… that's one of the biggest groups I've ever seen."

I can hear several 'wows' from those girls closest to me. Gratified by their reactions, I lower the binoculars, waiting for the next group to crowd up around me. I continue to show the suns to each small group in turn. "This is something y'all can put down in your observation journals, you know."

After allowing the kids sufficient time for some furious journal scribbling, Jason herds our group together and marches us toward our evening camp destination. He is a good and knowledgeable guide. He knows a lot about camping and nature, but I doubt he knows much about teenaged girls. At times he seems almost embarrassed by all the attention, yet overall he appears to be handling it quite well.

Long after the sun sets that evening and we're all gathered around the campfire, the girls begin to tell ghost stories. Jason is helping and even encouraging them. I've never been a fan of ghost stories. Personally, I prefer to stargaze. Tonight though, when I look up at the stars, I notice something different. At first, it looks like wispy clouds at sunset that are being blown around by the wind. But we're way beyond sunset. The colors are growing deeper and brighter as I watch. Then I realize what I'm seeing; an aurora and it's building into a massive one at that. It's everywhere.

Slowly, I take a deep breath and rise to my feet in awe of the amazing display above me. Laura, the girl who is fully engaged in regaling us with a highly-detailed ghost story, stops talking and follows my gaze skyward.

"Look, everybody. It's the Northern Lights!" Enthusiasm is evident in my voice. I can't help it. Living down south, seeing the Northern Lights is an extremely rare event; and we *never* see them like this. I hope this is a sign of good things to come on this trip.

Kids and adults alike stand... we all stare, transfixed, at the show unfolding above us. The myriad of colors is remarkable... red, green, blue, yellow and violet. They dance across the sky until it is covered in great rippling sheets. It is absolutely mesmerizing.

It's wonderful to see the kids so completely engrossed in something other than television or their cell phones. This will be an outstanding entry in their journals. I have seen a couple of auroras in my time, but never anything this beautiful, or of so many colors; it must be a really intense solar storm. The thought of soon having to sustain ourselves on fish and wild plants is well worth the tradeoff for me, at least for tonight.

CHAPTER 2

In the middle of the afternoon on the third day of hiking we arrive at our goal… the multi-night campsite. We are none the worse for wear. The campground, on the other hand, is nothing more than a small meadow by a wide, meandering stream. A lot is lacking, in my estimation. I would have preferred an actual campground, complete with showers or at least wooden sleeping platforms, but instead we are roughing it in the depths of a recently-designated National Forest.

Camp is set up with a little more thought and care than the two previous nights, since we are going to be here for six nights. A few girls have even picked grasses to place beneath their sleeping bags to create a softer surface. I watch them and decide to do likewise. I've been able to feel every irregularity in the ground at night and I had some difficulty sleeping last night due to the discomfort. I guess I'm what people would call 'soft'. I couldn't agree more.

After arranging my sleeping bag, I strike out with Elise and Anastasia to search for firewood. I keep a wary eye out for venomous spiders and snakes, but apparently they aren't hanging out in this heavily-wooded area where shade and cooler late afternoon temperatures are prevalent. We return with armloads of firewood, as do the other groups who likewise volunteered for the assignment.

I study the piles of wood with my hands on my hips, as Jason and a couple of volunteers build the fire pit. "That isn't a good sign, is it? Finding so much dead wood and kindling everywhere, I mean," I ask with a deeply-furrowed brow.

Jason pauses in his work to look up at me, then over at the abundance of wood. "Oh, we'll be fine," he says with his usual cheerful smile. "We'll just have to be extra careful with our campfires, and no looking at the sun through binoculars without close adult supervision. We're probably the only people out here for a hundred miles around, so there shouldn't be anything at all for us to worry about."

"If you say so," I remark as I walk away, biting my lower lip. I vow to keep a close eye on the campers. I wish I hadn't shown them how cool it is to look at the sun, even with the pinhole viewing card.

Little did I know then that none of the kids would show any further interest in looking at the sun for the duration of our trip. Nor do they pay any additional attention to the night sky. I'm especially disappointed in that. I've always found the stars so fascinating. My family never shared my interest, though. I guess I shouldn't have been surprised about these kids.

They are very curious about the life forms found in the creeks or studying insects, though. Several of them are interested in birdwatching. Maybe there is hope for the class producing a scientist or two yet. I know that girls their ages show more interest in makeup, clothes and boys. I just don't get it, personally. When I was a girl, I wanted to be outside, following wildlife and observing nature in my journals... something I've gotten far away from as I grew older. My sister Noel was always the boy-crazy one between the two of us.

CHAPTER 3

This camping trip has been a long but successful accomplishment for our sizable group of campers. The students have conducted innumerable experiments, filled their journals with observations and sketches and we have all worn ourselves out from days of hiking. Several of us made walking sticks, some with less success than others, to help traverse the mountainous terrain. And thankfully, there were no broken bones, just a few skinned knees and elbows, and the occasional mosquito bite.

We're all looking forward to reaching the solar storage shed; it has been the day's primary topic of conversation. The shed will be filled with hotdogs, beans and all the fixings for a pre-welcome home dinner. Tomorrow we will hike to the spot where we were originally dropped off. There, the crew from the Expedition Company will pick us up at noon to take us back to Camp Correll. And tomorrow night, it's a STEAK dinner! I'm so excited I can hardly contain myself. After our meals over the past ten days, I can hardly wait to get into that shed to get at those hotdogs.

"Alright, everybody, listen up," Jason says, halting the convoy as we approach the shed. "I want a show of hands; we need volunteers for gathering firewood, building a fire pit, setting up camp and unloading the food from the shed. Keep in mind the fact that we can't all do the same job. Now I know there are some of you that haven't gathered any wood this entire trip. It won't hurt you to get a little dirty. Tomorrow we'll be back at Camp Correll and we can all take showers."

Seriously, Jason? I'm hungry enough to do almost all the chores myself. Just get on with it already, Jason. He has started pacing back and forth in front of the kids and looks like he's going to make a long, drawn-out ordeal over this. I try to hide my impatience. Then I decide it'll probably be better to volunteer for something just to get the ball rolling. "I'll take a group to gather firewood," I say, dropping my backpack and sleeping bag. "Whoever wants to help can just come on with me."

I see the momentary irritation on Jason's face. He gets over it quickly enough and winks at me. "Thanks, Cole. Okay, you heard the lady, everybody who wants a nice big fire to cook those hotdogs and s'mores with, get going with Cole. I'd prefer for it to be those who haven't gathered firewood before, though. I know there are a few who still need that experience. You see, girls, there are lots of things you need to know how to do in order to survive in the wild…"

I let out an exasperated sigh; here comes another lecture. Several kids come over to me. Most have gathered wood before, a few have not. I don't really care at this point. We set out for some nearby trees as Jason's voice rings out behind us, breaking the other kids into groups for various assignments.

As has been the case on our entire trip, it doesn't take long to gather a sufficient supply of firewood. We return with armloads of the stuff. We are approaching the others, who seem to be milling about in circles, rather than unloading supplies from the shed.

"What's going on?" I ask Jason when we're close enough. He's been watching us on our approach to the fire pit, his usual smile absent.

He rubs a hand across his face as I deposit my wood on the ground. "I don't know what happened, Cole, but the shed is empty."

It takes a couple of seconds for that bit of news to get processed by my brain. "What? Empty? You mean there's no food?" I guess that was kind of obvious when Jason said the word 'empty', but I'm so surprised I can't avoid saying it.

"No, there's no food. Nothing at all," he says.

I look around, as if I might see Jason's coworkers on their way right now with the food we had been promised. "What do you think happened?"

13

"I don't know, Cole. It looks like they never came; our trash is still in there from last week, too."

"Do you reckon someone might have stolen it?" Anastasia asks.

"No, I don't think anyone stole it. The padlock is on the door, and it was locked up nice and tight," Jason says with an apologetic look on his face. "I'm really sorry; I don't know why they didn't bring our food. They've never missed a drop before."

The kids are verbalizing their displeasure with growing volume. I look over at the teachers, who are standing in a tight circle, talking amongst themselves. They look more than just disappointed.

"That's okay, Jason," I speak up so the teachers can overhear. "It isn't your fault. We are all just disappointed, that's all. We have plenty of rations left over, so we'll just eat what we've got with us."

"I know, but I still feel bad about it," Jason adds.

"It's okay, y'all. Don't worry about it; it's just one more night. And then tomorrow night, we'll be having steak for dinner," I say loudly enough for all to hear, and with as broad a smile as I can manage. "And the day after that, we get to go home! Let's finish getting camp set up, and then we can eat and maybe get to sleep early. That way, we can get up earlier and get back to the retrieval spot. Who knows? Maybe the Expeditions people will come by early to pick us up, too!"

I really don't want Jason to be made out to be the bad guy here. He had nothing to do with whatever happened. And now I'm really looking forward to that steak dinner tomorrow.

CHAPTER 4

I sit on the trunk of a fallen tree while we wait for the retrieval and admire the selection I had made a few days earlier of a sturdy, almost six foot long piece of red cedar. I believe I have done a nice job of turning it into a walking stick. When I had come upon it, the wood of my staff was already weathered to a silvery color; it is smooth, with only a long, narrow strip where the bark clings stubbornly in a deep groove. I had personalized it with a few long strips of leathery, dark green grasses which I braided together. Then I wrapped the braid around one end of the cedar for a decoration, leaving the ends to dangle. My hair is likewise braided against the surprisingly hot weather for an early spring day in this part of the country.

Nearly all of the females with long hair are wearing it bound in some fashion to keep it off their necks, which are sparkling with sweat. The shadows are telling me it is late afternoon. We've long ago eaten our jerky and dehydrated fruit lunch. Our exhausted group sits or lies back in the wildflower meadow and waits while Jason attempts to spot his coworkers arriving in the distance through his binoculars; but it appears he's having no luck, despite checking repeatedly every fifteen minutes or so for the past few hours. Finally, he gives up and sits down near the edge of a smaller cluster of girls and Regina to wait for his long-overdue companions to pick us up for a return to civilization. I'm sure he is anxious to be free from all the female attention.

As the day continues to grow later, I can't help the rising feeling of suspicion in me. If one vehicle had broken down, the others would still have come for us. They had a long line of Hummers and several ATVs back at Camp Correll. Plus, there was the empty storage shed to add to my growing concerns.

Jason has us set up camp for the night, just in case. Good thing, too, because the retrieval doesn't happen. During our evening meal, a bright meteor shoots silently across the sky, causing many exclamations of wonder from everyone. It's the brightest we've seen on our trip.

We watch for about fifteen minutes to see if there are more, but the girls grow impatient with the exercise since none are forthcoming. Tolerance for this activity is in short supply after nearly two weeks of stargazing, especially with no more of the brilliant displays of aurora to watch. One by one, the campers all make their way to tents or sleeping bags and lie down for the night.

Jason adds a couple more pieces of wood to the fire. I watch the others as they settle in and turn to Jason. "So, what do you think is going on with your friends, honestly?"

He sighs. "I'm sorry, Cole. I really don't know. This just isn't like them. Maybe they got their days all mixed up or something. I have no idea."

"Okay. So if that happened, they should be here by lunchtime tomorrow to get us," I say in a serious voice, getting to my feet.

"Yeah, should be," is all the response he gives me.

"We'll see what happens at lunchtime, then," I say and walk away to try and turn off my worried mind so I can get some sleep. I don't hold out a lot of hope.

CHAPTER 5

I awaken to the first hint of dawn. The horizon is just beginning to show a warm yellow-orange glow and the stars are fading away. I yawn and watch the sun come up. Nearby, Jason rolls over onto his back and rubs his eyes.

The granola bars I munch on had tasted much better at the start of our trip, before they had been crushed and baked by the temperatures seeping into my backpack. Still, it is far more appealing than the insects championed by Jason a few days ago. That was just plain gross.

One by one, sleepy heads begin popping up. The girls busily prepare themselves and their gear for the return trip home and munch on granola bars or pop tarts. They sit in small groups talking about the restart of school after the long spring holiday break, coupled with their big field trip. Regina, ever the teacher, even dares to bring up the required research paper to result from the trip. That seems to be making the girls even more anxious for the Expedition vehicles to arrive and retrieve them from the situation, however temporary the distraction would prove to be.

The hours seem to crawl by, as everyone grows more impatient for our transports to arrive. Worry begins to set in as noon comes and goes. Jason motions for the adults to gather with him a short distance from our charges.

"Bruce Correll and the other guys were supposed to have been here waiting for us yesterday by noon. Something must have happened to stop them from coming to get us". He pauses and looks off in the general direction of Camp Correll. "Our company has a great reputation. We've never missed an extraction or even been late for one."

It's easy for us to see he is concerned, and that he's trying to downplay it all. "It takes upwards of three hours to get to Camp Correll from here by

17

vehicle, what with the rough terrain and all. It's going to be a lot longer on foot. A Hummer going over rugged terrain travels at about ten miles per hour... with the terrain around here, though, plus carrying younger girls, it's probably closer to five or six miles per hour. We don't have many roads out here. The campers like bouncing along through the woods and fields better than driving on roads."

I decide to add to where Jason is going. "Our best pace is that of the slowest hiker. We'll be doing good to get about two miles per hour, with breaks and all; if that. I say we need to get going, and maybe we can get there by sometime tomorrow afternoon; before dark, anyway. We can't travel too fast because some of the girls are a little beaten up."

"Some of us adults are, too. I agree with Jason and Cole," Regina states firmly. "Whatever happened, we can't stay here waiting for who knows how long. We need to start back. The parents of those kids will be getting worried because they haven't heard back from their daughters by now. We would have had our cell phones back and reception at the airport we're supposed to be flying out of this afternoon."

"Jason, can you find the way... can you lead us back to Camp Correll on foot?" I ask.

"Sure I can; no problem. I can't use the GPS on my phone since there's no signal out here, but I do have an old fashioned backup," he says with a grin as he pulls a tattered paper map from his back pocket. "I was a boy scout... always be prepared. Not that I need it, though." His smile is so contagious.

"Then gather up the girls, and let's get moving," I nod my head toward Regina.

Before we vacate the designated extraction area, we leave behind a message, spelled out with large stones and sticks. Just in case anyone from Camp Correll does come looking for us. Then at Jason's suggestion, we herd the group of teens at a westerly angle, toward a tributary of the wildly-meandering creek we had fished along successfully when we were much farther to the northeast, at our weeklong campsite. That way, we will at least have the possibility of fishing for dinner, even though it will put us even later arriving at Camp Correll. We are beginning to run a little low on supplies.

The girls are relatively subdued in the hours we spend hiking to the creek. They set up camp like the experts they have become. There are no complaints when their presence is requested along the creek for fishing duty. Even when it is time for cleaning the catch, there are no protests.

The fish we catch and feast on that evening taste like a delicacy, especially since it was pretty late in the afternoon before we captured enough of them to be able to share small amounts amongst the group. This part of the creek must not be as appealing to the farm-raised stock as the densely-populated one we had stayed by for the main part of our trip. The wild plants don't taste as good as the fish, but we eat until we can't hold any more because those grow abundantly in this particular area. It's obvious we won't be able to make it even halfway to Camp Correll by nightfall, but at least we have a solid meal. We tell the campers to leave their baited lines in the water, securely moored on the banks of the creek, in the hopes that we might catch more fish for breakfast the next morning.

Regina, DeShondra, and the other adults are assisting the girls in setting up their tents and sleeping bags by the light of the campfire. I take advantage of the distraction to pull Jason aside for a private conversation.

"Can you think of any reason why your friends wouldn't have come to get us today?" I whisper, my facial expression as stern as the anger and growing fear welling up inside me. I'm trying to remain calm so the girls won't know anything is up.

Jason searches my eyes. "No, honestly I can't. We all love what we do, and we appreciate that we get paid pretty well for doing it. Bruce took over the business from his dad when the old guy retired eight years ago. He's done a great job of modernizing it and making sure we please our customers so they'll not only come back, but they'll tell their friends about us. That's how he's been able to hire on four new people in the past three years. He would never leave us out here." He pauses and looks around at the campers before finishing. "I think something's happened... something bad." He hesitates. "Worse than something like car trouble."

"Like what?" I look from side to side, just as Jason had done. I don't want any campers to overhear and get any more worried than I am sure they already must be.

"Well, there are all kinds of rumors about these mountains and what goes on here. We hear things sometimes, just stories; but now it's got me thinking."

"What stories? Come on now." I put my hands on my hips because I just have a feeling he's going to say something I don't really want to hear… or believe.

"We've heard that there's drug running through here sometimes. There are tons of good places to hide. A couple of our guides swore they were shot at last year when they were scouting out new campsites for the tourists. We had to shift our sites because of the new National Forest. Bruce worked out a deal that let the federal government take possession of the land while giving him exclusive rights of continued use for the next fifty years. They just wanted us to keep clear of where that Fountain of Youth plant grows. That's why our guys were scouting new spots in the first place." He finishes the sentence with downcast eyes. "Nothing ever came of the gun shots. The Sheriff and the Fish and Wildlife guys couldn't find a trace of anyone. And it was far away from where we are here. It was northeast of Camp Correll, actually. We haven't had any problems at all before or since. But the two guys involved did quit, though. It shook them up pretty bad."

"Why didn't you tell me this sooner? We're about a half day's hike from Camp Correll, which is ridiculously isolated, by the way, and now you're suggesting… what? That drug dealers have gotten to the Camp and killed your friends? That would mean there's a chance they might still be there when we reach Camp Correll with these kids." My anger is beginning to flare and my voice is rising, so I stop talking to listen to the response.

"No, no, no… that's not what I'm suggesting. You wanted to know the possibilities, so I'm giving you the only one I can think of." He shrugs his shoulders.

"Yes, and it's a good thing I asked. Is there anything else you want to tell me?" I put my hands back on my hips. I don't like his withholding information and possibly putting the girls… and all of us, at risk.

"No. The only other things they talk about being around here are ghosts." He casts his eyes downward again. "Those stories have been around since way before I started working here. Most of us have seen things we can't explain. I even thought I saw one once."

"What?" My teeth are tightly clenched by this point. "Now you're telling me that ghosts are running around here, causing problems?" I have had very little patience for the ghost stories Jason and the kids had been gleefully telling each other around the campfires for the past several nights, let alone this. "That's bull!"

"No, that's not what I'm saying. But obviously something has happened; otherwise Bruce would have met us yesterday at the retrieval point," he finishes defensively.

"Obviously," I agree and turn to stride a few paces away in frustration before turning on my heel and returning to where he stands, waiting patiently, watching me with those intense blue eyes.

"Listen, first thing in the morning, hopefully before the sun comes up, I want you to point me in the direction of Camp Correll. Then I'm going to scout ahead, all the way to the Camp. Let the girls wake up on their own, no rush. Get some more fish out of the stream and cook them up. Make fish jerky, pick some more plants and roots, something, anything. Keep them all busy, especially my niece. Don't tell them anything if you can help it. And keep your eyes and ears open." I stare at Jason without blinking. "If something bad happened at Camp Correll, I'll come back and we'll head off on a different path to get out of here."

"I should be the one to do that, Cole, not you," Jason begins to protest.

"Look, don't pull any of that manly crap on me. Besides, you need to stay with the girls to keep them safe; and if for some reason I don't come back, you have to lead everybody here to safety… you'll have to find another way out. And well away from where your guys got shot at before, too. It'll be a long trip getting to a town outside this forest, I'm assuming; and you're the best person to do it. Probably the only person who can do it," I say, placing a hand firmly on the young man's shoulder with a confidence I'm hoping I can impart to him. "You'll be fine, and so will they."

"And so will you." He gazes into my eyes, trying to believe in both me and in himself, I suppose.

This might be far more responsibility than he has ever had before in his young life, I realize. I know it is for me.

"Hey, just don't take off in some random direction without me before my time is up, that's all. I'll never be able to find you." I leave him and walk over to kneel near my niece and open my sleeping bag for the night. I need to calm my restless mind for tomorrow's journey.

CHAPTER 6

If I hadn't been so tired, I never would have gotten any rest. I'm anxious, even in my sleep; and I nearly bolt out of the sleeping bag in one motion when Jason touches my arm to wake me up. There is only the barest tinge of light in the sky. Jason has allowed the fire to burn itself out and is using a small penlight, as the thin sliver that is the current moon phase hasn't yet risen. Its light would have been too feeble to offer much if any assistance, anyway, even if it was visible now.

"I'll take care of your pack and sleeping bag for you," he offers in a whisper. "It'll lighten your load, just in case you need to move fast – but I'm sure everything will be fine," he adds quickly when he sees my eyes widen.

"Right," is all I can manage in response to that. I get to my feet and stretch gently, then pull on my shoes and tuck my large bowie knife into the holster on my belt. "Turn off that light so my eyes can adjust to the dark, please."

"Oh, I'm sorry." He quickly extinguishes his light, then hands me a fistful of beef jerky packets, some dehydrated fruit and a pack of granola bars. I can barely see them in the glow from the fire's dying coals and the visual after-effects from the penlight. I stuff them into one of my pockets and strap on the two canteens of freshly-treated water he hands me next.

"I want you to take my gun," he offers as we move farther from the campers so as not to disturb them.

"No thanks, I'm one of those "weirdoes" who don't like guns. I saw my Dad use them once in a while when I was a kid, but that's as close as I've come to using one. There was a whole traumatic incident when I watched a deer he shot die, and I was only five years old at the time. Besides, you might need it to protect the kids, and that's way more important. Don't worry; I'll be just fine without it. Besides that, I don't believe you can shoot a ghost; not successfully, anyway," I smile at him in the growing hints of the coming dawn.

"Then at least take my map. It has some extra terrain details sketched in on it. It might make all the difference." He extends his hand, holding the tattered map, which I gladly accept and tuck gingerly into a back pocket, along with his penlight. I reach down and pick up my walking stick.

I know he has worked in this area long enough that he wouldn't need the map in order to navigate the kids to safety if I don't make it back. Sunrise is close enough for me to see my feet a little bit better now, along with potential obstacles in my path. I know it's time to get started.

"Okay, point me in the right direction. I've got my trusty little compass ready."

Jason stands alongside me and points to the southwest, where the landscape is relatively free from trees for about a half mile or so before the forest begins to encroach. "Just follow the compass, and you'll be fine. You should get to Camp Correll by around noon or somewhere in there. You'll be able to get back to us before nightfall, anyway. If you don't take too much time checking things out, that is. Just take a quick look and come straight back, okay Cole?"

Jason has picked up one of my curls and is rubbing it almost absentmindedly between his fingers as he's been talking to me. He leans his head in next to mine and gives my cheek a tender, lingering kiss. I couldn't have been more surprised; that was totally unexpected. There's enough light now for me to see an encouraging smile on his face. I think the kiss may just be due to the fact that he no longer believes he'll ever see me again. He could be right, of course.

"If I'm not back by sometime early tomorrow morning, I want you get the girls out of here *quick* – understand?"

He doesn't hesitate. "You can count on it. I'll keep them safe. I promise."

CHAPTER 7

The cloudless sky is growing brighter by the minute, soon to deliver another beautiful, unseasonably-warm day and providing my path with illumination. I know when I get closer to Camp Correll, I'll have to slow my pace; but for now, I want to make some time before the sun climbs too high overhead. I'm determined to reach my destination as far ahead of noon as possible. I plan on having lots of time to look around and still make it back to the kids before dark. I don't want to have to think about sleeping alone in the woods because I was too slow and couldn't make it back on time. Plus, Jason has me spooked with his stupid ghost stories. Damn him.

Through the morning, I eat with one hand while I hike, the other hand using my trusty walking stick to move aside the prickly briers that litter the ground in places. I don't have the stomach for much food or water, as my uneasiness is growing rapidly, robbing me of my appetite. The cover of the forest is gradually giving way to a slightly more open terrain. I have been traveling for well over five hours, I'm sure.

I slow now, because I can tell from the shadows cast by the trees that noon is only perhaps an hour or so away. Camp Correll must be very close. It sprawls across such a large area that I know I have a good chance of finding it using the compass, Jason's map, or even simply dumb luck from stumbling across it by accident. I double check my compass, but find I am fairly well on track. I have a decent inner sense of direction. My father had taught me well about such things as following a map, using the sun and stars for navigation... and just plain using my head. That was back when I was young, living on our large family farm in the Low Country of South Carolina. We didn't have much money; but my sister Noel and I never realized it growing up, living off the land as we did.

Recalling my childhood lightens my mood; but I move even more cautiously now, taking care to keep to the larger tree trunks and spots of heavy underbrush whenever possible. It is the same effort I had put into sneaking up on wildlife – mostly birds – around the farm so I could photograph them. That was my favorite thing to do when I was younger. I know it is vital that I be as alert as possible, just in case something is indeed wrong. The little voice in my head has the hair on the nape of my neck standing on its end.

Reaching the crest of a low rise, I see why: Camp Correll spreads out before me in the distance through the sparse tree line, just as I remembered it. There is no smoke curling upwards from the chimneys this time. Maybe it's just the warm weather, though. Even the nights had been warm enough to go without a fire really, unless you need one for kids to roast s'mores and tell ghost stories by. I hate the thought of ghost stories; I'm glad I didn't really pay attention when the kids and Jason were telling them around the campfire. I don't need anything else to make my nerves jittery. Upon closer inspection, I can see the vehicles are parked in a long row, just as they were when we were here almost two weeks ago. No human activity is evident anywhere. I don't even see the camp's friendly black lab mascot, Molly. Jason had said that dog was outside nearly all day, every day.

The only sounds are the multiple trills of birdsong and a pair of squirrels chasing each other through a pine tree near the edge of the forest, with bits of bark falling to the ground in the scuffle. I crouch behind a tree and the underbrush surrounding it, watching for a good twenty minutes. I want to wait to make sure that no one is around before I attempt to go any closer. Patience is a virtue I don't always have in sufficient quantity, but I'm certain I will make an exception this time.

I figure it must be approaching noon, and I know I need to get moving in order to get back to the others before dark. Jason's tiny penlight I am carrying will be of little benefit then. I leave my walking stick and supplies by the trunk of the largest tree so I can find them easily enough when I return. I keep the canteen that is nearly empty to refill at the Mess Hall if I can, leaving the other one behind, and make my way down the low hill toward the nearest Camper Cabin. I use trees for cover as long as I'm able to. Eventually, though, I have to cross the wide-open expanse of grass between the forest and that first building.

I move quickly over to the Camper Cabin, crouching low in case there's anyone inside who could potentially see me through a window. I wait only a moment, trying to listen to everything around me, despite the sound of my own breathing, which seems rather loud in the relative quiet. I'm so nervous. It's really hard for me to calm myself. I slowly raise my head until I can see into one of the windows, using my hand to help block the outside glare on the glass.

No one is inside as far as I can tell. The building is one large room, save for the restrooms at the other end. The multiple rows of beds are all made, apparently awaiting the long-overdue return of our group of campers. We had occupied this one and the next two over. The wildflowers in a vase on the round table nearest the window I'm peering through are still holding their fading color, although the stems are beginning to sag with most of the water having dried up.

I turn and look behind me, up along the rim of the geographical bowl that Camp Correll sits in. As far as I can see around me from that vantage point, there is no sign of anyone, anywhere. I move around the side of the cabin and make my way cautiously toward the main structure. In between are ten of the Camper Cabins. There are even more in a row off to the west of these, but for now I decide against exploring them in the interest of time. Besides, each cabin I pass in this row is as empty as the first one was, in pristine condition, nothing seeming to be amiss. The buildings farther back to the west, closer to the woods, seem equally unoccupied from where I stand. The browning grass crunches beneath each step I take.

Where in the world did everybody go? I hate being here alone. I feel like someone or something is going to jump out at me any moment, from any corner, like in a horror movie. It doesn't make any sense. Why would they up and leave us like this? At least, it looks like that's what happened. I just can't figure it out. It makes no logical sense.

I'm careful in my approach to the Headquarters Building, which the camp staff had nicknamed The Head - not very funny, if you ask me. The girls had not found it amusing, either. But then, what do you expect from twelve guys, the oldest of whom is the owner at the ripe old age of twenty-six? That's not too much younger than I am, but I'm definitely more mature than that.

I decide to pass by the Mess Hall and save it for later. I continue to keep a sharp lookout all around, although I no longer expect to find anyone in the area. Everything I have found hints at complete desertion, by many days. The long row of windows on the side of the Headquarters Building I come to first, which is near the vehicles, confirm my gut feeling, revealing that part of the building to be unoccupied, at least as far as I can tell from the outside.

When I come to the closest vehicle, a Hummer, I reach up and touch the hood. There is no heat emanating from it, indicating a lack of recent use. I don't know if that really means anything or not. They do it on television all the time, though. But I know the next thing I see does have meaning. The gas tank door is open, and the cap is hanging loose. It's the same with the other vehicles. The last one I come to has a hose hanging from inside the gas tank. There are several Hummers missing from the parking area line-up. Why would they siphon the gas out of all the other vehicles?

I go around to the front of the two-story structure and up the wooden steps, then onto the expansive porch, where we had sat rocking in the chairs to enjoy the evening air the night before we headed out on our journey. I cringe when the weight of my foot accidentally presses on one of the boards at just the right angle, causing it to emit a small but high-pitched squeak. It sounds so incredibly loud, echoing off the nearby cluster of trees planted years ago to help shade the porch. I quickly look behind me, checking my surroundings, but still no one makes an appearance. I close my eyes and exhale a deep sigh of relief, then step slowly forward and twist the doorknob. The front door is unlocked; so I push it open, gradually, and walk inside. The huge room is clean and neat with everything in its place. There are no sounds or voices or other human activity that I can detect, so I wander cautiously from room to room. A thorough search of the downstairs proves to be futile; every door is wide open, with no one inside.

After closer exploration, I find that the entire structure is vacant, even the upstairs. The rooms on the second floor are primarily living quarters for the owner and his staff. In contrast to the Camper Cabins and the downstairs areas of this building, the rooms upstairs are all in disarray, with closets and drawers left open. Most of the clothes are gone, along with any suitcases that I assume had been there and no medicines of any kind are in any of the bathrooms. I have searched in vain for signs of people at Camp Correll; and there are no clues to indicate where they all had gone, or a reason for the apparent emergency evacuation. Everything conveys the impression that all is fine. There's no indication of a wildfire or any kind of an attack, whether by humans or animals… maybe there was a ghost, after all.

Nope. I don't believe in ghosts. I'd better keep searching then.

One flashlight was cast aside on the floor downstairs, beneath the check-in desk. It has a belt clip on the end, so I attach it to a loop on my pants. Notepads and pens are in abundance at the reception desk as well, but they have left no notes behind. It's like they took off in a big hurry. I don't understand why they would abandon us like this, let alone risk the business they were so proud of and professed to love so much.

I'm nearly out the front door when I think to check the big safe. That's where we adults had stored our cell phones and valuables for safekeeping while we were on the camping trip. I go to the walk-in closet around the corner from the front desk. The door is open a crack, and it is dark beyond. The door creaks loudly when I push it slowly open. This whole place is like being in a horror movie… only no horror, at least not yet. I swallow the lump in my throat and look around me. I don't see anyone coming my way. And I still don't hear anything. My heart is pounding anyway.

The light switch does nothing at all. I activate my new flashlight, but it only seems to add to the sense of mystery and fear. I go to the safe and give the partially-open door a tug. I shine my light inside, only to find it empty. Are these people thieves, too? It's not like we brought a fortune with us, just a little spending money for the gift shop near the airport on our way out. Plus the cellphones. I turn away and the light plays across the floor. A flash raises my hopes. A cellphone! Someone must have dropped it and been in too big of a hurry to pick it up. There isn't supposed to be any reception at all this far out anyway, but it's worth a try. I hold it in my hand, examining it carefully. The face has been smashed, and the power button has no effect. Great, just great.

The Mess Hall is next on my list and a top priority. It is a stone's throw from Headquarters. Our breakfast on the morning we headed out was held there, as was the wonderful steak dinner the night before that. I'm getting hungry just from the memories. The cook here was outstanding at his work.

I peer out, a bit fearfully, from just inside the front door of the Headquarters Building. My eyes scan the trees and the vehicles, but I see no one. I still keep my guard up as I make my way to the Mess Hall. The massive garden behind the building stretches all the way back to the forest. Jason said they grew more food here than they needed to get the staff and guests through the entire year. They had an abundance to sell to the local stores and restaurants. They even had extra to freeze or can for getting them all through the winter with their skiing and cross-country excursions, plus fresh produce from their large greenhouse. The main entrance to the Mess Hall is wide open. The large number of windows are allowing plenty of light inside for me to see everything with ease.

This building is in a very different state from the others. Where there had two weeks prior been an abundance of food and tables so clean you could have eaten off them, a large portion of the substantial stores of food are gone and scraps are smeared on some of the tables and floors. Several chairs have been strewn about, along with the vases of wildflowers, now dead, the water spilled and long since evaporated. In the kitchen, cabinet doors are open or broken, hanging from their hinges. The door to the walk-in refrigerator stands wide open. I slowly step into what should have been refrigeration, only to note that there is no hint of cold air, but plenty of rotting meat, milk, and eggs. The stench is overwhelming. I rush out of it before the smell makes me vomit.

"No power," I whisper out loud to myself. Strange, because several workers had told our party how there was a backup generator with enough fuel to give them the capability to run everything in the compound for more than three days. Finding several empty backpacks, I fill the largest of them with some of the edible morsels left behind: multiple packs of dehydrated fruits, vegetables and meats, along with several sleeves of saltine crackers. I can't take everything, but it's a start for our group. And I take several of the water treatment filters I find, along with a good first-aid kit. I also think to grab one of the few knives remaining… a small, serrated meat cleaver, the blade of which fits perfectly in the back pocket of my pants. It makes me feel better to have an additional weapon.

Before leaving, I make sure to eat as much food as I can possibly hold, and drink a full bottle of water. Now I almost feel sick. I decide to walk around and check for anyone in the cabins out back. I need to make certain I've searched everywhere. Just as I suspected, they are also vacant. The five outbuildings they use to store equipment and supplies seem devoid of recent activity. The plants in the greenhouse are dead or dying. But it's obvious some of the tools have been removed from one of the smaller sheds nearest the Headquarters building. I have no idea which ones, just that there are empty hooks in suspicious places on the wall. I didn't really pay that much attention on our tour to be able to figure it out. The gasoline cans are all gone, too.

Before leaving, I decide to return to Headquarters to retrieve all the vehicle keys. One by one, I try each of them in the vehicles that had been deserted. None of them will crank. The gas gauges read empty. It is the same for the ATVs parked nearby.

CHAPTER 8

I take the same precautions in leaving Camp Correll that I had used in approaching. Before I leave the front porch of Headquarters, I scan the tree line as far as I can see, but I cannot detect anyone. Nothing is amiss… yet everything is.

The large backpack I wear is actually too big for me. I have stuffed it to the gills, but since most of the items are dehydrated, the pack is fairly light. The powerful flashlight I had picked up in the Headquarters Building is clipped to the outside of the pack. Two large bottles of water are the heaviest items I carry inside my new pack. My walking stick and packaged provisions from Jason were right where I had left them. My newly-filled canteen balances well with the one I had stashed here when I went exploring. One rests by each of my hips, so that helps. I stuff Jason's food packets into a side pocket in my backpack and take my walking stick in my free hand. I look back toward the compound, but there are still no signs that any other humans are around. The birds are still singing, the pair of squirrels is still scurrying up and down the trees and they have even been joined by a third. The new addition is busily scratching through the leaf litter in pursuit of last fall's acorns.

Turning away, I sigh with a measure of relief and begin my journey back to the campers. It remains a mystery what has happened to the workers at Camp Correll; but the entire area appears to be deserted. At least I had been able to get in and out without any problems. Maybe it would be safe enough to come back through this way with the campers. If we are all careful, that is. We would have shelter, plus there is enough water and dehydrated food to feed us and replenish our supplies before we attempt to hike out.

I am consumed with my thoughts on the return hike. What could have happened to the camp workers and owner? What about the missing vehicles? Who had siphoned off the gas from the ones that remained? Could that have been done by the same person or persons who had trashed the mess hall and taken the lion's share of the food? This area is so isolated, it had taken nearly three hours just to drive the dirt roads from the nearest village to Camp Correll, and that village wasn't even where the airport was located.

Maybe one of the workers trashed the food and took off, and then the others went after him. People go crazy sometimes; you hear about it on the news almost every day now, it seems. The isolation could have gotten to one of them. I don't think I could take it long-term myself.

Then I think about what Jason had told me, about the gunshots last year and rumors of drug smuggling. But as vast and relatively isolated as this National Forest is, why would anyone choose it for such a purpose? Didn't drug dealers or whatever they were need customers? Why travel through a huge expanse of forestland, using bad roads - or in many cases out here, no roads at all - to move their cargo? It would make it so slow because of the terrain, even if they stuck to the service roads. It just does not make any sense, at least not to me. Of course, I don't have any idea how drug smuggling works. Still, I keep my footsteps as quiet as I can manage, with all the dry leaves and twigs seemingly everywhere. No rain on the trip had meant good weather for the kids, but it's a real hindrance if you are trying to be quiet.

After nearly an hour of travel, I feel like I'm far enough away from the Camp Correll complex to stop and sit briefly for a break. I find myself wishing I had worn my watch on this trip. I had wanted to relax as much as possible for these two weeks, which included not bringing a timepiece. I look at the shadows cast by the trees around me and guess a time of somewhere around two or three in the afternoon. I know I need to make better time, so I decide to resume my hike after only a few minutes. I don't feel the need to eat anything, since I had gorged myself back at the mess hall. I should be able to go without stopping until I get back to the campers, sometime after dark – except for a couple of quick bathroom breaks, naturally.

As I begin to regain my feet, I hear a cry of pain that is emitted so loud and sharp, and so completely unexpected, that my quick swivel toward the direction of the sound causes me to lose my balance and fall over backwards. I have a momentary sense of panic as the hair stands up on the back of my neck. It was a frightening sound; the sound of something horribly unpleasant happening to someone. As I scramble to stand, I begin scanning the far horizon in search of the person who had cried out. I wait for another sound to give me some bearings, my gaze darting amongst the forest that lay to the north, searching for a speck of color or some movement. There is nothing to see but trees and more trees. The voice had sounded like a man's, but he was definitely in distress. I know it is possible that the situation could be dangerous, but I have to see what is happening. This is too close to Camp Correll.

I move quickly at first, jumping shrubs and fallen logs, moving toward where I thought the noise had emanated from. After a couple of minutes I slow to a snail's pace, trying to be as quiet as possible, careful of where I place each foot. There are no more noises to guide me, so I hope I am still heading in the right direction as the minutes tick by. Then, just beyond a thick clump of trees, I catch sight of a movement and spot the man who had cried out in pain.

It's immediately obvious as to why he made the noise when I get close enough to him to see him clearly. He is tied around the midsection to a large tree. He has obviously been brutally beaten and his olive skin is bruised and bleeding. His head, with its neatly trimmed pepper-with-a-sprinkling-of-salt hair, is leaning back against the tree trunk, as if for much-needed support. His breathing seems labored, as I watch for the shallow, regular rise and fall of his chest. He is dressed in a tan t-shirt, camouflage cargo pants, and hiking boots. On his belt, next to an empty gun holster, I can just make out something oblong and shiny gold. It takes me only a moment to recognize that it's a badge.

He groans in misery. "Why don't you just go ahead and get it over with?" he mumbles.

A very thin man with shoulder-length brown hair, just under six feet tall, rises to stand in front of his captive and looks him in the eye. "Hey, don't you worry about that, Rios. You'll be dead soon enough," he chuckles.

Another man strides into view. He is shorter, but very muscular, and clearly of Latino origin. "Get to work digging the grave, Harrison. Do it over there, away from all these damned roots," he points, barking orders in an accent so thick it's very hard for me to understand him. "I'm not going to be late for the handoff because of this guy. We have worked too hard, and there is too much money on the line."

The man called Rios groans again and closes his eyes.

"Call me when you are done so I can bring him over to you." He moves close to the man tied to the tree and shoves the barrel of a large handgun into his victim's bruised cheek and watches him wince in pain. "Then I will shoot him in the back of the head, you can cover him up, and we will get out of here."

"Why do I have to do all the hard work, Carlos? This isn't fair. You never do any manual labor," the thin man complains in a voice that is decidedly high-pitched.

Carlos turns slowly to face his companion, the anger on his face evident even from a distance. "Because I am the one in charge, you idiot, that is why. Just go do what you are told," Carlos orders again, this time with added authority and a not-so-subtle hint of a threat.

The man called Harrison doesn't have any further questions. He simply picks up his shovel and walks toward a small, sunny clearing a short distance away, whistling all the while.

I am terrified and have no idea what to do. My capacity for rational thought has temporarily abandoned me. I know there is nowhere to run for help, and no one to get help from out here anyway. It is entirely up to me. While the man named Carlos continues to talk, threaten, and periodically punch the officer, I carefully place my backpack and canteen belt on the ground, so that my actions produce no sounds. Then, clutching my walking stick, I dart as quietly as possible from one tree to the next, until I'm close enough to clearly hear the groans and heavy, pained breathing of the poor man tied to the tree.

"You know, Rios, your father married your American mother and moved away, but he still has a few extended family members back in Columbia. I know where they are. I may have to pay them a visit when I get back home. I'll be sure to give them your regards," Carlos laughs.

Cautiously, I peer around both sides of the wide oak tree I am hiding behind, checking on the locations of both Harrison in the distance and Carlos. I glance briefly at the defenseless victim and see he appears barely conscious. Suddenly though, to my surprise, he opens his eyes slightly; but they rapidly grow wider. Due to the angle of his head, he is looking directly at me.

I'm in a panic, completely terrified that he is going to inadvertently react somehow to seeing me and give away my presence. I quickly think to motion to him for silence with my free hand, then angle myself back flat against the tree, out of sight. I wait a few seconds to see if the tortured man will say anything to give me away, but nothing happens. The walking stick and the element of surprise are my only weapons. I'm so nervous I can hardly stand it. I have never gotten into a real fight before in my life. I slowly lick my tongue across my lips to try to ease my nervousness. I take a deep breath then dart from cover toward my target.

The officer tied to the tree must have guessed at both my plan and the timing of it. He calls out to the Latino man in front of him in a low, broken voice, "Hey, Carlos, look at me."

The distraction gives me time for the five strides I need to cross the open distance between us.

Carlos never sees me coming. I reach him with my walking stick poised for the attack. In one grunting motion, I throw all my force behind my swing, and the wood strikes him across the side of his head. Blood spurts out as he falls into the cushioning leaf litter without ever having uttered a sound.

Wild-eyed with adrenaline, I glance quickly toward Harrison, who already seems to be taking a break from his work. His head is rotating in our vicinity; so I quickly duck behind the tree that also conceals the officer, my back pressing up against him as I try to avoid being seen. I desperately clutch my walking stick and shift it lengthwise in front of me so that it will not be visible from the thin man's vantage point. I'm trying to reason with myself and calm the pounding of my heart, which is so loud I'm certain it must be audible for several miles in every direction.

"Carlos!" Harrison calls out, breaking into a run. He must be able to see his partner's legs protruding oddly from the base of the tree. As the man approaches, I quickly side-step around to the far side of the tree. I am carefully keeping pace with Harrison's frantic steps, so I can avoid being seen. I must have the element of surprise again in order to stand a chance.

Harrison reaches his partner and sees the blood pulsating along the side of his head and streaming down across his face. The head has an abnormal indentation at one temple. The thin man kneels. "Carlos! Carlos!"

When the Latino shows no response, Harrison looks up at the officer. "What did you do to him, Rios?" he demands, rising.

I dart from cover behind the tree faster than Harrison is able to get to his feet. He sees me out of the corner of his eye and turns his head away while simultaneously throwing up an arm defensively to block me. I smash the arm with one determined blow from my walking stick. I can hear the crack of the bone.

He screams in pain and falls back into a sitting position against his partner's limp body, cradling his broken arm. Adrenalin rushing through my body, I neither hesitate nor show mercy. After all, they had obviously shown none here. My second blow is directed firmly at Harrison's head, which jolts to one side with the sound of a sickening snap.

I feel my body begin to shake from the combination of adrenalin and fear as I look around for another attacker, ready to swing my weapon again. Seeing none, I step closer to the man imprisoned on the tree. "Is there anybody else?!" My teeth are clenched, and I continue to scan the area.

"I'm not sure. They talked about another man, the last guy's brother. But these two are the only ones I've seen," he says in a raspy voice.

That does nothing for my nerves. There could be others, anywhere out there. We have to go. *Now.*

"I'm going to cut you lose; just hang on." I lean my walking stick against the tree and examine the ropes. I pull the little meat cleaver from my back pocket. In a few swift, firm blows, the knife chops through the ropes, and with the final strike it firmly embeds itself in the tree's thick bark.

As the ropes fall to the ground, so does the officer, landing unceremoniously across the two broken men in front of him. Abandoning the knife, I kneel by the man and help him to rise, though only with difficulty. His body frame carries muscular pounds. Average for his height, I suppose, but heavy for me. Once I have him on his feet, I steady him against the tree by pushing my weight towards him. The task is made more difficult by the fact that he is almost a head taller than I am.

"Hey, you've got to help me out here, mister," I manage to say through gritted teeth to the slipping form in my grasp. I let go with my right hand and lift his chin away from my shoulder as he moans in response.

"You're way too big for me to carry, so you have to stand up. I know you're hurt; but you have to try, please. I need you to help me."

I lean away slightly as I feel him trying to right himself. I continue to press my hands up against his shoulders for support until he raises his own hands to grasp my elbows. His dark brown eyes open halfway, looking weak but not quite as bad as I had thought they would in his condition. I slowly back off from supporting him, allowing him to lean back against the broad trunk of the tree and stand on his own. I watch intently, ready to spring forward should he start to slide or tip to one side or another.

He closes his eyes for a moment and coughs, which obviously hurts him badly. It makes me wince for him. Then he begins moving his limbs slowly and carefully, one by one, as if making sure they still work. He uses his tongue to check his teeth. It looks to me like they are still in place, even though his mouth is bloody. He straightens himself and takes a cautious step out from the tree, keeping one hand on it for balance. He bends away from me and coughs, spitting out as much of the blood as he can without falling over from the effort.

I watch him, concerned about his condition, but even more worried that somewhere the two bad guys have a buddy or more, who will soon come hunting for them. I look down at the pair of prone figures on the ground, searching for movement from where I stand. I know that with the situation being what it is, both the officer and I, not to mention the kids out there somewhere in the forest, would likely be better off if I made sure the two men were dead. My left eye twitches at the thought. I have never killed anything bigger than a spider. And more often than not, I would capture the occasional spider in my apartment and place it outside in a nearby shrub where I believed it would be happy. I turn away, knowing I cannot do anything more to them unless they are presenting an immediate threat. At the moment, they both appear lifeless. They are at least too badly injured to cause anyone any harm for some time to come.

The officer is standing more or less upright now, although still bracing himself with one hand against the tree.

I step forward, closer to him and speak firmly to gain his full, undivided attention. "We've got to get going. And there's no way out except to walk. And don't even think about asking me to leave you behind, because it's never going to happen. So don't waste your breath."

I see I have his focus with those statements. He looks as if he has no confidence in his ability to follow my directive, though. I square my shoulders. "Look, I'm here with a large group of kids. They're waiting for me to get back from scouting the big camp back there." I hook a thumb in the general vicinity of Camp Correll. Surely he must know of its existence.

"There's no time to lose. I'll help you. Hang on a second." I reach over and pick up my walking stick and hand it to the officer.

"Use this. Use it on one side and me on the other. Just let me go get my bag," I say as I turn and leave him to dash over and retrieve my bloated backpack, which I shift easily to my shoulders. I quickly strap on my canteen belt. Water is doubly important now. Returning to the man's side, I take his pack away from him as he is closing the top compartment and I help him to his feet. I struggle with his pack; it is smaller than the one I found at Camp Correll, but heavier, too, and rests at an awkward angle over the top of my own backpack. I remove it and decide to carry it in my free hand instead.

"There. Now we're all set. I want you to take a quick drink of water." I hand him one of my canteens, and pause a moment to think as I gaze up at him. "What's your name, anyway? I'm Nicole Gerringer, but my friends call me Cole." I smile up at him with what I intend to be a reassuring expression.

In spite of the pain, he tries to smile at me. It comes out as more of a grimace, though. He hands me back the canteen. "Alejandro Rios... but everyone calls me Alex."

Hopefully, Alex's condition isn't as serious as it appears to be to my eyes. I only know some elementary first aid and no more than that. I'm fairly certain no one else in the camping group knows any more than I do, with the possible exception of Jason. We have to get back to the others before they give up on me as lost or dead and move on, leaving me behind. The man I am looking at might die if that happens, but I'm realizing quickly there is no way he can move fast enough. And I cannot risk leaving him here. I'll just have to work it out as we travel. The first priority is to simply get moving.

"Okay, Alex. To state the obvious, we've got to get out of here. I know you're in pain, but..."

"That's okay, I understand," he groans. "Just get started, I'll do my best."

I push myself up against his left side and hold onto him tightly, more afraid of him falling than that I might cause further aggravation to his injuries. If he goes down, I don't feel confident that I will be able to get him back up again. His weight is substantial on my light frame, but not as heavy as I think he should be. I realize he's doing his best to avoid leaning on me too much.

We proceed cautiously, heading ever deeper into the forest. The terrain is becoming more difficult to traverse and the trees in this area are thicker with branches and brambles that impede our progress. I stop once to remove my compass and check my bearings. We are off course to the north from the path I had taken to Camp Correll. It doesn't matter, because I know we will never reach the campers in time, not at this pace. Jason will leave early, maybe even at first light, just as I had made him promise to do. I'm guessing he will take the group on a northerly heading, the most difficult route, but also the shortest way to civilization. Or at least a small village. There are no sizeable cities around here. The girls are tough enough; they can make it.

My impatience is growing with each hour and each excruciatingly slow step, though. Sometimes I can be calm in stressful situations, but I'm worried about my niece and the other girls. The circumstances we are all in, knowingly or not, are very troubling. Everything is wrong. I am gravely concerned about the presence of the smugglers; but there is something else, something nagging at me that I can't quite put my finger on. We continue along; but I can't shake that sensation that there is something much more insidious going on, right in front of my eyes.

I'm attempting to focus my thoughts on the here and now, concentrating on each step and trying to select the best path with the firmest ground and fewest obstacles and to keep us moving in the general direction of the campers. Or at least where I project they will be by sometime tomorrow. I intend to angle over and cut them off. I can't play it safe; I must take a gamble. I'll look at everything more closely on the map later. Right now, I'm going from memory. I'm also trying to keep my senses attuned to any sounds made by other people, like the smugglers, for instance, just in case there really are more.

I snap back to the present as my foot crushes a small, dry branch with a loud crack that seems to echo. I stop us short, and I am wide-eyed as I scan the surrounding area for any pursuers who might have heard. The only sound besides the labored breathing of the man next to me is the territorial calls of a native songbird. No one else appears to be around. We pause long enough to make sure we are alone before resuming our slow journey forward.

Less than an hour later, I find myself experiencing the stress of the extra load I am supporting. My breaths are coming faster and my legs feel weak. I stop to allow us both to rest for just a few minutes, and to share a bottle of water.

I help Alex lower himself carefully to the ground. It is easy to see the relief in his eyes as he sinks back against a tree trunk.

He sighs deeply with exhaustion and pain. I kneel beside him and drink a little of the water while I wait for him to open his eyes. When he does, he looks so very tired. I feel bad for him. It would be a different situation if we were closer to civilization and medical care. I hold out the bottle of water. With a shaking hand, he takes it and gulps it down thirstily.

"We're far enough away now that I'm going to try and fix you up a little bit, okay? I'm not a doctor, but I'll do the best I can. I know a little first aid." I smile, hopefully not showing the hesitation I am experiencing. Blood isn't my favorite thing to deal with, but I can do it if I have to. And in this situation, I definitely have to.

He nods and even manages a slight grin.

I unzip my backpack and hand him a pack of dehydrated fruit. "Eat all that fruit; it isn't much." Next I remove the first aid kit and extra bandages in case I need them. "Do you need me to help you take your shirt off?"

"I think I can manage it, but thanks," he says with confidence, although his voice is weak.

As he works to remove it, I can tell it is difficult for him. Most likely he's going to be too proud to let me assist, but at least he isn't complaining about me wanting to patch him up. That part he can't handle on his own. I reach over and help him get the shirt over his head.

In spite of the fact that he has several places where I can tell bruises are already beginning to form, and some cuts with dried blood, I can't help but admire the well-chiseled muscles adorning his chest, arms, and abdomen. Wow. It's enough to make any red-blooded American woman drool. I take a good, hard swallow and a deep breath before I try to touch him. It wouldn't be seemly to be drooling like a St. Bernard while I'm trying to render aid to him.

"Here, drink some more water while I'm getting everything ready," I say as I hand him the fresh water bottle I just opened. "Take these Tylenol, too. They may not help a lot, but even a little bit of pain relief will be good for you."

He takes them without question. "Yes ma'am."

Opening an antiseptic wipe, I caution him, "I just want to warn you, this might sting, Alex."

"That's alright, go ahead," he states as though it's nothing. Maybe to him it is.

I swab the area of what looks like a knife wound as gently as I can. Strange, but I seem to be the only one wincing. His muscles tense up momentarily but then relax. There isn't a lot of blood coming out of it, which surprises me. The wound is wide, indicating to me that it penetrated more than the inch or two where the point of the knife would have broadened farther up the blade. Maybe it just didn't hit anything vital, which would be great, or maybe the wound has been there long enough that most of the blood flow has ceased by now. As it is, I imagine it's hurting, but not nearly so bad as when the knife went in.

"I'm so sorry all this happened to you. I wish I could've gotten there sooner," I say.

"I'm just glad you got there when you did. You saved my life, Cole. You're my Guardian Angel. Thank you."

I smile at that. "You're welcome."

"You know, you were pretty impressive back there. Where did you learn to handle yourself like that?" Alex asks.

"Actually, I've never done anything like that before in my life. I was scared to death."

"I never would have known. You had me fooled."

I give him a shy smile and resume my work. The hydrocortisone ointment is next. I rub it in gently over each injury I find. Then I apply an absorbent compress bandage to the worst of them, the one from the knife. It still isn't bleeding much, but I figure I should cover it just in case our hiking starts the wound to bleeding again. I hold it firmly in place with a solid wrapping of adhesive cloth tape. It doesn't look too bad, if I do say so myself. "There. How does that one feel?"

He looks better now, with what cleaning up I've been able to do, even though there's more work to be done. He's definitely more alert. He moves around gingerly, without getting up. "Hmm, are you sure you aren't a doctor, Ms. Gerringer? It is Ms., right? You aren't married, are you?"

His eyes are still looking a little on the weak side, but his gaze is too intense for my taste. "No, I'm not. And damn it Jim, I'm a geographer, not a doctor." It is only a little joke on my part; very little, apparently.

"Jim?" he asks.

"Sorry, that's an old Star Trek reference. I couldn't resist." I have to remind myself, not everyone is interested in the stars, nature, photography, or even Star Trek. Go figure; I guess it takes all kinds after all, like my Mom used to say.

With narrowed eyes, he mercifully skips over my failed attempt at humor and asks, "Geographer, huh? That's interesting. You'll have to tell me more about your work as we're marching off toward those kids of yours. Wait, how many kids are we talking about here?"

Raising an eyebrow casually, I reply, "Sixty-six." Seeing the shock, then confusion on his face, I laugh and decide I'd better explain. "None of them are mine, per say. They're from a private, all-girls school back in Georgia. I'm directly responsible for eleven of them... and one of those is my niece. There are six chaperones, one of which is me. We also have a guide from the Wilderness Expeditions Company. He's the only man with us, so he should be happy to see you. It increases the odds for him."

"Don't you mean decreases? He might not be so happy to see me come strolling in with you, arm-in-arm. You might still be helping me walk if we get back to them soon enough, you know."

At first, I just don't get it. I can be a little dense sometimes, especially when it comes to the kind of intimations Alex is making. Then it hits me, and I know I must be blushing. Damn it, I hate when that happens. "No, I'm sure you'll be fine by then; and that isn't what I meant at all. All I meant was, he won't be the only male in the group anymore. It probably isn't easy for a young man like that being around a bunch of young teenaged girls. He's outnumbered, is what I meant."

"Oh, I see," he replies with a grin.

He has a really intriguing smile. Okay, snap out of it again, Cole. "Where else does it hurt?" I ask but immediately set to work wiping away the rest of the blood on his face and neck without waiting for a response. I can see with this guy I'm going to need to maintain my composure. The only way I can think of to do that is by focusing on something – in this case, trying to treat his injuries as best as I am able.

"Pretty much everything hurts at least a little," he says, still smiling.

That's alright, smile as much as you want. I'm not going to look at your face anymore. After a couple of minutes of wiping and bandaging another wound, this one minor, I've done about all I can. "Okay, you're clean now. But I can't do anything about those bruises. Does it feel like anything might be broken or sprained?"

"No ma'am. I think I'm fine in that respect. I don't know what kind of a geographer you are, Cole; but you make an outstanding Florence Nightingale."

"Do you have another shirt in your backpack?" I ask. I am determined to remain all business. At least for as long as I can, anyway. It would help if I didn't find him so attractive.

"Yeah, I have a few of them in there."

"Good, 'cause this one's toast. Even if I beat it against a rock all day I'll never get the blood stains out." I look at the label. "Hey, alright, it is one hundred percent cotton. Sounds good to me. I'll just bury it here under the leaf litter. Maybe it'll just decompose," I rummage around in his pack and pull out a tightly rolled tan t-shirt.

"Excuse me?" He asks with a measure of surprise.

"Hey, if I can find a logical enough reason not to carry extra weight, I'll take it, no matter how small the weight is," I explain as I begin to scoop out a shallow hole by hand. The dirt is powdery dry on top, but quickly changes to an almost rock-hard quality below. "We're supposed to hike out everything we take in on this trip. You know, save the environment." I mound the loose soil partially over the shirt then pile on leaves, pine straw, and a couple of substantial tree branches that were lying nearby. There always seem to be plenty of branches lying around everywhere I go. "There, that should hide it, just in case."

Wiping off the dust from my hands onto my pants, I help Alex get his clean shirt on, being as gentle as I can. Then I retrieve the backpacks and stand up to put them both on my back this time. Although it is awkward, I think it'll let me support Alex better. "Okay, it's time to get going. We won't be able to catch up to the others today, but we can get a little more ground covered before nightfall." I extend a hand to him.

Alex uses my walking stick more than my hand to get to his feet. I watch him closely as he wobbles slightly before righting himself. I'm hoping his injuries aren't more extensive than what meets the eye.

CHAPTER 9

The long shadows being cast by the trees let me estimate we are already several hours off the schedule I need to keep us to for any hope of a rendezvous with the kids before they break camp in the morning. Of course, I knew that already, though. Glancing over at my new companion, it's easy to see how bad off he is. He looks pretty beaten up to me, but of course he won't admit it. He keeps saying he's fine every time I ask. I don't want to catch up to the kids but end up killing him in the process. I believe the walking has taken a toll on him; I know it has on my back.

Obviously, he needs to spend more time resting than this latest break will allow. I know when we move out he'll need for us to continue to maintain our slow pace of travel. It's going to be hard, but I have to get us on track, or at least as close to it as this injured man can manage. Yet I'm growing more concerned about him by the minute. Right now, he appears to be unconscious, leaning against a tree where he sits with his eyes closed. His complexion remains decidedly pale beneath his tanned skin. I watch his chest rise and fall. He's still breathing regularly, though. If he is asleep, I hate to wake him, but I have no doubt he needs fluids just as much as rest.

We've been here for at least a half hour. While there is no way to make it to the kids before dark, we have to get moving again. I stare at him, my face close to his, looking him over carefully before placing a hand on his shoulder to give it a gentle shake. His eyes open slowly. I hand him the water bottle so he can drink his fill, which isn't nearly enough by my estimation.

"Do you think you can eat anything?" I ask.

Alex sighs and looks over at me, still seeming a bit weak, but certainly in better condition than he was when I found him. "No. I'm really not hungry, Cole. Thanks anyway."

47

I hand him an opened bag of mixed nuts and seeds that I've been lightly snacking on while he slept. "Start with this. You have to eat, even if you don't feel hungry."

"Yes ma'am." He takes it and places a small handful in his mouth.

"How long has it been since you ate? And I don't mean the dehydrated fruit I gave you a few hours ago, I mean a real meal."

Alex shifts the food to one side of his mouth. "Early this morning. I had a big breakfast at my campsite, before I started hunting for those two poachers on my way out. I still can't believe I let those guys get the drop on me."

"Nobody's perfect. So what are you, exactly? A forest ranger?"

He swallows his mouthful before responding. "I'm a Special Agent with the Drug Enforcement Agency. We've been working with the US Forest Service for the past several months on a joint operation. We've actually had a few agents stationed here on rotation for the past six months, as soon as the scientists discovered that the Native Americans in the area were right, that they had found a cure the whole world would want.

"This is my first time being sent to this part of the country in my job," he continues. "I've been assigned to help protect that plant, the one you might have heard of in the news. It was the reason the President established the new National Forest two years ago, to help provide some federal protection for the plant. There have been sporadic episodes of drug running through this forest in the past decade or so, up until recently. We thought we had it under control six months ago. Now we think they've expanded their operations into poaching. The plants are just starting to emerge from their winter hibernation, and someone's been digging them up. The plants apparently can't be detected until they grow up above the surface in the spring each year."

"You are talking about the potential cure for Alzheimer's, right? I've heard a little bit about it. From an article I read, it not only obliterates Alzheimer's, but it has shown early indications of having some impact on reversing the aging process, too… at least in mice. I heard a couple of the researchers even got fired for testing it on themselves. It makes the brain cells more youthful in appearance and in their functions or something like that, and even seems to have an impact on other types of cells in the body, too. It's been nicknamed the Fountain of Youth plant." I sit down cross-legged in front of Alex.

"That is only a rumor… speculation. But then, they don't tell us everything. We were told to protect the area where the plants grow at all costs and keep everyone away." He pauses to put more trail mix in his mouth.

"Are you out here all by yourself?"

"Yes. We're very short-staffed, what with government spending cuts and all. They were sending someone in to partner with me, but something must have happened because she never showed for our shift. I was actually on my way out, because with an operation like this, you need backup. I came across those guys back there by accident. Well, sort of by accident. Even though we're not supposed to be out here alone, I saw evidence of recent poaching. So my brilliant plan was that I would try to stop them before they could dig up any more plants. This stuff is important. I've seen people with Alzheimer's… it's a terrible disease. It robbed me of my grandmother." He puts more trail mix in his mouth.

It's a good sign that he is eating. But we have to leave soon.

"You know, when you finish that we need to get going again. I'm sorry, I know you need to rest; but I can't leave you here alone, and I can't wait around. I have to try to get back to those kids." I am pretty sure he knows I'm serious about not leaving him behind. He should by now, since I'm sure I've said it more than once.

After a swallow of water, he responds. "I know. I can make it, don't worry. And in fact, now I'll start carrying my own backpack."

I turn and take a few steps away as he continues to drink more water. I know we'll never be able to make it very far. The sun is sliding lower and lower in the western sky. Soon we'll have to stop for the night. I can't risk traveling with Alex in the dark. He's barely vertical in the daylight. And I'm not willing to take a chance on using my flashlight, knowing there could be bad people out there somewhere, perhaps even searching for us at this very moment.

This situation requires some forethought. Which way would Jason take the kids out of here? Carefully, I pull the worn map from my back pocket. He will leave with the kids sometime tomorrow, in the morning, so I will have to guess at the direction he'll take and then angle our path in such a way that we at least have a chance of coming across them later on as Alex is doing better and is able to travel faster. If he isn't substantially better by tomorrow morning, I may have to give up on my plan and hunker down somewhere with him. I'll have to tend to him instead of catching up to the kids.

After studying the map, I think my initial guess was correct. Jason will most likely take them out of the forest to the northeast. It's the shortest distance geographically, even though the terrain is rougher. The girls can make it and so can Alex. I have to believe that. I put the map and everything else back into my pack.

"Okay, let's see how far we can go before it gets too dark to see. I'll let you carry a backpack tomorrow, but you'll take mine, not yours. Yours is too heavy. Tomorrow we'll see how strong you feel, and I'll decide if you're ready to carry a backpack." I can tell he doesn't like that, but there isn't time to argue. I stuff the empty water bottle into my pack. Mine is far and away the lighter of the two packs, so I don't believe there's anything I can do to further lighten the load he will carry tomorrow. I know I'll have to allow him to carry one of the packs then, just to avoid doing some muscle damage to my own back.

He stands unsteadily, and I wait for him to stabilize himself with the walking stick before I put his arm across my shoulders. Alex looks at me with what appears to be a mixture of gratitude and frustration at having to be helped. At least we aren't going to walk more than another hour, so we should both be okay for that relatively short amount of time. I need to find a source of water before nightfall, too.

We start off slowly, of course. I am sure he must be in a lot of pain. I wish he would admit to it, though; and let me know exactly where it is so maybe

I can help him better. Most men keep too much bottled up inside… like pain, for instance. I find a fallen tree limb, long but thin, that I can use to move aside brier vines in our path, saving us the time of going around. In some areas, the briers are quite prevalent.

I estimate what feels like an hour, more or less, then find us a good place to stop for the night. At least to me, it seems good. It's a relatively dense cluster of trees with a few well-placed shrubs that should give us sufficient cover should anyone come looking for us. Just in case. At least, that's my hope. Alex lowers himself gingerly to the ground.

I haven't known this man very long, but I'm sure of what his reaction will be to what's coming next. He won't be happy about it, but it has to be said. "I'm going to leave you here while I go searching for water. We're going to need more than what we've got left."

"Cole, I can come with you. I'm really not that bad off."

"Yes, you are. And you're staying here. I'll be back before you know it," I say, placing the backpacks on the ground next to him.

"No, I can't let you do that." He begins to rise.

I simply put a hand on his shoulder and push down; stopping him with surprisingly less effort than I had thought it would take. "See? You need to rest. I hiked out all this way and farther, by myself. I can handle this." I squat in front of him. "Look, I know you are probably used to being the strong one and handling everything yourself, most likely. But things are different now; you're hurt, and I need you to get better. Walking around unnecessarily isn't going to make you better. Stay put and rest."

Getting to my feet, I add for good measure, "And I mean it. You aren't in charge here, in case you haven't figured that out already. I don't mean any offense, that's just the reality of the situation. At least for right now it is, anyway."

"Understood," he looks up at me. "And I had already figured that out. Even if I hadn't, I'm completely in your debt. You saved my life back there, Cole. You could have easily been killed right along with me." He pauses then asks,

"Why did you do that? Why did you risk your life to save mine? The odds were totally against you, and you didn't even have a gun."

Shrugging, I reply, "I didn't need one. And the odds weren't totally against me. The way I saw it, they were in my favor. I had the element of surprise. Those guys had no idea I was there."

"And no idea who they were dealing with," Alex says with a slightly-crooked smile.

I return his smile this time, before heading off deeper into the woods.

Surprisingly, it takes me less than a half hour to find some water. It's a small stream, and the water looks clean enough. I fill the bottles and canteens but use the filters, just to be sure. You never can tell about the purity and safety of water anywhere nowadays. Then I head back. It's nearly dark and getting hard to see where I'm putting my feet.

Alex is waiting for me right where I left him. He must be somewhat better, because I can tell he is on alert. He has already spotted me before I see him. I look around me before going into the cluster of trees. We seem to be alone.

"Here you go, Alex," I say as I sit down beside him and hand him a bottle of water.

"Thanks," he replies softly.

He actually has a slight grin on his face. Surely it's a good sign that he keeps on smiling. "We need to settle in for the night as soon as we've finished eating."

I reach into my backpack and pull out two packs of jerky. "Here you go; eat this. I'll stay up a while to keep watch."

I can see he is about to protest, so I cut him off before he's able to get started. "You need to rest a lot more than I do. Go ahead and get some sleep. I'll wake you up when I can't stay awake anymore. Don't worry; it won't be long. I'm a real sleepy-head." I smile and start eating my jerky slowly. Eating will help me stay awake. I really am so very tired.

He sighs in apparent resignation. "Okay. But you have to promise to wake me up. I'm trained for this kind of thing, and you're just a civilian. No offense," he adds quickly.

I'm probably getting on his nerves by now. I can understand that… sometimes, I get on my own nerves. I move the petite bite of jerky to one side of my mouth. "None taken. I'm not a crime fighter and I don't want to be. I admire people like you who keep the world safe for the rest of us. And it's a job I don't ever want to have; it's too dangerous and demanding. I promise I'll wake you up in a little while."

Alex smiles again, a little broader this time. He has a nice smile, kind of crooked, a little skewed to one side. I find him quite attractive, too. But we're in a serious situation out here, so I know that is the last thing I need to be thinking about. I watch Alex as he reaches for his water; he isn't wincing as badly when he moves as he had earlier in the afternoon. He finishes his jerky quickly and lies down in the pine straw. Sleep comes almost instantaneously for him.

At least now I'm no longer afraid he's going to die on me; that has been my biggest fear for most of the afternoon. I'll be glad when he's able to carry his own pack, though. Or at least when he's just able to move faster. That's the most important thing, now that he seems to be on the mend, that is. I have to catch up to the kids. I am so worried about them being out there without me. I'm not a great outdoorswoman or anything, but it's the not knowing that's getting to me. Lots of people have accused me of being a control freak at times; I guess they're right. Hey, at least I can admit to it.

As the night wears on, it becomes a real struggle to keep my eyes open, as tired as I am. I have nearly finished the packet of jerky. Soon it will be gone, and there won't be a distraction to help keep me awake. Plus, I don't believe anyone is after us, at least not in the dark. And if those two bad guys are dead, like I assume they probably are, they won't be telling anyone else about Alex and me. I continue nibbling on my jerky for another half hour, until it is finally gone. I lean my head back against a tree trunk, but only for a minute… then I'll get up and move around for a while.

Simultaneously with the sound of a loud twig snap, my head slouches over to my shoulder suddenly; and I jerk myself awake. What was that? Was it a real sound or in my dream? Dream... oh, no, I fell asleep! I wasn't supposed to do that. I can't afford to do that. Is there someone out there? I listen for a couple of minutes and don't hear anything besides a few crickets. It must have been a dream. I look over at Alex and see him sleeping peacefully.

Well, I'm awake now, for sure. I can't tell what time it is. I try to remember the timing of the moon phase we're in now, what time of the night it would be at this location, with the stars positioned as they are right now; but I can't seem to recall. Besides, we are nestled in amongst trees which are blocking my view of the stars and the moon, if there even is one. I think it is so low in the sky right now it won't matter anyway. I stand up and walk around in our sheltered area slowly, first peering out through the trees and then staring out into the darkness. I still don't see or hear anything unusual. I sit again and let out a deep sigh of relief. I have to remember it's like with the kids – I am responsible for someone other than just myself. Alex needs protection right now, too.

About another hour is all I can take. My head keeps flopping over as I doze, then I'm startled awake again. It's all too aggravating; and it seems useless to think there's any way I'm going to be able to stay awake any longer, no matter who is depending on me.

I gently shake Alex's shoulder. "Hey, I'm sorry; but I can't stay awake anymore. You're going to have to take over. If you need to sleep, though, please keep sleeping... you need your rest. I really don't expect there's anyone out here but us." I don't wait for a response. I sink down beside him and close my eyes. I fall asleep without knowing if Alex stays up or not. I am too tired to care at this point.

Pain in my left arm wakes me. I open my eyes and try to move my fingers. Immediately I can feel the numbness, then the pins-and-needles sensation starts attacking. I lift my head and sit up, rubbing my arm.

"Here, try one of these."

The voice startles me. I turn to see Alex sitting nearby, holding out a granola pack and smiling. His dark brown eyes are sparkling now, the weakness from yesterday mostly gone. I believe maybe he really is getting better.

"Thanks." I take the granola. "How long have you been up?"

"I stayed awake from the time you woke me up. It was only a couple of hours ago. You ended up being on guard most of the night, you know. You really shouldn't have done that. You need to get more sleep."

Finally, I get the granola pack open. It's hard to do anything with any amount of precision when you've got the pins-and-needles thing going on. "I didn't realize it was that late. Besides, you needed the rest a lot worse than I did." I am still so tired. I think I could sleep for another day, at least. But what I've said is true. "You won't be any good to anyone if you don't get some rest. How do you feel?"

"Much better than I did about eighteen hours ago. I'd be dead if it weren't for you, you know."

He's looking at me intently, in a way that makes me uncomfortable. My parents had raised my sister and me to be humble, not seeking reward or credit for what we did. And to always try to help others and do what was right.

"We already talked about this yesterday. I couldn't just leave you there to be beaten to death and shot. Besides, anybody would have done what I did."

"Not anybody, Cole, not by any stretch of the imagination. I owe you my life. I won't forget what you did," he says with a steady gaze.

I'm still a little uncomfortable; but a warm sensation is filling me, too. I'm sure he means what he said; and it's gratifying to me, even though this man is still far from a hundred percent recuperated. I manage a nod and a smile in response.

"Do I need to check any of your bandages or anything before we head out?" I ask, hoping the wounds are healing.

"I think everything is fine. It doesn't feel like I'm bleeding anymore. But far be it from me to object to having a beautiful woman check me out." He gives me a wink.

My eyes narrow at him in spite of my grin, but I don't say anything in response. It has been a long time since anyone said I was beautiful, whether he was serious or not. I slide over next to him and gently lift up his shirt to study his wounds. The bruises have darkened and deepened overnight. I touch them lightly. "Does any of this hurt?"

He's smiling at me with a gleam in his eye while I examine his injuries. "No, boss lady. I really think I'm fine. And like I said, it doesn't feel like I'm bleeding anymore."

At least not where we can see it, I consider to myself, ignoring the look he is giving me. Hopefully if there is some internal bleeding, it's minor. His face remains pale beneath his olive skin, though not nearly as bad as yesterday. I change the bandage on the knife wound, but it isn't bad. I'm able to simply refold the bandage and reuse it. Who knows what the future has in store for us, and our bandages are in limited supply.

As soon as we've finished breakfast and have gotten everything put away in our backpacks, we load ourselves for the day's trek. I have transferred everything I consider to be too heavy into his pack for me to carry. I help him put on my backpack. It doesn't seem nearly so large on his broad back, but I'm worried it will prove to be too heavy for him as the day wears on. Today is promising to be as warm and sunny as all the previous ones on our trip. That still concerns me. The campers will be careful, but clearly there are more people out here than just our group. And then there's nature… storms are still a possibility at some point, but hopefully not today. The only sure thing about the weather is that it will change, at least eventually.

"How are you feeling?" I ask after we've been walking for a few minutes. I know there must be some pain, soreness, and discomfort for him now that we have started moving around again. I am almost afraid to hear his answer. He is moving very slowly. I think my patience is going to be tested again today. I'm torn between helping this man and finding the kids. But at least the kids have the other adults, and especially Jason. I am confident he'll take good care of them all.

"I'm okay. Everything is stiff and sore, but better than yesterday. Don't worry; I'm going to try to avoid slowing you down too much today."

I glance over at him and see he is indeed trying his best, plus, he seems to have a good attitude. I need to do the same thing myself, I know. I give him what I hope is an encouraging smile. "If that backpack gets to be too much for you, just let me know. I'm trying to get you well, not make you break down."

"Break down… I don't think I'm quite that bad off. I'm really feeling a lot better. You did a good job on me yesterday," he says.

"No, I just meant breaking down as just a figure of speech. Seriously, let me know if you need a rest or water or anything, okay?"

"I will, boss lady; don't worry," he says.

"Why do you keep calling me that?" I ask with slight aggravation in my voice.

"I'm sorry, Cole. I don't mean it as offensive, just respectful." He raises one eyebrow and isn't smiling now. "You are the boss, in more ways than one. What you've done for me… you have my complete respect and admiration. That's what I mean when I call you 'boss lady'."

"Oh… okay, then, I guess. But you can just call me Cole, and that'll be good enough." I give him a sideways glance, "Or you can just leave off the 'lady' part."

He smiles at that. "I'll try my best, boss."

We trudge along until about noon. He isn't putting much of his weight on me. He's only using me for balance now. The forest has been really dense all morning, providing us with deep shade. That helps us both to keep cool and to preserve our water supply. The terrain is becoming hillier and more difficult for us to traverse. We will need more water by day's end. We stop to take a lunch break, and eat jerky and dehydrated fruit and drink plenty of water. I know from the map that we should come across a water source before the day is over, if not sooner. I especially am determined to be sure that Alex drinks plenty of water.

Alex decides it's time to resume our trek before I think he should, but he doesn't listen to my protests. "We have to find your campers, remember? And I'm thinking I can walk the rest of the afternoon without leaning on you. I'll just be using the walking stick."

"Alex, I know I need to get back to the kids; but I want to make sure you're alive when we get there. If you pass out, I'll have to drag you."

"You're not strong enough for that," he says.

"Maybe, maybe not. But it's not such an emergency that I'll leave you behind. Don't even try to argue with me about it, either. You'll lose." I resettle the heavy pack on my shoulders, then add mine on top of it and move off.

"I can believe that," he declares, under his breath.

I still heard the comment, though.

"Cole, give me one of the backpacks to carry," he calls out to me, insistent.

Walking backward as I answer, I grin mischievously and simply say, "Nope," then turn around to watch where I'm going.

"Seriously, Cole."

"No," I call back over my shoulder. "If you're going to hike without me helping you, the least I can do is carry your backpack. Besides, I'm the boss, remember?" I can hear his grumbling behind me. I'm almost enjoying this.

Our pace remains slow throughout the afternoon. I decide it's probably better not to talk too much, so we can conserve both energy and water. We hike in silence for the most part. Occasionally, I hear a low groan behind me. I know Alex is still in pain, but I know he also wants to walk on his own. It actually is faster traveling this way. I'm managing to avoid having my mind wander by keeping a sharp focus on the sound of Alex's footsteps behind me. That way, he doesn't have to feel like I'm watching him as closely as I am. His steps are irregular, but they keep coming. I still wish he would tell me everything, every ache and pain. But then, I'm not letting him know how much my back and legs are hurting, either. The double load yesterday and today, plus having Alex leaning so heavily on me yesterday, is really adding up. My feet are shuffling, and I have to be careful not to trip over roots, rocks or even areas where the ground is level and I'm just not paying attention. Maybe tomorrow will be easier for both of us. And maybe we'll be back with my group for added help. I can always hope.

Late in the afternoon, we come across what I think anyone would classify as a babbling brook, sprouting from somewhere deep underground. It is located in one of the most idyllic settings I could imagine, too; much like in a fairy tale story. There are a few large, gnarled shade trees in the tiny meadow, which is lush with greenery and wildflowers stretching several feet outward along both sides of the water. Dense forest rims the tiny piece of paradise. Birdsong fills the air, as does the light scent of perfume from the flowers. The plants farther out are more scorched from the heat, lack of rain and absence of close influence from the brook. I remove the backpacks, and we settle by the water to fill our canisters. I produce the filters for treating the precious liquid.

"Are you sure we have to treat the water here? It looks so clear and we're so far from civilization. Can't we just scoop it up in our hands?" Alex wonders aloud.

"You never can tell about water anymore, even though this obviously comes from underground," I assert. "I'm sure a hundred years ago it was different, but humans have polluted just about every corner of the globe now. It's such a shame. I got into geography to try and make a difference in the world, to save it, to save the environment and animals... from humans, really. Instead, I have a government job where I sit in a windowless cubicle and make maps all day. I don't do anything to help the environment except volunteering for an annual litter cleanup." I don't know why I suddenly decided to share that with a stranger.

"Participating in a litter cleanup is probably more than most people do. I'm ashamed to say it's more than I do. I never give it much thought, aside from recycling what I use when I'm in a place where they have the facilities for it." Alex surveys the area around us as if he never really saw it when we came into this meadow a few minutes before. "This is beautiful; and it's worth protecting. When they discovered that Alzheimer's plant, they decided to protect it and this forestland. From humans," he smiles.

"The government said that if they hadn't stepped in, people would have trampled everything to get to that plant. But it looks to me like they haven't done a whole lot besides giving it a name. My group was supposed to be the only ones with permission to be in here," I say in a whisper.

"I think you're right about that. And hopefully they'll do more to keep the poachers out of here once we get back to civilization and report on what's happened," Alex states with confidence.

After the water has filled our containers, we consume all we can hold then refill our water supply again. Using what I have learned from Jason about plants, I harvest a meal's worth for us and we eat them raw. I am still hesitant to build a campfire. Besides, I don't have any cooking utensils with me and the nights are not cold, so there's really no need; especially since I'm not all alone out here.

When our hunger is satiated, I harvest more plants, rinse them clean and place them in a bag inside Alex's backpack for use the next day. That is when I see the gun. I decide not to mention my animosity for the weapons and instead allow myself to feel gratitude that he has one. It may make a difference sometime.

Alex is preoccupied looking at some of his wounds and didn't notice what I had seen. "Hey, do you know what would really help you? This water is chilled, coming from underground like it does. It would probably do your body some good, especially wherever you're sore. You could take off your clothes and soak a while."

That got his attention. "Take off my clothes?" He looks shocked.

I beam deviously, on purpose. "Don't worry, I won't look. Seriously, it would give me time to scout our surroundings. I can get up someplace high and see if I can catch any sight of the girls."

My suggestion darkens his expression. "No, I don't think that's a good idea at all. I don't like the idea of you going off by yourself. It isn't safe. I don't need to soak anything, so you can just stay right here with me."

It's easy to tell he believes he has the final say in the matter. He doesn't know me very well yet, obviously. I let out an audible sigh.

My eyes narrow momentarily. "There's nothing to be concerned about. I won't go far. You'll have about an hour at the most, maybe a little less. Then I'll be back, so make sure you're decent by then. I'll also be scouting out a place for us to camp for the night. It's getting late and we won't get much farther, but I don't think we should stay out here in the open."

He watches me stand, and I can tell he isn't happy. "Just soak whatever parts of yourself you feel comfortable soaking while I'm gone. I won't be far away."

"What if you come across someone?" He is clearly concerned, but surely he must know he can't stop me and couldn't hope to keep up with me.

"I'm a whole lot more likely to come across a bear than one of your bad guys," I reply before thinking about it. Then I realize I haven't been giving bears much thought lately. Even though we have been surprised not to have seen one for our entire outing, I need to be more aware of the possibility, for sure. That's the main reason Jason carries a gun, with lots of ammunition to spare.

With a hard swallow, I straighten my back. "Just keep your eyes and ears open. Everything will be fine. I'll be back before you know it." This time I don't smile; I just turn away. Taking a running jump on the moist ground, I hop over the brook easily enough. I make a point of not looking back until I'm out of his sight and it takes an effort, peering between the trees, to see him.

It isn't long before Alex is lost to my view amidst the deepening forest. I'm trying to be careful to watch for signs of bears. The man I left by the water would probably be more at risk than I am. Jason taught me what to look for; and Alex is in the open, wounded and slow moving. He is also sitting by what may well be a popular watering hole for the animals in this area.

And on top of all that, I told him to take off his clothes and soak. I probably shouldn't have left him alone. That doesn't stop me, though. The thought of those girls out there, somewhere, is what most concerns me. Yet I can't stop worrying about Alex, too.

I have my bowie knife holstered on my belt and the walking stick in my hand. Alex has the gun in his pack in case I can't get back to him in time. Realistically, it is unlikely that anything will go wrong. Of course, who would have thought the events of the past few days were realistically possible? Certainly not me. Otherwise, I would never have agreed to come along on this trip. No, that's not true. I would have still come, if for no other reason than to watch over Elise. And now there's Alex who needs me. He is right; if I hadn't come along when I did and hadn't made the decision to jump into the middle of his pending execution, he would be dead right now. No, I would definitely still come on this trip, with no hesitation.

The time seems to tick slowly by as I walk. I realize that progress made hiking on my own isn't really all that much faster than walking today with Alex. He's in good shape in spite of his injuries, and he's doing an excellent job of traveling faster than he probably should. We are very likely moving about as fast overall as the girls are, since we aren't stopping as often, or for as long as they tend to do. That gives me cause for hope and lightens my spirits substantially.

Climbing a very steep hillside, I have to use my walking stick for traction. At the top I'm above most of the surrounding land, but it isn't much of a vantage point. I find I'm unable to see much of anything due to my surroundings – trees and hills, seemingly without end. I consider momentarily trying to climb a tall tree, to get even higher up, but I know it wouldn't do me any good. The girls could be close by, but clearly I wouldn't be able to spot them what with all the extensive vegetation.

I wait for my breathing to slow to normal and then get as quiet as I can. The only sounds I hear are those of the creatures surrounding me. No human voices or twigs snapping underfoot; nothing… despite the fact that I am listening very closely. I want so desperately to hear the girls somewhere out there.

The futility of searching for them in this huge expanse of nature finally hits me. I look up at the blue of the sky for some divine inspiration or maybe simply consolation. I turn to leave, but stop and look up again. Something is different about the sky. It isn't the clear, deep sapphire blue it has been for almost two weeks. It is softer, more like the skies back east when the humidity is up, kind of hazy. The wind has picked up some, too. I realize my skin has felt less like dry paper today than it has been feeling for the past two weeks. There is moisture in the air now. To the west, there is a small white cloud, floating slowly along, all by itself. How long will that be the case? With enough heat and moisture, the atmosphere will destabilize and coalesce into thunderstorms. With thunderstorms comes lightning. At certain times of the year, the west is notorious for dry thunderstorms - lightning and little to no rain. Numerous forest fires are started that way each year.

I take a deep breath and decide it's time to head back. I manage a controlled slide most of the way back down the hill. It's nearly impossible to do otherwise. I lose my balance at the bottom and nearly topple over in a summersault. Even though I am deep in the wilderness, old habits die hard… I still glance around reflexively to see if anyone saw my clumsiness.

That hill would be good to have at our backs for the night. The base of it where I stand now is flat, steep, and has relatively few trees. It's probably the best we will be able to find under the circumstances and it will have to do.

Now I just have to get back to Alex and get him across the brook, hopefully without getting his shoes wet. I wonder if he decided to soak his body in the brook like I suggested. I hope so. It should help his muscles feel better. I wonder if he is dried off and dressed by now. I think I'm returning a little sooner than I thought I might. He could still be soaking. I can't help imagining seeing him naked. It's not like I'm doing it on purpose or anything; it just popped into my head all by itself. I've already seen him with his shirt off and it's not like I'll ever be able to get that image out of my mind… no, definitely not. I'll make sure I check carefully before I get too close. I certainly don't want to embarrass him or anything, not that I think he's the type to get embarrassed about such things. But I could be wrong about that. It's a peaceful walk back to the brook and its meadow, which has fallen into shadow with the lowering of the sun in the sky.

When I get close enough to peer out between the trees, I see that Alex has already managed to get himself to this side of the brook on his own. I smile to myself. If anything happens and we get separated, maybe he's well enough to take care of himself after all. That is certainly good news. He also happens to be fully dressed, but his clothes are a bit moist in spots, indicating that he did take advantage of the water.

Alex rises to his feet when he spots me approaching through the trees. He collects all our belongings and carries them to meet me halfway. His hair is still noticeably damp.

"Hey, you certainly seem to be feeling better," I say to him, hoping he can see I am impressed.

Nodding his head, he hands me my backpack, the larger but distinctly lighter one I took from Camp Correll. "I do feel better; that cool water really did seem to help." He looks at me. "Thanks for the suggestion. All I was missing was someone to scrub my back. What did you find?"

"Nothing. I couldn't see or hear the kids. You can't see much of anything around here except trees." I know my voice plainly expresses my dejection. "I think I'm going to have to just trust the adults who are with the kids to get them out safely. It's unrealistic to keep believing I can ever find them in this damned forest."

Alex allows the walking stick I have just handed him to fall to the ground along with his backpack, and steps forward to place his hands on my shoulders. "It'll be okay, Cole. We'll find our way out and get help. If the kids aren't already out of here, that is. They'll probably beat us out, you know, as slow as I walk. You'd be able to move a lot faster without me; you know that, right?"

"Okay, you've stopped making me feel better now. Time to go," I step away from him and retrieve the walking stick, which I hand back to him. Then I grab his backpack and put in on, leaving him with mine. "I found a decent place to camp for the night. If we stop talking and get moving, we'll make it before it gets dark."

I take an angry step toward the trees and am stopped short by Alex grabbing my arm firmly and turning me to face him.

"Listen," he says in a serious voice. "I know you're worried about your niece and the others. I appreciate that you're taking such good care of me and that you don't want to leave me behind. I wouldn't have made it without you, and I'll do everything I can to help you get back to those kids."

"Okay." I look into his eyes, the anger fading from me. We're both trapped in a stressful situation and our tempers are bound to flair. I take a deep, slow breath and release it just as slowly. "Let's get going then."

CHAPTER 10

I awaken with a start at first light; actually, it's a bit earlier than that, even. It's becoming a habit for me to wake up at the first sign of dawn out here in the wilderness. I really don't like the wilderness much anymore. That isn't really accurate, though, I suppose. It's more like I miss civilization, or at least a soft bed, or even a restaurant. I would almost kill for a cheeseburger at this point. I love cheeseburgers... and pizza. I'm kind of over salads for a while, I think. I need to stop myself from thinking about the food I know I can't have; that's just making matters worse. I sit up slowly, trying not to make too much noise. I know Alex needs to rest as much as possible.

As he sleeps with his head lying on one arm, I try to watch for his steady, regular breathing; but it is too dark to see that clearly just yet. He appears to be getting stronger almost by the minute, thank goodness. Even last evening, as we ate some of the plants and roots I had gathered earlier, he consumed more than I thought he would, and he smiled even more than he had the whole rest of that day. He seems to be a happy, positive person. It'll do me good to be around him.

The birds are beginning to move around in the trees. I can hear them rustling around up above us. As the sun rises, they will be singing their little hearts out as they dart from one branch to another. I have always loved hearing them sing. It makes everything seem better and the mood lighter, at least for me. I miss their songs in the wintertime. I look forward to spring each year, watching for every little clue that the seasons are changing. The swelling buds on the earliest blooming trees, daffodils and crocus breaking through the surface in the gardens, the sounds of the spring peepers, croaking away, all are good signs. Then all the flocks will return, bringing their lovely songs with them.

After a good while, I can tell the sun must surely have risen above the horizon by the increase in the level of light all around. The hill behind us is blocking the view of the sunrise. From what I can see overhead through the tree branches, the sky looks clear, except for a little of that haze I noticed yesterday evening. Aside from the chirping of the earliest-rising birds, it is relatively quiet.

It's easy enough to hear Alex stirring behind me.

"Good morning," he says softly, sounding as though he's still half-asleep.

Turning, I see him smiling at me. "Good morning. You certainly do sound like you're feeling better." I don't want to let on what a huge relief that is for me.

"Yes," he says, stretching gently. "I do feel better. The pain is a lot less today, probably thanks to that cool water. And I'm actually hungry… starving is more like it."

"Well I'm glad to hear that." I pause just a moment to grab my backpack in order to retrieve granola bar packs for us, along with the remaining water in our bottles. "Do you think maybe you could cover a little more ground today than yesterday?" I don't want to appear too impatient with him; I know he's doing his best.

Smiling, he responds with a firm nod. "Most definitely, boss. And who knows? Maybe we'll find your campers today."

"As soon as you finish up your water, I'll take it and run back to the brook for a refill. Then we can get going."

He nods again, his mouth full of granola. I toss him the bag of nuts and seeds to munch on, too – extra protein.

When we finish our water, I leave him eating while I jog back to the brook for more water. I just wish I had more containers. Or that it wasn't quite so warm. It's too bad this brook isn't a regular stream that would be big enough for fish to live in. I was so tired of them before but would love some now, especially prepared over a fire. Jason is an excellent cook. I say a quick prayer for the kids, that God and Jason are keeping them safe.

Just as I finish my prayer, two butterflies float upwards in front of me, just having finished feeding on a flower. They are creating an invisible, twisting braid in the air as they dance. I take that as a sign that everyone is okay. I have to think that. I can't let my sister down. My niece is okay, I'm sure of it.

It's time to get moving, so I head back for the trees at a jog. When I reach our campsite later, it makes me smile when I see Alex. He has everything ready to go. He is wearing his own backpack, and I can't help but notice the gun in the holster he has strapped to his belt.

"Just in case we need it," he says, following the direction of my gaze. "We can't be too careful. After all, someone told me there might be bears in these woods." He flashes that devastating smile of his.

"Really?" I can't help but smile back.

"She seems to be a very reliable source."

"Hopefully she's not. That way maybe we won't see any bears," I say, passing him to pick up my backpack. I slip into it and hand him a water bottle.

"I don't know about that. Personally, I'd trust her with my life any day of the week," he says.

"Let's go to the left, so we can avoid this hill. It is way too steep, and I don't want to try it again. I almost fell more times than I can count climbing it yesterday," I say seriously, in an attempt to change the course of the conversation.

"Hey, you're the leader. Whatever you say, boss."

I shoot him a reprimanding look; but instead I have to smile again, because he is smiling so warmly. It's nice to travel with someone who has a good sense of humor. And it doesn't hurt that he's a DEA agent. Now that he is healing up, I feel much safer with him around. I have no plans to let my guard down, though. I believe my hearing is better than what most people have; and my eyesight is excellent, too. Growing up the way I did, surrounded by nature, I can't help feeling as if I'm sensitive to everything around me, like when I would track animals. Maybe the sensitivity is only my imagination, though. I just wish I was attuned enough to find the girls.

Once we are clear of the steep hill, the terrain becomes more passable, so that we are able to shift to the northeast again. When we stop for a brief lunch of greens and a stick of beef jerky each, I review the tattered map and attempt to figure out where we are. Using the long, steep escarpment we camped by and the meadow with the brook, I find our approximate location. I need to make sure we're still heading in the right direction.

"If we continue to the northeast, I think we'll have our best chance of catching up to them. That's where we were heading yesterday, too. I'm not going to get my hopes up, though. They have a really good head start on us, I'm sure. But the closest community outside the National Forest is up here," I point to the northern edge of the map so Alex can see. "It should be quicker for them to get out that way, even though the terrain is a lot more rugged up there."

Alex places a hand on mine. "We'll find them. Try not to worry so much. If you are close enough to being finished with your lunch, we can eat the jerky while we walk. It'll save us a little time. Your kids may have gotten a head start on us; but they will spend more time stopping to take breaks to eat, get water, and rest. Now that I'm feeling better, we can catch up by covering more ground than they can."

"You know, you're right about that. The most they have been hiking on this trip is about six hours a day, taking all that into consideration," I add, a renewed sense of hope coming over me with confirmation from Alex of what I was thinking all along.

"From the looks of this map, I'm guessing it will take a couple more days to reach the perimeter, at least. We'll find them. I promise." He smiles again.

His confidence is probably more contagious than he intended. "Let's go then," I say and slip my hand from under his as I get up, holding the jerky between my teeth while I fold the map and stuff it in my back pocket. Grabbing my backpack, I start walking. I don't take the time to look behind me to see that Alex is following; I just assume he is.

I don't hear him directly behind me; but I know he is there, somewhere not too far in back of me. The man suggested we get a move on, so I am. I hike as quickly as I can, until he calls out for me to slow down.

"Hey, hold on up there, please. I'm not that much better yet, Cole. I'm sorry."

I stop and turn to wait for him. When he reaches me, I'm busy trying to remain calm. I know I was pushing it too hard for him. I really don't want to leave him behind; but I keep wavering back and forth from assuring myself that the kids are fine to needing to get to them, especially now that this man can probably look out for himself. "No, I'm the one who's sorry, Alex, I wasn't thinking," I lie. I don't want him to feel bad that he can't keep up with me, at least not yet. Hopefully he'll be able to soon, though.

"It's okay," he says, not seeming as winded as I thought he would be. "I know you want to reach your kids. Under normal circumstances, I would be able to leave you way behind me. They keep us in good shape for this job."

I look him up and down, without really realizing I'm doing it. Under the bruises, he is quite ruggedly handsome. I remember from seeing him without his shirt on that his body doesn't carry an ounce of fat but has plenty of well-developed muscles. "Yeah, so I noticed."

He smiles that great smile of his again. Damn. I'm really starting to hate it when he does that. It makes me uncomfortably warm and tingly inside. Along with distracted and confused. All I can really come up with on the spot is that I have to change the course of this conversation. I seem to be doing that a lot lately.

"Come on," I say. "I'll keep it to a slower pace now."

I notice he has a hand on his side. I recall his largest bruise is there. Now I am concerned about him again. "Are you okay? You're holding your side. Do you need to rest?"

"No, I'll be alright. But thanks anyway." He reaches out and rubs a hand along my arm and smiles that smile that devastates my resolve so easily.

Damn it. Cut out all the smiling, can't you? "Okay, just let me know if you need to stop." Part of me wants to check him over, but I don't think I trust myself to be touching him right now. I suppose I must be over that whole episode with my ex-boyfriend, the ordeal where he left me wanting to be entirely free of romantic entanglements, as I find myself wondering what it would be like to kiss Alex. Come on, Cole. Cut it out and focus.

This time, I make sure he is close beside me as we travel along. And I keep an eye on him the whole time. I keep flashing back to the beating he was taking when I found him. I'm afraid I have reached my peak in nursing capability, though. I don't know what else I could possibly do to help him if he has internal bleeding or more extensive injuries that I can't see. I glance over periodically to look at his side. There is no fresh blood on his shirt anywhere, and he's no longer holding his side. I don't know if that's a good thing or not. He could easily be putting on a brave face for me.

We walk in silence for a while before I decide it is time for a brief rest. "Okay, let's stop here and sit on this log for a few minutes. We need a water break."

Both of us groan as we sit down, me because I'm so tired and sore, Alex because he is injured. I pull out the water bottles, and we finish them off before getting back to our feet. Time is of the essence if we are to have a chance of finding the kids. That thought just won't stop running through my head, twenty-four-seven, it seems. Wait, seven... it hasn't been seven days yet. Wow, I can only imagine how crazed I'll be if this goes on for a full week; but I know it won't. I have to be more positive. We'll find them way before then. If they even went in this direction, that is. And naturally, the sun is getting lower in the sky far too fast for me. I know it has to be too soon for him when we start walking again, because it is definitely too soon for me.

"Cole, do you want me to carry your pack for you? Just for a little while, to give your back a break. You've been overloaded for the past couple of days. I'm just offering..." Alex's voice trails off.

I realize he's trying to be helpful. "Thanks anyway, but I've got it. It's not all that bad. I'll just be glad when we stop to sleep for tonight." I sigh audibly. "I'm really beat."

"I know you are. So am I, but we'll make it. Tomorrow I might be recovered enough to carry you if you need me to. You can sleep with your head on my shoulder." He wears a broad grin and there's a definite gleam in his eyes.

Okay, now he's moved on from being helpful to a gray area. I simply smile, shake my head without any comment, and focus on the path ahead of me.

We continue to travel the remainder of the afternoon with no incidents. Alex shows every indication of doing well; but we have both slowed our paces, maybe more for ourselves than for each other. Eventually, the sun does get too low in the sky; and we start looking for a place to camp for the night.

"You know, maybe we could have a small fire tonight," Alex says. "Just for a little while. If you want one, that is."

"You know, I think since we've done without one for the past two nights, we'll be okay for a third night. If we had something to cook for dinner, then that would be different." I look around. "I believe maybe we'll have some moonlight to help us see until around midnight, but I wouldn't swear to it. It's been so hard to see the sky through the trees I haven't really even bothered looking to see if I could find the moon. But it doesn't really matter anyway. Personally speaking, I plan to be asleep by then."

Alex smiles. "What a coincidence... so do I."

We find a decent spot to sleep. The few clouds in the eastern sky float off. So do I, once I finish my jerky. I am beyond exhausted.

Early the next morning, I wake up before my companion, as usual. Even before most of the birds. I get up as quietly as I can and start walking, but carefully though, because the sky isn't bright enough to see all that well yet.

Exploring alone has all the earmarks of a good idea. I believe that sometimes I think better when I'm by myself. Alex has proven himself to be a nice and trustworthy person in my estimation, anyway. Plus, he has a side benefit. Having a second person who is armed will be helpful to our entire group. Alex is strong and, I assume, good with his gun. He will provide protection for me now and for the kids when we catch up to them. I have never liked leaning on anyone ever, even when I was growing up. It's preferable to me that I be able to take care of myself. Living alone, as I have been doing for the past four years, I have come to rely on myself. I had even taken a short series of self-defense classes at one point, right after the big break-up, when I knew I'd be living alone for the foreseeable future.

Walking along, searching for any signs of the campers, I feel safe enough. I'm not that far away, and I know Alex would come as fast as he is able if I were to call out for him. Besides, we are so far away from Camp Correll, I have very little concern that anyone seeking Alex and perhaps even me, too, is still after us. Any poachers no longer pose a threat. We are out here alone.

Those thoughts stop me short… I don't think anyone is looking for us. Indeed, someone should be looking for us. In fact, lots of people should be out there, searching. I don't know about Alex, but definitely the rest of us should be a high priority on a search list, the kids in particular. We are overdue. Way overdue. The parents of the kids should have gotten terribly worried by now, and there should be search parties coming soon. We should be seeing search and rescue planes looking for us, but where are they? Why haven't they been flying overhead? I'm trying to reconstruct everything in my head now. When was it that we were supposed to be at the airport for our return flight to civilization? We would have been in contact with all the families by cellphone at that time. We had assured them that would happen, without fail.

Thus, without those calls having been placed, the parents would have become concerned and contacted the airport first, I suppose. Then the local authorities would have been notified. Word would have been passed along quickly that there is a group of missing children out in the wilderness somewhere. They would have begun searching immediately, frantically.

Without thinking about it, I look to the sky, pale blue, but brightening slowly. Searchers by air would not be overhead this early in the morning, but it shouldn't be much longer. We need to get out into the open so we can have a better chance of being seen from above. In spite of the early hour I look around for planes anyway and notice something different. There are several clouds scattered about in the still hazy sky. They are glowing pink from the sunrise. The air is noticeably moist. There is even a little dew on the ground.

Great. It will be a warm, humid day. Yesterday was humid, too, but not all that bad. Plus, we were in the shade of the forest. Today, we need to be out in the open, in the hot sunshine, where I hope search planes will see us easily. Humidity is something the girls and I are used to, but I would prefer dry air while we are stuck out here in the middle of absolutely freakin' nowhere. In dry air, there won't be a chance of thunderstorms building. Rain would make traveling more difficult with Alex and any tracks the kids might leave behind would be washed away. I need to relax and stop worrying so much. Rescue should be coming soon, after all. As for the weather, we'll have to wait and see what happens later in the day.

After a few more minutes, I decide to go back to where I left Alex. By the time I reach him, he is just beginning to stir from his deep sleep. Good, now I won't have to explain myself. I have a feeling he would not like the idea of me going off on my own, especially without him even knowing about it.

"Hey there, sleepy head," I say cheerfully. "Let's get our breakfast and head out. We've got to be getting really close to the kids by now."

He sits up slowly and runs a hand through his short, tousled hair, then rubs his eyes. "I don't mind sleeping outside, but it would be a lot better if I had a sleeping bag, at least."

"I know what you mean. I miss mine. I never thought I would say that. But what I miss most of all is a real bed." I sigh and sit down near him to dole out the food portions for breakfast. "The air has a lot more moisture in it today; it's going to seem warmer because of it." The warmth doesn't seem to be bothering him much; but I want to let him know, just in case.

"Really? I can't tell, but maybe after we get out of here and start hiking I'll notice." Alex yawns and reaches for the granola I'm offering to him.

"I'm sure you will. It hasn't really been all that oppressively hot for the past couple of days, but hopefully it won't be too bad today," I respond. "You just be sure and let me know if you need to slow down or take a break while we're hiking, okay?"

"Don't worry, I will," he says through a mouthful of granola. "But I feel even better today. It should be a breeze."

"Just don't overdo it," I warn. "You're doing good. I don't want you to have a relapse or anything."

"I won't. But the same goes for you, Cole. And there's to be no more sneaking off without me knowing what you're up to, either."

I cannot believe it. How could he possibly know? My face must be showing my guilt as well as my puzzlement.

He points to my shoes. "Your shoes are wet, showing you've been walking around in the weeds for a while. I don't want you wandering away without me. What if you had come across a bear?"

"Well, I didn't want to wake you up. You need to sleep, and I wanted to scout the area ahead of us a little," I say as I look down at my shoes. "Besides, I didn't really give much thought to bears. I guess I should have."

"Just don't do it again, okay? Promise me, please." He is looking at me very sternly.

I hang my head, more due to the fact that I am upset with myself at having been caught than for feeling bad that I had left camp without letting him know I was going. "Okay." He is sharper than I've been giving him credit for. I don't know that I won't try to get away with it again. I'll just have to be more careful when I do it. Next time, I won't get caught.

"I'm better now, Cole. I can go where you go, at least most of the time. And especially after today, I think. I'm getting stronger all the time."

"I'm glad to hear it," I hesitate for a moment to swallow some water. "Alex, I was thinking while I was walking around out there; and something important occurred to me. Our kids should have been in contact with their parents by now, but we haven't been able to do that. The parents are going to know something's gone bad wrong on this trip, and they're going to want to move heaven and earth to find their kids. There should be search planes in the air today."

"That's a good observation," Alex says.

"They're going to be up there, looking for all of us. We have to hike out in the open as much as we can today. We have to give them every chance to see us. If they pick us up first, we can tell them about the kids; and they can start searching for them. We may be all back together before dark!" I smile as I explain it to him.

"Good, that would be great. But this is a huge area, and I don't want you to get your hopes up too high. They may not find us until tomorrow. Or maybe they'll find the kids first and have trouble spotting just two people hiking out here. It seems pretty heavily wooded to me. But we'll listen for the sound of an airplane engine or a helicopter, okay?"

"Okay. I'm so excited, Alex! I'll do my best to try to stay calm; but I can't make any promises." I smile at him and he smiles back. For the first time in days I'm really looking forward to the future with hope.

We finish eating in silence, then pack up and start walking. We stay silent through most of the day, listening. Instead of stopping for lunch, we eat as we hike. When we get to the occasional open area, I look at the sky, both for search and rescue planes and to study the clouds. They have been steadily accumulating on the western horizon, and now they are building upwards.

When I stop to study the clouds and inhale the wind deeply, Alex contemplates me with more curiosity than he can stand.

"What in the world are you doing?" he asks finally.

"Can't you smell it? The smell of rain," I reply, smiling. "Rain would be wonderful. It will take away some of the fire danger."

He tries sniffing the air, his nostrils flaring. "I don't smell anything." He looks over at me. "Are you sure? Is it possible to smell rain?"

"Yes," I say, putting one hand on my hip. "I'm positive. I grew up on a farm in South Carolina. Rain is very important there, too. It's all a part of being close to nature. I know what I'm talking about. You'll see soon enough. Let's walk while we can. There's not really any cover out here if it rains hard or for a long time. We can shelter under the trees, but eventually the rain will get through."

"Rain would be good," Alex agreed. "I could use a shower right about now."

A smile comes over me as I look at him and start walking. "Me, too! You at least had that bath in the brook. I'm starting to get ripe."

He shakes his head in disagreement. "I think you're just about perfect."

"Thanks, Alex." I don't know what else to say to that; so I just keep walking.

We have been walking for about an hour more when I hear a long, low rumble in the distance, very faint, that stops me in my tracks. "Uh-oh. Did you hear that?"

"What? I didn't hear anything."

"It was thunder, and we have no protection out here," I say with concern.

"We'll be okay. We can still go under the trees," Alex says.

"No, we can't. That would increase our chances of being struck by lightning," I respond. He looks as if he doesn't believe me.

"Lightning goes for the highest target. Around here, that would be the trees. The lightning hits a tree, travels down the trunk and into the ground. Anyone under the tree will be hit and most likely killed. So, no, we can't do that. We need to be out in the open, it's the best we can do. If you feel the hairs on the back of your neck stand up, crouch down like this." I squat on the balls of my feet in demonstration and cover my head with my hands.

"That way, you are a smaller target and the least possible amount of your body is in contact with the ground." I stand and look around again. "It isn't the best solution. It's an older and imperfect one, but it's all we can do. Unless you count prayer. Prayer never hurts."

"Okay, if you say so, Cole; but I don't know if I can squat down like that. I think you're a lot more limber than I am at the moment. Let's get going. Maybe the storm will miss us." He starts walking and then stops. "What about your kids? Do they know what to do?"

"Hopefully. Some of them should, anyway. I'm sure Jason knows what to do, though. He'll protect them as much as he can."

"Oh yes, your Jason. It sounds like there isn't much he can't do." Alex has his brow furrowed.

"Jason is the group leader. He's been doing this kind of thing for years. He works for the Wilderness Expeditions Company," I explain. "The kids will be fine with him. As good as they can be out in the wild, anyway. He has done a really good job of keeping us all safe and fed. I think he's about as knowledgeable about the wilderness as they come – and strong. It's kind of funny, too… a good number of the kids and women in our group have a crush on him." I smile at the thought of that.

Alex makes a noise under his breath that I cannot quite catch.

"What was that?" I ask.

"Nothing," Alex says as he starts walking off without waiting.

A moment later he turns to me, still walking. "But you know, come to think of it, maybe the kids have already gotten out. They would have contacted the authorities to search for you. We might get rescued before we make it out of this park on our own. I wonder if Jason will be leading the rescue party?"

"Maybe. That would be nice," I say. Alex turns quickly toward me, frowning.

Oops. That's when I realize what he said. "Well, not necessarily the part about Jason; but the part about the kids being safe and the authorities looking for us." I try to sound hopeful, although I have little faith in his idea. I just know the kids are still out here, somewhere. But maybe that's just my negativity talking.

A crack of thunder makes me duck instinctively. The western sky behind us is dark and angry-looking. The breeze coming out of the storms is cool. They seem to be strong storms and still building.

"There isn't any place to shelter, so we may just as well keep on walking," I say to Alex.

"Fine by me," he replies with a quick glance to the angry sky.

The storm continues to rumble and occasionally we can see the lightning flash in bright, jagged forks across the near-black clouds. It makes me so very uncomfortable that I can hardly hold myself together.

Alex must be able to tell I'm afraid. He walks close beside me now and reaches out to rub my shoulder comfortingly. "Try not to worry; we'll be okay. I'm sure the kids are fine, too."

"Thanks," I say as I glance his way.

After about an hour, the storms begin to die off as the sun sets beyond them. The storms are losing their energy source. I watch as the clouds cease to build and eventually start to break up, passing overhead without having deposited even a drop of rain, at least not for us, anyway.

We stop to camp for the night. I place my pack on the ground then step out from the trees we have just moved into so I can see the sky. I had smelled rain earlier, but all we had received was lightning.

"What is it, Cole?"

I jump at the sound of Alex's voice so close by my shoulder.

"I'm sorry. I didn't mean to startle you," he says, reaching out from behind me to rub my arms soothingly.

"That's okay. I guess it's nothing. I was just noticing how we never got any rain, but there was a lot of lightning. It was kind of a dry storm."

"What do you mean, it was a dry storm? It was dry for us? Maybe it rained somewhere else and didn't have enough left by the time it reached us. But then, you seem to be the expert between the two of us. I don't usually pay much attention to the weather, since I usually have to work no matter what's going on outside." Alex is looking at the sky now, too.

"Maybe, but if a storm produces a lot of lightning and little to no rain, it can start a wildfire, especially when it has been as dry lately as it has been here," I tell him.

"Well, it seems like there isn't anything to worry about right now. There isn't any fire, and the storms have gone. Let's eat and then get some rest." Alex finishes as he walks back into the trees. "Come on, Cole. You need to sleep."

I look to the western sky, wondering. What Alex doesn't know, but I do, is that it is far too soon to tell for certain. I am beat, but I don't know how I'm going to sleep tonight. It is definitely far too soon; we'll have to wait to see what tomorrow brings us on the winds.

CHAPTER 11

Indeed I was right – sleep does not come easily for me, and when it does come, all I can dream about is the kids and lightning.

Early the next morning, we decide yet again to eat while we walk. I'm still trying to keep my pace slow so that Alex doesn't overdo it. As we trudge along, I can swear, however faintly, that I can smell smoke coming in on the breezes. Surely, it must just be my overactive imagination combined with fears from last night. I decide to keep my suspicions to myself. Alex doesn't seem to be aware of anything except moving himself forward at his best possible pace.

Later in the morning, our path is overtaken by a dense section of the forest and the smell becomes masked. I allow myself to forget about it. What seems like an hour later, the forest thins just a bit, and we can hear the sound of water flowing over rocks. Alex and I look at each other and smile, as our water supplies are nearly depleted.

The stream is only a short walk from where we first heard it. The water is rushing across a bed of rounded rocks, making miniature waterfalls in several places as it rushes down a gently sloping hillside. We stop to refill our water canisters. We sit for a few minutes, allowing ourselves a brief respite. I pull out the map for a check on our location. This tiny stream doesn't show up, at least not these meager headwaters. It does continue onward from here and might increase in size as it courses along through the landscape.

"Can you tell where we are?" Alex asks.

"Not exactly. I don't know where this water goes to, or if it's even on the map. But you know, come to think of it, this might be it on the map, farther down that way where it gets wider." I point to the south. "I've been checking the compass periodically, and I believe we might be able to really start looking to see the kids sometime today. I hope so, anyway. Regardless, we're still getting really close to that village or whatever you want to call it… a crossroads, maybe."

"That's good news. Whoever gets there first can send out the call for reinforcements for the rest. We'll all be out of this before you know it, and you'll be back with your niece," Alex comments.

"That'll be great. And speaking of a reunion, I think it's time to get going," I say with a good measure of tiredness in my voice. This feels like it's never going to end. At least it looks as though we're getting near the edge of the park now. Maybe we'll get to that village sometime tomorrow, I hope.

After we have walked about another half hour, the trees thin even further and the terrain becomes increasingly rugged. I stop to allow both of us to catch our breath. That is when I notice how much more concentrated the smell is; the unmistakable scent of smoke from a fire. And it's far stronger than it was before, probably because the direction we were hiking in has now shifted more to the north, coinciding with a shift in the wind. I am sure I can even see the smoke in the air all around us, very faintly, a barely-perceptible, whitish haze that fills every bit of space.

"Can you smell that?" I ask Alex.

"Smell what?"

"Smoke. I thought I smelled it earlier this morning, but now I'm positive."

"What, do you mean like a campfire?" he asks.

"No, like a wildfire," I answer.

His brow furrows. "I don't smell anything to indicate something that big. Are you sure your mind isn't just playing tricks on you, Cole?"

"I'm positive. I know what I smell. I'm quite familiar with what a wildfire smells like. I was in a wildfire once when I was a kid. It's something you never forget."

He sniffs the air more deeply this time. "Yeah, I think so... maybe... but it might just as easily be a campfire, you know. Maybe your kids are nearby." He says hopefully and strides off, stepping around the rocks of various sizes and configurations that are embedded in the ground.

I catch up to him and notice how he grimaces when he steps over a large obstruction in his path. I take his arm to stop him. I look first at his side, then into his eyes. "What was that all about?" He can't possibly miss my expression of concern.

"Nothing. It's just a little pain in my side. It's no big deal, really."

"I thought you said before that it wasn't anything serious?" I move to completely block his path now, the potential fire momentarily forgotten.

"It only happens once in a while. It's not bad, really. I might just have a bruised rib or something, that's all."

My head shakes from side to side. "'Or something.' If you're hurting like this, you should tell me." I decide to help myself without asking. I pull on the shirt from where it is tucked into his pants and lift it up so I can examine the bruise closely. Then I place a hand on his rib cage and apply firm but light pressure, but he doesn't wince.

"This doesn't hurt?" I ask.

"No. I'm telling you, Cole, I'm fine," he says earnestly. "Certain ways I move or really deep breaths. That makes it hurt. But it really isn't that bad. And it's not like we're running a marathon or anything."

He removes my hand from his rib cage and holds it up to his lips, then kisses it lightly. A slight nervous tremor passes through my body.

"You are my angel, do you know that? You saved my life, you nursed me back to health and now you're still trying to take care of me, all while you're trying to find those kids. You're an amazing person, Cole." It appears to me that he is looking at me with genuine sincerity.

I pull my hand away from him and choose to ignore both the kiss and the burning in my cheeks. We certainly don't have time for any of this, and I'm glad for that. He's making me quite uncomfortable. And now the smell of that smoke is registering in my brain again, distracting me from having to deal with wherever this thing with Alex might or might not be going. The smoke is stronger now, carried by an increase in the wind speed.

"No, I'm just an ordinary person. Anybody would have done the same thing in my place, like I said before." I turn my back to him and pull out the map for a closer examination. Something on it that I remember suddenly stands out to me... potential salvation! "Hey, where we just got our water... if we follow that downstream, it flows due south and empties straight into the river!"

"What difference does that make? I thought we didn't want to go that way. I thought your theory was that the kids are heading north." He asks from over my shoulder.

"That isn't the objective anymore. I'm trying to find a way to keep you safe."

"What? What are you talking about?" Clearly, I've confused him. I tend to do that with people from time to time. I believe my thought processes are a little off.

"We can't keep hiking, not knowing where the fire is or which direction it's moving in; so I'm going to go find out what's going on. That way, I'll know which route we need to take and how fast we need to go. The wind is blowing this way so the fire could be coming this way, too. I can't take a chance on bringing you with me; you're still hurt. There's no possibility you'd be able to keep up with me. I can run, and you can't."

"I might be able to. And I don't like the thought of you being out there alone. If we separate, I can't protect you," Alex says with genuine concern.

It occurs to me to bring up the fact that I have been essentially protecting him all this time, rather than the other way around; he as much as said so himself a minute ago. But that would probably be a bad idea, so I suppress the urge. "I know. But if there is a fire out there, bears won't be stopping to attack me. They're going to be running for their lives. The wind is blowing in this direction, and that's not a good thing. What I need for you to do is take all the gear and head for a safe place. And the only place where it might be safe is the river."

"What about you? You expect me to just let you go like that?" Alex asks, reaching out to take my hand in his.

That surprises me at first. Then I think about what kind of person he seems to be, and I know I need to allay his fears. "Look, I'll be fine. I won't get too close. I just need to check it out. You have to head for the river. It's way south of here, but it has an oxbow...", rats, that's a term he might not know, "...a long twist in it that shoots pretty far up this way. It looks like maybe it's something like a fifteen or twenty minute walk from here, if you move quickly enough. At least that's my guestimate from looking at the map." I pull it from my pocket and hand it to him.

"The river should be wide this time of year," I continue. "In spite of the dry weather, it's running on snowmelt. All the streams around here are proof of that. If not for the snowmelt, a lot of them would be dry right now. If the fire is coming this way, I just hope the river will make a good enough fire break. Oh, and it has a really wide flood plain to its north side, too. There shouldn't be much of anything in the way of trees, so that will help stop any firebrands from drifting across to the south side of the river and starting new fires on that side, unless the wind gets too strong. And what makes this whole scenario even better is that the peak of the river's bend up this way is also marked on the map as having a ford."

Alex looks at me with confusion plainly evident on his face, so I explain.

"That means it's shallow enough to cross safely there. You know, as in fording a river. At least, I hope it'll still be crossable with the extra water from the snowmelt. You'd better get going, because if the fire is heading this way, I'll probably beat you to the river," I finish with an encouraging smile and put a hand on his arm. "I need you to do this. You have to. There's no other alternative, Alex."

I remove my backpack, but keep the canteens and my bowie knife. I hand him my pack with the water bottles included. "Just get back to the stream we just came from and follow it down. I'll hurry so I can catch up to you way before you can get to the river."

"Why don't I just wait for you here? If there is a fire, it can't be that big, not yet. We don't have to be so far apart." His expression plainly shows his worry for my safety.

"If there is a fire, it has been growing since yesterday afternoon; and the conditions out here are super tender... really dry," I correct myself. "We might not have time to outrun it, not if you're here waiting for me. If you get a head start, we'll have a better chance of making it. I'd rather have to walk farther and retrace our steps to get back to this point from the river than to have to try outrunning a wildfire and have you collapse or something along the way. Or I could even get injured while we're running together and then I'll slow us down," I add in, so he doesn't believe I'm just thinking of him as a burden or anything like that. "If I get hurt and you try to carry me then, there's no way we'll be able to get away in time. This is for just in case. Alex, the air is getting smokier; and the wind is picking up. We may not have much time. Walking is always better than having to run in a situation like this."

Alex is considering what I told him, and I know he sees the logic. I also know he is reluctant to leave me.

"If you follow the stream, I can find you again," I implore him. "Please, you need to go now."

His jaw is firmly set. He drops my backpack and the walking stick and places his hands on my shoulders. "Okay. But promise me you'll be careful. And if it turns out to be a campfire, you'll come back and get me first. Don't approach anyone. Don't trust anyone. Please."

"I promise," I say slowly. He is looking into my eyes in a way that makes me feel warm and... uncomfortable, again. So I pull away, again. "Don't worry about me, I'll be fine. I'll probably be back with you in less than forty-five minutes. Just walk for at least fifteen minutes. Then, if it makes you feel better, you can stop and wait for me to catch up to you. More than that would be better, though. I'd like you to get all the way to the river. As it is, a fifteen-minute walk should put you really close to it; so you might as well just go on all the way."

I turn and start off at a fast pace away from him before he can say anything else. I glance back a minute later, before I re-enter the forest. He is heading toward the stream at a southwesterly angle. Alex appears to be intending to intercept the stream farther to the south, in order to give himself more distance from the fire, no doubt. I step into the trees and don't look back a second time.

CHAPTER 12

I know I must have been walking for well over ten minutes; but it seems like it has been a lot longer than that, just due to my lack of patience alone. I find myself wondering how far Alex has managed to get by now. With every step, I grow more certain of the close proximity of the wildfire. I need to see where it is and how large it is. The thick, acrid smell of burning vegetation is so strong now, but I still haven't located a sufficient vantage point from which to see it. And in what direction is it moving? Lives are at stake, and the trees and hills are blocking my view. It's much easier to see things where the land is flat, like on the coastal plain of South Carolina. I miss my childhood home.

My biggest fear is that the girls are in its path and won't know until it's too late, especially if they think they are clear of it and the wind shifts. But maybe they went to the south instead of the north. Surely if they went to the north, Jason would have smelled the smoke long before now and gotten them to safety, somehow. Unless, that is, they are a lot farther ahead of us than I am projecting. In that case, they could be running this way right now. All I can control is what happens to Alex and me in the here and now. I just have to hope for the best for the kids.

I break into a slow jog because I know time is of the essence. Ahead of me lies a high ridge extending about as far as I can see in both directions. The tree cover on it is sparse, which I think will make it an easier climb. I am so wrong. My calves are working overtime to get me up it, as my hands and feet dislodge small rocks and a good amount of loose soil. I forfeit almost as much ground as I gain. I grab for each shrub or bit of weed along the way, trying to help pull myself up.

When at last I reach the top, I can see for quite a long distance, not that distance is really needed for locating what I came up here to find. The terrain expanding out below is a long, open, flat plain of high, pale grasses, blowing in the gathering winds like waves on a rough sea. Spanning down along the length of the meadow is a long line of smoke, towering high above the landscape as far to the east and west as I can see. At its base, the smoke is a mixture of yellows and oranges, tongues of flame leaping forward along the ground. It is a good-sized fire, feeding voraciously on the meadow's dry vegetation. I watch, mesmerized, for long minutes. I wait so that I can determine the fire's path. At first, it doesn't appear to be moving at all. After a few more tense moments, the reason for the apparent lack of motion becomes abundantly clear.

Unbelievable. It's moving due south-southeast, directly toward me. I watch for a moment longer, just to be sure. There is no doubt. It is rapidly consuming the dry grasses. It will likely reach the ridge I stand on in moments. There is no time to worry about where the girls might be right now. The flames are speeding across the flat land at an astounding rate as the winds continue to build. I look around me to judge the wind speed based on the movement it is causing in the trees. It looks to be gusting at least fifteen to twenty miles an hour, about half of that sustained, though. If only the gusts would cease. That's faster than I think I can hope to run. And definitely faster than I believe Alex can run.

Once before in my life I have seen a wildfire, when I was a child, as I had mentioned to Alex. Those memories flood back into my mind in a quick flash, like some unstoppable force. The fire had taken flight many miles from our farm, in drought conditions, much like here. A negligent man was burning rubbish rather than taking his trash to the county landfill. And in spite of the no-burn order that had been issued the day before.

The weather had been windy, but less so than it seems it is on its way to becoming here today. I can still remember seeing the smoke off in the distance and eventually the smell of burning vegetation, then the fear brought by bits of ash falling from the sky. My parents had packed our most important belongings in two of our vehicles, preparing to flee. Our two horses and our dogs were the only animals we could take. The cows wouldn't survive, my father told us, which had made me cry. My sister Noel's cat was nowhere to be found, hiding from the flames, our mother had said. He'll be fine, cats know what to do, she told us. We hadn't known if we could believe her, but we had no choice in the matter. Staying and searching for the feline was not an option.

By that time, the orange glow was much closer, only a few farms over. Then the airplanes began flying past our farm toward the flames, dropping water and fire retardant. A crew of firefighters came and used one of the long, bare fields of a distant neighbor's farm as a fire break for the main part of the fire. That fire break, coupled with the airplane drops and the lessening of the wind late in the day had allowed the fire to be contained before it could reach our farm.

Fighting back the deep-seated fear those memories still hold, I inhale a deep breath as I turn to flee. I know from real life experience, as well as from research when I was a student in college, just how fast a forest fire can move... easily faster than a human can run, especially uphill. And I have several hills to climb before I get back to Alex, as well as thick forestland to traverse.

The ridge I'm standing on could easily double as some kind of big kids' slide, except for the rocks and occasional trees and shrubs. I take a couple of steps down, but then begin a rapid and frighteningly uncontrolled descent. The next thing I know, one of my feet knocks against a firmly planted rock, which causes me to stumble, then fall and roll head over heels the rest of the way to the bottom.

Coughing up dirt, I bound to my feet. There is no time to dust myself off or check for injuries. There is nothing to do but hope for the best as I begin to run. Nothing feels broken as I sprint toward the base of the next hill.

Running is far from being my favorite activity, nor is it my strong suit; but there's no option now. And I cannot afford a misstep. A twisted ankle or broken leg and l will be dead, but still I have to move as fast as I can... faster than that even. Alex can only go at a comparatively slow pace, and it is impossible to consider leaving him behind. I have to move quickly to make up as much ground as I can, in order to give us a chance to have the time we need to escape the flames and reach the river. It is the only hope and the only thought occupying my mind now. I haven't seen the river except on the map. I'm praying as I run that the water source is significant enough to halt the fire's spread.

In the woods, I find it quite difficult to get traction on the pine straw. It's so dry and slippery; not to mention flammable, of course. I can still smell all around me the smoke from the wildfire advancing on me from behind; the air is growing thicker with it. When the fire draws even closer, I know from personal experience the smoke will sting my lungs worse than the exertion from running the distance I have to cover to reach Alex and the river. I slide down another steep hillside, this one with a dry creek bed at the bottom. When I'm close enough I jump it, landing awkwardly on the far side in unexpectedly soft soil and rocks. Losing my balance, I fall to the ground. There is some pain in my palms and knees, but I manage to stumble to my feet and keep hurtling myself forward, dodging brambles, small boulders, and areas of loose rocks.

The forest becomes denser, and the tree branches slap me all about the upper torso and head. I try to cover my face with my hands for protection. The pines aren't too bad, but the hardwoods have only tiny, young leaves emerging, which provide no cushion for the impact of the bark against my flesh, my arms and face being well-exposed for scratching and cutting. Some trees are also overgrown with brier vines. One thin branch whips across my right cheek, slashing, and I can feel where a thin stream of blood is trickling down my face. More briers rip at my pant legs as I pass through them. Some seem to reach up to grab at my feet as I leap over them. I'm no athlete, but pure panic is giving me speed. I've never run so fast in all my life.

Not too far in the distance behind me, I hear a loud, explosive, whooshing roar. I stop briefly, holding onto a tree trunk and gasping desperately for a breath. My lungs are burning so badly; I'm not in shape for this. I turn to glance behind me toward the sound, to the top of the hill I had just come down moments before, afraid of what I might see.

A very tall tree up at the summit is alight, ignited by a random, solitary firebrand which was caught on the wind and carried ahead of the main fire until it found the dry boughs of this dead pine. The flames lick their way through the tree's branches in mere seconds, sprouting more firebrands that waft along on the winds, falling into the branches of trees farther down the hill.

The sight fills me with dread. The fire is now leaping from treetop to treetop down the hill! A new, even nearer wildfire has been started. It will soon be too close to outrun, and it will overtake me. I must get to Alex, and I'm running out of time.

CHAPTER 13

Choking on smoke and fear, I continue my pace, but I feel as if I can't make it much farther; and I begin to wonder if I'm even going the right way. Maybe in my blind panic I have gone down a different path and missed Alex entirely. It has been a long while since I left him, and I think I have covered a sizeable distance in that time. After another few minutes, my pace is slowing as I come into some rather thick smoke, which is being blown in from the new fire behind me. If I'm not careful, I will run the risk of needing to bolt blindly for the river and accidentally leaving Alex behind.

I stumble again and slow further; I stop briefly to take time to look around. I see no signs of Alex. I pull a handkerchief from around my neck and cover my nose and mouth with it. I walk now, as fast as I can. Running is not an option. I need time to catch my breath or else I am afraid my heart may simply explode in my chest. My legs are unsteady, but I think my chest hurts a little less as the time is ticking by. I can see the stream, off to my right, not too far away. But where is Alex?

I break into a slow jog, unable to move faster than that for the moment. The stream doubles back on me sharply in its journey to join up with the river. Within just a few minutes, smoke begins to overcome my handkerchief. It looks as though the white haze is a thick fog. The fire must be moving a lot more rapidly than I am. I begin to run again and almost immediately my lungs begin to protest and I reduce my speed back to a jog. If I don't find Alex soon, we may not make it to the river in time. I decide to continue along the stream, trusting that he followed my request and got closer to the river.

Then, just ahead of me, I see a wonderful sight. Alex is sitting on the ground, calmly waiting for me, his handkerchief over his lower face. I yell a warning to him, but little sound comes out and he isn't looking in my direction. I break into a run.

As I get closer, he must hear the breaking of brittle branches under my feet because he suddenly glances over his shoulder. The expression on his face as he scrambles to stand, grabbing the backpacks and walking stick, lets me know he sees my urgency. I slide to a stop, skidding on the pine straw; but all I can manage to say is "Fire!"

He nods and takes my arm. "We'd better get to that river you told me about then."

We move as quickly as Alex can manage, which is a lot faster than I thought he could go and almost faster than my lungs can handle at this point. The threat of imminent death is an extreme motivator. Within a few minutes we reach the river. It is indeed swollen with meltwater, wide and spreading across to fill its rocky banks, but none of its floodplain yet and not moving overly fast. It should be possible for the girls to have made it through, if they have already gone this way. Alex and I will certainly emerge thoroughly soaked on the other side. The water is crystal clear for a few feet out and I can easily see the smooth rocks along its bottom. The rocks are larger and more numerous closer to the center of the channel, where the water is also a lot deeper. It's not easy to judge the depth exactly from where we stand.

Alex drops the backpacks and in one impressive motion, hurls my walking stick in a clean arch to the other side of the river. He removes his gun and holster, checking the safety. He places them inside his backpack and shortens its straps to make it ride as high up on his back as possible, then does the same to my pack.

We look back over our shoulders to where we had emerged from the trees onto the floodplain. We can't see the fire, but the smoke is continuing to grow thicker, obscuring everything beyond the tree line. I worry about the firebrands crossing the river, just as we are about to do. Where would we go then? Maybe we will have to try to shelter in the middle of the shallow river. Would it offer enough protection? I am uncertain, but I doubt it.

I face the river again and retrieve my backpack, at the precise moment that I hear a terrified scream, far in the distance. I stand bolt upright. It was a girl's cry and it came from behind us, in the direction of the fire. Then, just as

Alex and I look at each other, me wondering if perhaps I had heard something else altogether, comes another scream, like the first.

I thrust my backpack at Alex and point across the river. "Go, get across! I'll get the girls; you help them get to the other side!" I turn and start running without waiting for a response or looking back. I race headlong across the grasses covering the river's expansive floodplain and over a low rise into sparse tree cover. Not far from me, the land rises into more heavily forested hills beyond.

I can hear them now. Young voices are crying out to one another, just out of sight. I sprint toward them and spot the first small group of ten or twelve girls and a chaperone, no doubt heading for the river.

"Over here!" I yell. "This way!"

The girls see me waving my arms as I approach, and they shift the path of their flight toward me. As we get closer to each other, I can see bits of soot mixed with tears streaking their faces. Some wear their bandanas over their noses; some do not.

I point behind me. "Keep going – the river is that way!"

They dash by me without acknowledgment and without slowing.

The screams Alex and I had heard are still coming, somewhere ahead of me in the smoke. I force my exhausted legs back into a run.

Emerging from the tree cover on the hill I'm approaching are at least forty girls and three of the adult chaperones. I wave them on, pointing toward the river.

"Elise!" I call out as I catch sight of her plunging out of the trees behind the group, helping a friend who is clearly running out of breath.

She dashes up to me and stops for a quick bear hug. I am happy beyond words to see her, but I know there are more girls to find.

I push back from her grasp. "Where are the rest?"

Elise points toward the trees.

"Okay, go! Keep running! The river is straight ahead. Get to the other side! Don't wait, just go," I say as I start to move away from the two girls.

"I will. Be careful, Aunt Cole!" Elise calls over her shoulder, coughing and taking her friend's hand again.

Just as I reach the beginning of the steeper hills, I can just make out figures coming toward me. As I get closer, I recognize Jason, DeShondra, and Regina, with at least another dozen girls in tow. They are half-sliding down the wooded hillside, dodging trees and undergrowth.

Jason carries a girl in his arms, as do Regina and DeShondra. He pulls up short when he reaches me. "Cole, you're alive!" Then he looks down at his passenger, "She couldn't go anymore. Here, take her. Two more fell behind. I've got to go back for them!"

"No." I can see that he's exhausted, just like the rest of them, but the girl he's carrying is too big for me. "You keep her. Just go on straight ahead. On the other side of that meadow is the river. You've got to help get the girls across. It's our only chance. I'll go after the stragglers."

"Cole, I can't ask you to do that. They're my responsibility." He could barely get the last words out between breaths.

"They're mine, too. Just go." I take off running up the hill into the trees, not giving him an option.

"Girls!" I yell as I climb, "Girls! Where are you? Over here!"

The smoke is getting much thicker, making it even harder to see and the heat is almost unbearable. I reach the top of the hill and see the two girls, coughing and struggling to get up the incline. No, wait... one of them is struggling while the other is trying to help her. As I plunge down the hill toward them, I recognize who they are. Anna is the one in trouble. She is holding her side. The fire is closing in behind them. They'll never make it at this rate.

I slide down to them and grab Anna, throwing her over my shoulder. Fortunately, she's small and lightweight. "Come on, let's go!" I yell to her little guardian, her twin sister Annie.

It takes a massive effort for me to remain upright and still keep Anna on my shoulder at the same time. She's throwing off my balance. I know Annie won't leave her, so I don't even bother to tell her to run. She has taken up a position at my elbow, doing her best to help balance both her sister and me.

Back at the top of the hill, I hear the explosion of the fire and turn to look back, just for an instant. It's in the trees immediately behind us, roaring up the hill with amazing speed. I slip on the pine straw as I shift direction and start to run, and I'm unable to recover in time. I fall, sliding down the hill, taking both girls with me. At the bottom, I regain my feet and reach for Anna. It seems obvious to me that we're not going to make it. The heat from the fire is blistering every piece of vegetation on the hill ahead of it, and the air is filled with burning embers and ash. Annie screams at me, pointing toward the fire, which has crested the top and is on its way down to us.

Suddenly, Alex is there, soaking wet and pushing past my arms to lift Anna into his. "Let's go, get moving!" He orders us into motion as burning heat sears the air.

It feels as if my flesh is about to spontaneously combust. I grab Annie's arm without question and force her into a run, practically dragging her. We dodge through the remaining trees at a breakneck pace and emerge onto the floodplain. It is an encouraging sight, because I know the river is close to us now even though it's nearly impossible to see with all the smoke.

We sprint through the grasses, terror lending us wings. We reach the river and plunge in without stopping. Jason is waiting in the middle of it and he wades out to meet us. He takes Annie's other hand and helps her swim across. The very center of the river is up to my chest and the current, while not strong, is still enough to knock me off my feet. I swim a few strokes before touching bottom again, as do the others. I don't know how Alex managed with Anna, only that he did.

Our little group is together, stumbling over the smooth rocks to the crest of the far bank, where I pitch forward, completely spent. I roll over onto my back and try to breathe. My eyes are closed in utter exhaustion and pain. I open them only when I detect arms around my neck, followed by a petite body on mine. Elise is hugging me as if she'll never let go. I wrap my arms around her and kiss the top of her head.

Everyone gets quiet, some shaking from fear or the slight chill from being wet in the breeze or maybe just from shock. We all watch as the fire burns across the floodplain meadow, less height to the flames now with shorter and much greener vegetation to consume as it approaches the river. We are all staring intently, hypnotized. A few in our group have gathered together to pray in a circle. The smoke still chokes us; but the fire is stopped, meeting its match in the water. The wind that blows isn't enough to push firebrands from the trees beyond across the meadow and river to the trees on the other side. There isn't as much force behind the flames now, either. The firebrands I watched light up the dead pine tree and start a new fire effectively snuffed out the larger fire coming along behind, robbing it of its fuel.

My body goes limp, and I let out a deep sigh of relief. Those who are standing suddenly collapse to the ground with happiness. A few of the girls begin to cry; others shout out with gleeful, hoarse voices. We made it. I can't believe it, but it's true. We have all survived.

CHAPTER 14

Elise is asleep, her head resting in my lap. I stroke her hair absentmindedly while looking across the river at the blackened landscape and smoke. The sun is going down; and the wind has shifted, coming out of the west now. That makes the air cleaner for breathing. Most everyone is lying down or sitting, and the majority of the kids are asleep. Jason has a few lines in the water, hoping to catch some fish. Fish sounds wonderful right about now.

Alex sits down beside me gingerly, holding his side with one hand. I never even noticed him approaching. We smile at each other. He places his hand on my free one. This time, I don't pull away. I know without him, Anna, Annie, and I might all be dead right now; I owe him everything. I have no idea how he managed to do it, either, considering that he's still not in the best shape.

"I used to do this when Elise was a baby," I whisper. "Sometimes she would get really fussy and I was usually the best one at getting her to sleep. I would hold her in my lap and rub her head like this. Sometimes my sister would call me in the middle of the night to come over and do it."

"You're good at it. You've got the touch," he whispers back, smiling at me.

Jason rounds up the other adults, who sit down to join us.

"It seems like all the kids are okay, which is amazing," Jason says softly.

"An amazing miracle, that's what it is," Regina corrects him.

"Maybe so," Jason agrees. "Whatever happened, it is a miracle, I'll hand you that. We're all back together, and we're all going to be fine." He looks at me and grins broadly.

"And we have a new member of our group," Regina adds with a sly grin. "And just where did Cole find you, Handsome?"

Alex, the tough DEA agent who had taken a serious beating from a couple of criminals and who had hiked for days in spite of bleeding and injuries, is blushing.

"She found me tied to a tree. I'm a Special Agent with the Drug Enforcement Agency. Some guys I was following got the drop on me. They were going to kill me and would have if not for Cole."

He is looking at me with genuine admiration. Everyone is looking at me now; I wish they'd stop. I'm not one for enjoying attention. I'd prefer to remain in the background.

"She rescued me single-handedly. I still can't believe what she did. She's really incredibly brave. Cole nursed me back to health while we walked, trying to get back up with all of you. Getting back to you guys is all she could talk about."

Jason is looking at me and smiling. "I can see Cole doing something like that. Good job." He winks at me.

"Do we have to be worried about these bad guys of yours?" DeShondra asks.

"No, Cole saw to that," Alex says matter-of-factly. "If there is anyone left, they're way over by Camp Correll."

Alex receives Jason's full attention with that statement. "What do you mean? Those guys who tried to kill you are at Camp Correll?"

"Jason," I say quickly, knowing he would be afraid for his coworkers. "When I got to Camp Correll, it was completely deserted. Nobody was there, and there was no sign of where your friends went. Maybe down the road toward town, I guess."

"No, Cole. They would never abandon us out here. I've worked with those guys for years. I know all of them; they're like my family," Jason maintains in loyal disbelief.

"Like I said, they were all gone. I'm not saying they just abandoned us here out of malice. Something happened. It looked like they grabbed some of their things and took several of the vehicles and drove off," I can't help but sigh in frustration.

"I'm telling you, they wouldn't leave us." Jason is staunchly determined to defend his friends, that much is certain.

"I'm just relaying information, Jason. All I know for sure is what I saw."

"And what was that, exactly?" he insists.

"Three vehicles were gone. The others were drained of their gasoline. Somebody siphoned it off and the hose they used was still sticking out of one of the gas tanks. The gas cans were all gone, and the generator was as dry as a bone. No power at all, anywhere. I checked every inch of that compound, every building, every room, every closet, even. It was like a ghost town." I pause for him to absorb that. "And the mess hall was trashed. A lot of the food was gone... or spoiled. Somebody left the freezer door wide open, not that there was any power to keep the room cold, anyway."

The other chaperones are looking at each other, clearly shocked and worried.

"What are we going to do now?" DeShondra asks.

"We're going to hike out of here," I respond without hesitation. "First thing tomorrow morning, we'll start out. After we have a good breakfast. I brought as many supplies back with me as I could. That backpack is stuffed. Alex and I didn't really eat all that much. We supplemented with native plant life, like Jason taught us to do.

"There is also plenty of food around here, and all we have to do is collect it. We'll stuff ourselves before we go and then stuff our backpacks. We'll head south, so we don't have to cross the burned areas. They'll still be hot and smoking. I don't want to take the girls back through that. Going south-southeast is our best option, toward one of the other area crossroads communities. It should keep us away from the fire that's still burning on the far northeast side of the river. And we're already across the river, so this way we won't have to worry about crossing it again. That's a little bonus."

"Sounds like a plan to me," Regina chimes in. "It looks like you're in charge now, Cole."

One of my eyebrows arch at the statement, and I study the faces around me. No one is verbalizing a complaint or appears as though they disagree... even Jason, although he has the appearance of being fairly distracted at the moment. "We'll be fine, especially now that we're all back together again. Jason, what can we do to help you catch plenty of fish for dinner?"

Jason seems to be at a loss. It's understandable that he's confused. We all are. I didn't learn anything of any real use to us while I was at Camp Correll. All I had succeeded in doing was deepening the mystery.

"Jason?" Regina asks, nudging his arm gently and smiling in encouragement.

He shakes himself out of his stupor. "Um, well, we lost some of our gear in the fire. We still have enough equipment to do a little fishing with, though. I could use some more eyes on the lines in the river. Regina, if you could be in charge of gathering plants and roots, that would help; you've got the best eye for plants I've seen on anyone in quite a while."

"Well thank you, Jason," she laughs heartily. "DeShondra, why don't you and Cole come with me? I would take Handsome over there," she nodded toward Alex, "but I believe he'll be better off fishing. That way he can sit down and relax. You look like you're still trying to recover from your fight with those bad guys of yours. You'll be at the top of my list for helping me out tomorrow, though. And don't you reckon I'll forget about you, either."

It makes me smile to see Alex blushing again. He's probably not used to someone like Regina. I love it! Gently, I lift Elise's still sleeping form from my lap and lay her on the grasses next to me as I stand.

"The rest of you can build a fire and set up camp for the night," I add. "I think we only need a small fire, just enough for cooking. And Alex, I'd really appreciate it if you could take it easy. We've got a few days of hiking ahead of us, and I know we'll need you back to a hundred percent. Please?"

He gives me that crooked grin of his. "I'll see what I can do for you, boss."

"Oh... my... goodness! What a sexy smile you've got there, Handsome!" Regina chuckles again. "And I don't see a ring on your finger. How in the world is it that some beautiful woman hasn't snatched you up already?"

"Uh, well, I, uh..." he stammers at first.

Regina caught him off guard — and I didn't believe that was even possible. It's enjoyable to me to see the shoe on the other foot now.

"I was married, but we got divorced years and years ago. I've been busy with work and haven't had time. And besides that, I've been waiting for the right woman to come along." Alex casts his eyes in my direction.

I can't tell if he's implying something or asking me for rescue from Regina. Whichever it is, I'm not planning to bite. It's better to let him squirm for a minute, I think.

"Oh, I see how it is now," Regina says with a jovial smirk.

"Let's get going, ladies," I say, turning from the scene. I've had enough of this game; it's time to get down to work. "We've got a lot of mouths to feed."

We separate into three groups for foraging, campfire, and fishing. I am so tired. I have no doubt that the others are, too. We work in silence, for the most part. There's an abundance of vegetation on our side of the river and whenever I glance back, it looks like Jason, Alex, and several of the girls are having at least some luck with the fish as well. I'm sure that after we eat, sleep will soon follow. I can hardly wait... that's the number one item on my wish list.

As the sun sets, we eat our dinner. It's wonderful to be able to sit down and take it easy for a while. And the fish tastes amazing. There isn't much to go around, but that's fine with everyone, I think. We're all so exhausted.

"They must be really tired," Regina says, motioning toward the girls. "All they did earlier today is complain about the food and tell us how badly they wanted to eat at a certain restaurant, or have their grandma's home cookin'.

And now look at them. They're happy to be eating a morsel of fish and some greens," she chuckles.

"They're tired, and they've been through a lot today. Poor little things," DeShondra says.

As everyone helps clean up, I scan the area for Jason. The sooner we get finished, the sooner we can all sleep.

Over by the river, Jason has returned with the fishing rods. He's kneeling to put them in a secure position to hold them in place until tomorrow morning, hoping to catch more fish overnight. I decide to follow while everyone else is distracted, since I want to talk with him privately.

"Jason, are you okay?" I ask.

Apparently he hadn't noticed me coming over because he acts as though I've startled him when he looks up from his work along the banks of the river. "Cole... yeah, I'm okay."

"Your friends are probably fine, you know."

"Probably," is his quick response.

"Most likely, they spotted those poachers and took off to get help. I bet they figured we would be better off at the rendezvous spot with you rather than taking a chance on picking us up and taking us back into the lion's den, as it were. Your friends must have surmised the poachers wouldn't be going in the direction of the rendezvous area. And they knew you would take care of us," I say, trying to help him feel better.

"Maybe, maybe not."

"So what do you think happened, then?"

"I don't know. I just don't understand them leaving us like that. I hope they're okay," he paused. "But they'd better have a damn good explanation for what they did when I catch up to them."

He stands and faces me. "Do you realize what could have happened if our whole group had gone to Camp Correll together and those poachers had been there? Or what could have happened if the poachers had found you while you were at the camp, all alone? It makes me furious. There's no excuse good enough for that – not for me. You were in a lot of danger, Cole."

I hadn't thought of the situation quite like that before. I guess I had been lucky. Very lucky indeed.

Jason steps closer to me and puts his hands on my shoulders. His incredibly blue eyes search mine. "I don't want you or anyone else going off alone anymore. It's too dangerous. I don't want anything to happen to you, Cole." He moves one hand from my shoulder to my hair, which he rubs between his fingers affectionately, smiling that compelling smile of his. Then he drops that hand to my waist and pulls me in suddenly for a long, tender kiss.

I am completely taken aback by his kiss and the way he's looking at me... and I find I have no idea what to say or do. I know I must be blushing; I can feel it.

He gently rubs a lock of my hair again. "I've seen the way Alex has been looking at you. It would be obvious enough to a blind man what he's thinking. I just want you to know I've been looking at you that way, too. I don't think you've noticed me. But I won't put any pressure on you. You've been through a lot, and right now I'm just glad to have you back with the rest of us, where you belong." His voice trails off and he releases me, turning back to his work of resetting the fishing rods.

Wow. Where did all that come from? I back away a couple of steps in utter confusion then turn and walk back toward the others. I don't understand this. I have dated several guys over the past few years after I was no longer attached to my boyfriend, but nothing much ever really came of it. Mostly because that was the way I had wanted it at the time, of course. Now, two attractive and wonderful men seem to be interested in me. I just don't get it. All this attention focused on me when I haven't even cultivated it, at least, not on purpose. All I can figure is that it must be something in the mountain air. I'm just going to lie down near the girls and go to sleep now, hopefully without talking to anyone else. I need some time to myself. And I desperately need some rest.

CHAPTER 15

As we hike along the next morning, strung out in a long, loose line, I do my best to avoid both Alex and Jason. I had offered first thing to bring up the rear, suggesting Jason take the lead. Regina and DeShondra are just ahead of me, walking on either side of Alex, keeping him preoccupied with conversation. When we had started out, the two of them had said they were going to stay near him, just in case he needed them for support if he got too tired. Sure, that's a believable excuse.

Now that I think about what they had said, it makes me smile. DeShondra had found a suitable walking stick for Alex, for which he had thanked her profusely. She had noticeably blushed beneath her dark skin. She is so cute and sweet, and a perfect teacher for those kids, from what I've noticed. They all seem to love her dearly; she's almost like the Pied Piper, but in a good way.

For my part, I'm both content and relieved to be hiking apart from the others. I'm doing my best to avoid thinking about both men. I'm concentrating instead on listening for noises behind us and watching carefully all around. Jason pointed out this morning that we have had no encounters with bears; and we were bound to be pushing our luck, especially since the fire had likely pressed most of the animals to cross the river as we did.

Come to think of it, we hadn't even seen any bear tracks, or deer, for that matter. Of course, the ground has been baked dry, so maybe that's the reason. Who knows? I just appreciate having the distraction and hope at the same time that nothing comes of it. Alex periodically looks back at me. I make sure I happen to be looking off in another direction when I notice his head might be starting to shift my way. I know I cannot continue to avoid these two men forever, but I am intent on putting it off as long as I'm able to. I consider telling both of them to leave me alone, that I'm not interested.

At first, that seems like a reasonable idea; but my thoughts keep returning to Alex, no matter how hard I try.

Yet that attention from Jason is hard to figure out. I'm trying to remember if there were any signals at all from him on our trip that I missed. I tend not to notice things like that because I'm never looking for them. I remind myself that this attention is most logically just a result of our current circumstances. I need to forget about all this anyway. Once we get out of here, and back to civilization, I'll likely never see or hear from either of them again. I certainly don't need that potential heartbreak in my life.

By the time we stop for lunch, everyone is tired and hungry. We eat mostly in silence. I assume everyone is still a bit in shock from yesterday. I focus on my food or my niece and her friends and block out the periodic inquisitive looks from my two would-be suitors.

With a concerted effort on my part, I'm able to turn my thoughts in other directions during our afternoon hike. That little voice inside my head is telling me to look around and pay closer attention, but to what? We are in an area with only young trees and wildflowers, evidence of a big fire in this part of the new National Forest years before.

Everywhere I look, things seem normal. I don't see any tracks save those from the people walking ahead of me, so I cannot figure out what's bothering me so much. Yesterday's fire appears to have burned itself out, or at least away, far to the east. It had been a big fire, but obviously not big enough to have brought out firefighters or even planes for dropping water or retardant. Wait. That's it!

I stop walking and stare up into the blue sky. It's cloudless today. There's nothing there. Nothing at all.

"What is it, Cole?" Alex asks, having approached without me having noticed, so engrossed am I in my thoughts.

His voice startles me out of my preoccupation. I look at him intently. "There are no contrails… anywhere."

"So, what does that mean? I don't think many planes fly over this part of the country all that often, do they? Or maybe it's just timing… there aren't any when you happen to have looked up for them."

"I don't know, but I would think there should be some. And the fire… no one came." I pause for a moment, hoping he will follow where I'm leading; but I'm unable to be patient enough. "No one came to fight the fire. No one came to help us."

"Maybe they didn't see the fire. We are kind of out in the middle of nowhere here. And as for our group, maybe they don't know we're missing yet," Alex reasons.

"You maybe… that might be understandable. But not the rest of us… no offense to you, Alex. Like I said before, the parents should have reported us missing by now. And the authorities should be looking for us. That means search planes. They would have seen the fire and at least sent in firefighters to try and put it out, especially not knowing where we were or what had happened to us." My voice is rising, and I stop to calm myself.

"Okay, that all makes sense, but maybe they're being cautious because Jason's coworkers have gotten to the authorities and told them about the poachers, and they don't know where those men are or exactly how many there are, or if there is a hostage situation." Alex has reached out to hold my free hand; and he's speaking softly, but firmly. I can tell he's trying to calm me down. I don't feel like calming down just now, but I know he's right.

"Maybe even those guys that work with Jason have been taken hostage or something," he is saying. "We just don't know enough to speculate; and I think we should keep this to ourselves, at least for now. There's no reason to scare the kids or anyone else. Let's just wait it out a while longer, okay?"

Nodding my head in agreement, I start walking with him toward the slow-moving procession ahead of us. "There's no sense in scaring the kids; you're right about that."

My mind is racing with the possibilities now. I don't believe there's any kind of hostage situation, although that is a possible explanation; just not good enough for me. It doesn't explain why no one came to fight the fire. Nor does it explain why I'm certain I haven't seen any contrails. At least not since sometime soon after we were dropped off by the workers from Camp Correll to begin this whole ordeal we find ourselves in now.

Maybe there has been another act of terrorism against the United States. When 9-11 happened, all air traffic, save for the military, was stopped; and there were no contrails in the sky for days. It was such a disconcerting sight. Perhaps that's the explanation for what's going on now. I feel a deep sense of foreboding coming over me. Something terrible has happened, something big-picture, maybe not terrorism, but something major… I'm certain of it.

We stop for the evening by a large stream that Jason says is another one the company always kept stocked with fish for the tourists, like the one we had camped at during our multi-night stay on the field trip. Everything is a fog for me; I'm just going through the motions. My mind is occupied trying to figure out the solution to the puzzle, but there are too many possibilities. Alex keeps looking at me as we set up camp for the night. I think he's concerned that I might be unable to refrain from telling the others about my theory, but I know he's right and any theories can wait. At least until we are closer to getting to the settlement we're heading for.

It's the same little village we believe Jason's coworkers must have gone to when they apparently abandoned Camp Correll.

The evening is uneventful, and I stay close to my pod of girls. We talk mostly about school. They are excited about getting home by the early part of next week, as Regina has been estimating for them all afternoon. I hope she's right.

"Okay, bedtime everyone!" Regina announces, much to my delight. I'm definitely ready for sleep.

Once I get my group settled, I snuggle into my sleeping bag. Actually, mine didn't survive the fire. Jason insisted I take his, and I didn't protest very hard at all. Alex lies not far away, on the outside edge of another group of girls. He faces out toward the trees, his head propped up on his hand. I wonder what he's thinking about, but I'm sure I know. I watch him for a few minutes, and then I start counting sheep so I can close my eyes and manage not to think about airplanes.

I awaken with a start and sit straight up, fully alert. I don't have any idea what it is that got my attention. It was not a dream; I was actually having a peaceful dream this time. I had heard... something. But what? No one else seems to have heard anything. It's readily apparent they are all soundly asleep.

Aside from the campfire, which is dwindling, everything is dark around us. The stars twinkle overhead. The only sounds are the occasional crackling of wood on the fire, insects, and a couple of owls.

The fire needs tending, I decide; so I go over and stoke it with more branches. After reassuring myself the fire is sufficiently fed, I return to my sleeping bag and stretch, trying to convince myself that I'm still sleepy. I scan the horizon before lying down. That's when I notice flashes of light to the east. It only takes me a moment to realize that it's what we call "heat lightning" down south, just the reflection of distant lightning off of clouds.

Thankfully, it's in the east, not the west. The prevailing winds are still coming out of the west, so we should be fine if those far-away storms start more wildfires. Our course out of the National Forest will keep us well away from where the lightning must be occurring now. If I listen carefully, I can just barely hear the sound of thunder. That must be what woke me from a deep sleep. There isn't anything else it could have been. Could it?

CHAPTER 16

Sure enough, smoke is visible the next morning, far on the eastern horizon. The wind is moving the fire away from us, so we have nothing to worry about today. We pack up our gear and snuff out the campfire thoroughly after breakfast and head out.

Although we have plenty of water and are hiking toward more, the day is growing hotter by the hour. Along the way, we gather edible food in the landscape and experiment with chewing on pine needles to slake our thirst and conserve our water supplies. Sweat is plastering our clothes to our bodies, as there is little shade in this more open area we are traveling through. It's surrounded by wooded hills, but the open area is more easily traversed and is a direct path to our destination, which is another wide stream sure to have a plentiful supply of fish. At least, according to Jason it should.

Again today, by my own choosing, I'm bringing up the rear and well behind the rest. Jason walks far ahead of the group, scouting the land beyond. I'm still enjoying my semi-solitary hiking. Jason is nearly out of my sight. Alex is relatively nearby, but Regina and DeShondra have him so deep in conversation I don't believe he could walk back here to me if he wanted to; he seems captivated.

Shaking my head at that thought, I smile. It's really quite funny, at least to me. I don't think Alex is quite as amused as I am, but he is polite and attentive to the jovial pair. They don't let much get them down, at least not for long. They are wonderful people to spend time with. Being alone and preoccupied with my thoughts is a more productive way for me to spend my time just now than being around either of the men. They are just confusing my emotions, and that's something I don't want to deal with. At least, I don't believe so. Once in a while, I still try to figure out why there are no signs of airplanes or search parties, but mostly I'm just trying to observe the landscape around me and appreciate the beauty and relative simplicity of this way of life before we get back to civilization. I'm choosing to ignore everything else.

There are a few butterflies, flitting about and trying to find nectar in the dry flowers. Occasionally, a large bird of prey will circle in the sky. No clouds are up there today, though, just a clear blue dome. The air is drier now, less humid. I look back at the well-trodden path I am following and periodically glance over my shoulder. There is still no sign of any problem.

No sign at all... except I cannot shake the growing sense that we're being watched. It all goes back to being awakened from my sleep last night for no apparent reason. There's still nothing for me to base my fear on. Yet it's there. I'm trying to chalk it up to the incident with the wildfire and feeling overprotective of the kids... but there's something more, something just out of the reach of my senses.

Later that evening, as we make camp by the stream that Jason told us about, I decide to let go of my thus-far unfounded fears. I don't want those thoughts to consume me. No one else seems concerned. With so many people around me and none of them noticing anything out of sorts, it must just be me and my admittedly often-overactive imagination. I go to sleep, tired and restless.

The same thing happens again in the middle of this night. I decide to walk to the far edge of the group this time, after stoking the fire. I sit well away from the nearest person, who happens to be Alex, and stare out into the darkness for at least an hour by my estimation.

I hear the sound of footsteps behind me and turn to see Alex approaching. He sits beside me.

"Hey, what's going on, boss?" he asks in a whisper so as not to rouse the others.

Sighing, I reply softly, "I don't know. Nothing, I guess. I thought I heard something… out there in the dark. I don't hear anything now, maybe it's nothing. I thought I heard something last night, too."

He turns from trying to pierce the darkness with his eyes. "You did? Why didn't you say something? Why didn't you tell me?"

I stare at him. "I don't know. Last night, I thought the storms off to the east were what woke me up. Earlier this afternoon, I felt like we were being watched; but I never saw anything. Then a little while ago, something woke me up. This time, there aren't any storms. I've been watching and listening, and there's nothing. Maybe it's just me. Maybe I'm imagining things, you know? I'm getting paranoid or going crazy out here or something."

"Well, so far, your instincts have been accurate every time," he says, putting a hand on my back and rubbing it, right where it happens to be a little stiff and strained. How could he know that? I think I should move out of his reach, or tell him to stop; but it feels so good. I must be more stressed than I thought. And I am enjoying his touch tremendously.

"In that case, I think we should travel differently tomorrow," I say. "Just to be on the safe side. We'll have the kids grouped a little tighter together. And we'll have two adults scout ahead of the rest of us. There should also be two in the rear, keeping watch. That would make me feel more secure, at least."

"The trouble is, we don't have that many adults who really should be acting as guards or scouts. There's you, me, and Jason. We need the teachers to stay with the kids and keep them calm and in line – that's where their talents lie. I'm not so good at working with kids," Alex observes, looking troubled.

"Then we'll have to make do. One guard in the rear. I'll take point with either you or Jason. It's the only way." I say matter-of-factly.

"Yes ma'am. You are the boss, after all," he says with a grin. "Go on, you go back to sleep. I'll stay up a while longer."

"Alex, you still need to rest," I begin to protest.

"Look, you may be the boss; but as your assumed second-in-command, I want you to get your rest so you'll be fresh in the morning and ready to go. I doubt you got enough sleep last night, knowing you. And all thanks to you, I think I'm pretty much back to a hundred percent."

I give him a look. I'm famous for the looks I give – among my friends and coworkers back in Raleigh, anyway.

"Okay, at least ninety-five," he suggests with another grin. "Tomorrow I'll be even closer to a hundred. Don't worry… I'll go to sleep in an hour or so… I'll wait just long enough to make sure everything is clear. You go on."

"Okay, but don't stay up long."

"Yes ma'am, whatever you say, boss."

He turns back to peer into the darkness as I stand to go back to my sleeping bag. The smile on his face is now missing… he's all business. I'm comforted with him on watch, and I fall asleep faster than I thought I would.

CHAPTER 17

Just like clockwork, the morning dawns bright and cloud-free. I eat breakfast amidst my pod of girls, but I cannot help but notice that Alex has pulled Jason aside for a private conversation. I watch as Jason listens closely and then begins scanning the horizon and the nearby woods with Alex. No one else seems to take any notice.

Now Jason knows. I see him nod in agreement as Alex spells out the plan. I feel better now that they both are aware. I just hope and pray I'm wrong this time.

After breakfast is finished and we pack up, we shepherd the girls into a tighter group and move out. Alex takes up the position of rear guard and Jason scouts ahead, far in front of me, although I'm close enough to reach him in case of an emergency of some sort. I keep the group in sight, where another teacher, Caryn, has taken the lead. She didn't even ask why.

We proceed this way until lunchtime. Jason makes sure to stop us out in the open, as we have kept carefully to in our travels all morning. The other adults comment that they like it this way better. If rescuers are searching for us by air, they'll be able to spot us more easily. And if there's another fire somewhere ahead, having people scouting beyond the group will give us more lead time to reach a safe place.

Alex, Jason, and I agree not to tell them what our real concerns are just yet. Not until we have evidence that we face another threat. No sense in worrying them needlessly.

Late that afternoon, Jason slows his pace so that I can't help but catch up to him. "Do you still think there is someone out there, Cole?"

I match my pace to his. "Yes. I don't know why, I can't explain it. It's just a feeling I've had for a couple of days."

"Okay, that's good enough for me. I trust you, just like Alex does." He gives my shoulder a quick little squeeze, then lengthens his stride and jogs off to get back to his place ahead of me.

It's kind of weird. Both these men trust me so much. I don't know what I've done to deserve it, but I'm glad for it all the same. And I'm very pleased to have two such capable men to help protect these kids.

As we walk along, every now and then I look up to the sky. There are still no airplanes, anywhere. This is all so wrong. What has happened?

The day passes uneventfully. We make camp and build a large fire, with plenty of wood nearby for keeping it going strong until morning. Jason puts Regina in charge of sleeping near the fire to tend it during the night. Alex, Jason, and I take positions so we are each a third of the way around the group, on the outside perimeter. I think the two men probably have more trouble sleeping than I do. It's comforting knowing they are watching, too. And the fact that each of them is armed doesn't hurt, either.

My dreams are strange. I hear a wild animal cry and wake up to see the two poachers I thought I had killed in my rescue of Alex, standing over me with guns pointed, ready to shoot. That's when I really awaken, and with a start, to see the sky is just beginning to turn a hint of blue with the coming of the sunrise. It takes a minute for my heart to stop racing. I look around the campsite to see that almost everyone seems to be sleeping peacefully. Alex and Jason are gone, though.

Then I find that if I squint my eyes, I can just make them out in the approach of dawn. Alex and Jason are walking back with... what is that they are carrying? When they get closer, I can see they have some rabbits. I have no idea where those came from or how they were caught. But even though my heart feels momentarily bad for the animals, I know it will mean a little bite of protein for each of us.

I get up and stoke the fire for roasting the meat. "And where did those come from?" I ask when the men are close enough.

"I went with Jason yesterday evening while the rest of you females were laughing your heads off about something. Jason knows how to set a mean animal trap," Alex compliments his hunting partner.

"I learned that a long time ago. I wanted to teach this group, but they wouldn't hear of it. But now that we need food, I think we can overlook where it comes from, right, Cole?" Jason asks.

"Hey, I've got no problem with it. I guess I can even help you get everything going. I'm starving." They can see I don't have enough enthusiasm to back up my claims, though.

Jason laughs. "How about you just find us some suitable branches to use for roasting these? Alex and I will take care of the rest while you're doing that."

I look at him with gratitude. "Hey, fine by me!"

After a late breakfast, we decide to keep the same positions as yesterday and march out. We have been walking for a while when it dawns on me. We may reach civilization as early as sometime tomorrow. Everyone is excitedly discussing the same thing, I think. I cannot wait to eat some real food and take a long shower. The thought is so strong I imagine I can even hear the water running…

Jason has stopped, so I step up beside him.

"Listen to that," he says.

For a few seconds, I try to place the sound but then realize it's the shower I thought I had imagined. "What in the world?"

"Come on," Jason says excitedly and runs ahead, with me right on his heels.

A wide, shallow creek comes into view not too far ahead, from amongst a rather extensive collection of rocks and boulders of various sizes. The sound that had grabbed our attention comes from where the water spills down over a drop of about twenty feet. The resulting waterfall cascades to create a deep, dark, noisy pool which is quite large. The creek slides out of the pool on the far side and moves across the brushy, rock-strewn landscape beyond.

"Wow," I say, "this is great!"

We carefully maneuver down the steep hill to the pool below. Jason helps me in a tricky spot at the end by putting his hands on my waist and lifting me down. We rush over and put our hands in to check the water temperature. It's almost warm, which isn't surprising considering the conditions. The rocks around it are quite hot, conducting the sun's heat and helping regulate the temperature to a higher level and heating the shallow water depth of the creek. Shallow water tends to be warmer anyway. In the pool, the water is a bit dark, but still clear enough to see down a few feet. I poke my walking stick into it and hit bottom at about four feet near the side.

"You know, we could all take showers, clean our clothes, and swim a little. It'll be big enough if we come in small groups," I say with enthusiasm.

Jason grins at the idea. "I guess it would be okay to take a break. This will set us back at least a couple of hours, you know, Cole."

I counter, "But like you said, it would be okay to take a break. The girls have been pining for a shower, and I know I've wanted one for at least a week."

"Okay. You wait here; I'll get the others," he offers, laughing.

"Sounds good to me," I reply. I can hardly wait.

I can hear the girls shortly before I'm able to see them. They are shouting to be audible over the ample noise from the waterfall. Everyone seems happy to have the chance for a shower or a swim. I walk over to the base of the hill, next to the pool, to help each girl down. The adults manage the last part more or less on their own, although some insist on Alex or Jason helping them. I don't have to wonder why that is.

When everyone is down, Regina takes over. "Okay, you two men. You're going to have to come with me. Let's allow DeShondra's pod to go first and then Caryn's pod will be next. All the rest of you come on. We'll find a spot downstream to wait for our turns. We'll give these girls some space."

Everyone obliges, although I think the rest of the girls are jealous. The stream is substantially deeper and wider on the far side of the pool, but the area surrounding it is so densely vegetated that we are forced to go around it rather than through. We decide to plop down on the far side of the trees and underbrush where it thins out. We are a few minutes' walk away, so we can't see or hear the others at the pool. That should give them sufficient privacy.

A moment later, Alex stands and begins pacing around restlessly near Jason.

I stroll over to him. "Hey, what's wrong?"

"I don't like this. If someone is following us, the group back there is unprotected."

That's something that hadn't occurred to me. "Oh wow, you're right. I didn't think about that. I'll go back."

He takes my arm midstride as I turn away. "No. You stay here – I'll go."

"Now wait a minute, Alex," Jason says, standing up. "Neither of us needs to be getting too close to those girls."

"Come on, give me some credit," Alex begins defensively. "I wasn't planning on getting that close. I'm going about three quarters of the way back up the way we came. There is a rock outcrop there. I'm thinking I can sit on one of those boulders and wait, just in case. I'll be close enough to hear them if they get into trouble, but not close enough to see them."

"That actually sounds like a good idea to me," I say. "I'll go with you, Alex. That way, I can go ahead to the pool and keep an eye on things and let them know to expect to see you around the bend when they're walking back here. Jason, you can stay and watch over the rest of the group. If that sounds okay to you guys, that is."

Jason shrugs. "Sure, I guess. Just tell them to hurry up and don't use all the water."

Alex chimes in, "Yeah, Cole. Tell them to get a move on, okay? Save some water for the rest of us."

"Such funny, funny guys. No problem, I'll pass the message along. Let's go, Alex," I say.

As we reach the outcropping Alex talked about, we part company.

"Cole," he calls out to me, grinning, "be sure and call me if you can't reach your back. I'll be more than happy to come get it for you."

"Do yourself a favor and don't hold your breath," I retort as I give him a coy smile. That actually sounds like a very pleasing notion, I have to admit.

CHAPTER 18

The last group of girls is mine, and they are splashing and laughing with delight. The previous pod's leader, Elizabeth, is walking her group alongside the creek as they leave the area. They will pass Alex in a moment. Elizabeth seemed to thoroughly enjoy her romp in the water with her girls. I think she had been looking forward to a shower as much as I am. Her long, thick, strawberry-blonde hair is absolutely soaking wet, leaving a streaming trail of water behind her. Her pod is making fun of her, but their hair is just as thoroughly doused. After all, we have no towels. Their clothes had dried quickly where they had been laid out over the warm rocks in the sun, but they are now wet again, up against the dripping wet bodies. Oh well, at least we'll all be clean for a while. Drying out will come soon enough in the warm early afternoon air.

I strip down to my underwear, swirl my clothes in the water and then lay them out on a large, flat rock near the waterfall to dry as the girls in my pod are climbing out already. That certainly didn't take long. They're having fun though, laughing and joking after their refreshing swim. It's hard for the kids to pull the damp clothes onto their wet bodies. It'll be a few minutes before they're finished. I will be nearly done with my little shower by then.

"Girls, why don't you wait just a few minutes and let your skin dry off first? That'll make your clothes go on a whole lot easier," I suggest to them. They choose not to listen; big surprise.

I shake my head and jump into the pool then leisurely swim over to the waterfall. When I look back, the girls are still laughing and gently pushing at each other as they prepare to start off down along the stream; but the waterfall drowns out most of the conversations.

"Be careful when you walk down that path! You girls could just wait for me, you know," I call out to them.

"We'll be careful, Aunt Cole," Elise yells back. "We'll tell Alex you're still here so he won't come yet," she calls from the far side of the pool as she pulls on her shoes.

At least, I think that's what she said. I find myself tuning out the girls and letting the invigorating water soothe my aching body. The girls are about to leave. That means I'll have the pool and waterfall all to myself! Even just a couple of minutes of this kind of alone time will be pure heaven. The water splashing down over my head is quite warm and wonderful. It smacks along the rocks and leaps into the water around me. It's quite loud, drowning out most everything else and letting me relax for the first time in a long time.

I glance back over my shoulder at the girls and see them squealing and pointing at the stream, then pushing past each other in their haste. Some of them seem to be almost laughing, or maybe they're yelling at each other... I can't really tell from here. They're making me angry... I told them not to play like that around the water and rocks, because it would be easy for them to slip and hit their heads. Good grief! Why can't kids listen to adults better than that? The next thing I know, they are all taking flight as a group, bolting down the path toward their friends.

I'll just let the teachers reprimand the girls when they go flying into the camp like that. And I'm sure they'll do it, too. All these teachers are nice people; but as teachers know, you do need to maintain some discipline. Maybe I'm just not that good at it, at least not yet. I shake my head and close my eyes, letting the water work its magic. I'm lost in a delightful reverie, but I can swear I hear someone repeatedly yelling my name...

"Cole! Cole! Cole!"

I open my eyes and turn my head to look behind me in time to see Alex, fully clothed, running toward the pool at a breakneck pace. Taking a massive leap, he dives in without hesitation. What the hell?!

That's when I notice it, only a few feet away from me. Completely out of place in this setting, but there he is, plain as day and unmistakable to a girl born and raised on a farm in the Low Country – a large alligator! I can only see the top of his head and part of his tail, several feet back from the head.

Oh my God! It's coming straight toward me. And Alex is swimming with powerful strokes toward the alligator.

The gator dives, still moving in my direction as he disappears from view. Alex takes a deep breath and dives, too.

"No, Alex!" I scream, but it's too late. He has vanished beneath the surface.

I can't see the gator, but I know how fast they can move underwater. I pilot my body toward the rocks at the edge of the pool, first swimming, then slipping and sliding, out of the water onto a nearby boulder. There I stop and turn back. Even though I know the reptile is close, I have to try to see what's happening. Where is Alex?

The water is churning, with silt and debris from the bottom mixing in, reducing visibility. Blood is in the water, too, now. I can't see anything at first, but then the tip of the alligator's tail slices through the air and goes back under the water. I can easily visualize film footage I had seen before in my life along with the stories I heard growing up, of an alligator's death roll. They drag their prey under the water and roll them over repeatedly until they are disoriented and easier to drown. Alex! Please, God, no! This can't be happening.

The alligator resurfaces, but this time he has the end of a knife protruding from the base of his skull. Alex pops up between me and the gator, gasping furiously for air.

"Alex!" I scream. "Over here!"

He looks my way and swims the few feet separating us, a small stream of blood trickling down one side of his face. He's pulling the dead alligator along by one of its legs.

When he reaches me, I climb down from the boulder and lean out to help him onto the rocky ledge I'm now kneeling on, just inches beneath the water's surface. He's breathing heavily.

"Oh my God! I can't believe you did that, Alex! Are you okay?" I ask, still holding onto him. I am shaking badly.

His eyes move upward slowly, taking in my dripping, nearly-naked body. I hadn't given a thought to the fact that I had been bathing; there had been only the need to get myself, then Alex, to safety. Now he is staring intently into my eyes.

He reaches up and places a hand at the back of my neck and then gently but firmly pulls my face down to his. He kisses me deeply and I feel a rapidly-mounting passion rising in me. There are feelings stirring inside me that I haven't felt in years, if ever I truly felt this way before. This kiss is so different, so full of life and meaning, affection and desire. I kiss him back desperately, not wanting this moment to ever come to an end. I rub my fingers over his short hair as my emotions intensify and I forget about everything else.

It is with obvious regret that Alex gently pulls back from me. "I don't want to stop." He gazes from my lips to my eyes. "But you'd better get some clothes on quickly, gorgeous, before Jason gets here. Those girls should be reaching him right about now, and I'm sure he'll be trying to get to you as fast as he can. I know I did."

My eyes blink repeatedly. Jason... oh, that's right. Alex and I aren't in our own little world after all. It had certainly felt that way while he was kissing me. Wow. I need to snap out of it. "Okay," is all I can manage to say at the moment.

I climb back up over the low boulder behind me and begin trying to pull on my wet clothes. It's even harder than it looked when I was watching the girls do it. I have just enough clothes on to be considered decent when Jason comes into view, bolting along the path. He slows to a jog when he sees that I'm in one piece and Alex is sitting nearby. At first, he looks perplexed. Then, when he gets close enough, he spies the alligator.

"Wow! I thought the girls were making all that up, but there really is an alligator!"

I'm surprised he's able to get all that out as hard as he's breathing.

"Are you two okay?" he asks, incredulous.

"Yes, since Alex was close enough to save me," I say, turning toward Alex, who is trying to pull the alligator's body out of the water. "It was unbelievable."

"Jason, how about helping me here?" Alex asks.

"Sure thing," Jason responds, rushing over to assist.

Together, the two men drag out the alligator and wrestle the weight over a low, protruding boulder. Then they stop and sit down to rest for a moment. They look at each other, then at me.

"Cole, I was born and raised a city boy," Alex began. "So I don't know anything about alligators except what I saw in a training film about them when I was stationed temporarily in New Orleans a couple of years ago. The agent in charge even told us how to kill one, because he used to hunt them. I saw it on a television show, too, not more than a month ago."

"Thank God for that," Jason says, wiping the sweat from his brow.

"And they say television is no good for you," Alex smiles that crooked smile of his. "I've seen alligator listed on the menu in a few restaurants in my lifetime; but you're from this guy's native habitat, aren't you? I mean, that sexy southern accent of yours gives you away."

A slow smile spreads across my lips as I realize where he's heading... plus the whole sexy southern accent comment doesn't hurt. "Yeah, you can eat 'em. They're pretty good, really. I've had them before. They actually have a good amount of meat on them, and he's plenty big enough that we can all get a taste of some fresh, unprocessed protein."

"That's just what I wanted to hear. But this guy is way too heavy for us to carry to the others," Alex says, looking at the gator and shaking his head slowly.

"Yeah, he feels like he's probably well over five hundred pounds, I think," Jason pauses, then looks at me as I struggle to pull up my pants. "Cole, why don't you go back to the others and let them see that you're okay... especially your niece. She was going crazy when I took off. Tell them to set up camp and then bring us firewood over here. Alex and I will stay behind and carve up the alligator for dinner. I think there are some plants between here and there that the rest of you can gather for our little celebratory feast."

"That's a great idea." I glance down at the alligator. "You guys have fun with him."

I'm happy that Jason suggested I go, before the men decide it would better for me to stay and help with the alligator carving after all. I put on my shoes quickly then head off at a jog for a reunion with my niece.

Within a few minutes, I'm in sight of the group. I wave my arms in the air as I approach. Elise breaks free from Regina and runs to meet me, leaping into my grasp. It's a good thing for me she's petite like my sister and I; otherwise, I think she would have knocked me over backward. I hold her tightly, reassuring her that I'm fine.

"What happened, Aunt Cole?" she asks.

"Alex came and killed the alligator. He saved my life."

"Oh my God," Regina gasps. "Then it was real? A real alligator?" She starts looking all around her with concern.

"How big was it?" Annie asks.

"Well, I don't know exactly, but pretty big. Something like eight or nine feet, maybe ten, I'm not sure. It was partly in the water when I left the guys back there."

"Wow," several girls reply all at once, their attention fully focused on my every word and expression.

"And guess what?" I ask with a smile, letting the drama build.

"What?" They ask me, their eyes wide in anticipation of more details.

"We are in for a real treat… we're going to have alligator steaks for dinner!" I say with enthusiasm.

Their excitement comes to an end. My idea is met with a loud chorus of groans and 'yuk' and 'gross'. "Oh, y'all don't know what's good. But you'll find out soon enough. We're supposed to set up camp first, and then we'll gather some greens and roots for dinner and some firewood. We're going to meet the men over by the waterfall to eat tonight."

"Do we *have* to eat the alligator?" One of the girls asks.

"No, if you don't want to eat it, you certainly don't have to," I say. "The rest of us will eat your share. Alligator steaks are good; you'll be missing out on a real delicacy, not to mention protein." Well, maybe not quite a delicacy… then again, out here where the selection of meat is limited under the circumstances…

"Alright girls," Regina steps in. "Let's get busy; we've got a lot of work to do. Get the camp set up first, then collect the firewood and stack it over here," she points to a level, open spot nearby.

"And remember, we need enough wood for a fire here and for cooking the gator over by the waterfall," I add. "We'll gather plants after we have gotten all the firewood."

The girls scramble in different directions to get the campsite ready.

Since all I have to do is spread out my sleeping bag, I leave the campsite in order to start picking up good-sized pieces of wood for the fire. I have several chunks in my arms and am about to turn back to camp when I stop to look at my surroundings. I am perplexed. I'm out away from the camp and its activities in a large, yet sparsely-populated grove of trees. Just beyond me, the tree growth becomes substantially denser. I peer intently into the trees. They are visually impenetrable after a few feet in; and their shade is deep, since the sun has gone down behind some tall trees to the west. That prevents me from seeing very far into the forest. The hair is standing up on the back of my neck, though.

What is it? What is in there? Or who? Is this just my imagination? If you think about it, I have thought for a while now that we were being watched. Then there was an alligator, of all things. But an alligator couldn't have been following us, watching our movements. What's going on? Part of me wants to drop the firewood and go into the trees to find out who is in there, if anyone. The other part of me wants to dash back to the relative safety afforded by the group.

I decide to compromise and keep my firewood while I move slowly back to the campsite. I make sure to keep a cautious eye peeled in the vicinity of the forest as I head back, not that I would be able to see anything in there, really.

The girls are talking about dinner when I get back to them. "Okay, girls, I want your sleeping bags moved closer to the tents and the tents closer together. Make a tighter grouping than this."

"Oh, come on, we just got finished, Aunt Cole." Elise is the first to complain.

This is not going to happen. I drop my firewood in the designated area. "I don't care. Do what I say. I want all of you in a tight group, close together. Hurry up now. I'll go get some more firewood."

The girls are busy rearranging things as I walk away. None of the teachers says a word to me. This time, I stay clear of where I gathered the other armload. It's probably just nerves, but I don't want to go back over there. There are plenty of other spots to collect from, anyway. And those places are also closer to camp.

I sure do hope I'm just being paranoid about this. After all, I think I have a right to be, after what happened to me today. It is certainly understandable, anyway.

CHAPTER 19

The alligator meat is pretty good, and after what we've been eating lately, it's a welcome change for most of us. Considering our current circumstances, I would even put it in the category of filet minion. It helps that the meat is so fresh. Marinating it would have done wonders, but beggars can't be choosers, as the saying goes. Everyone takes at least a bite. The men eat the leftovers; and they roast more on the fire for the next day, so none of it goes to waste. We certainly can't afford to do that out here, in our situation. We chuckle and make jokes and eat our fill. It is dusk when we return to our campsite.

The first order of business is to start a fire. The girls sit in groups both large and small, talking off to one side of the camp before taking to bed. They have been such good sports throughout this ordeal. I watch them, sure that they are missing their families back home in Atlanta, but none of them seem to be voicing those feelings to each other. I think they realize we're in a really tough spot and that we are trying our best to get them home. And keep them safe. Plus this day has offered plenty of distractions for them.

I approach Alex, Regina, and Jason at the fire they are stoking for the night with my arms folded across my chest. "Jason, do you have any idea where that alligator might have come from? After all, this is definitely not their native habitat. And I don't believe he was anyone's pet that got too big so they released him into the wild. They can't survive in this part of the country unaided by humans."

He rises to his feet. "Well, I've been thinking about that. Actually, Alex and I were discussing it while we were carving up our dinner over by the waterfall."

"Go ahead, tell her," Alex prompts as Jason hesitates.

"Well, there's a wildlife sanctuary not far from here, Cole. That's the only place I can think of that the alligator would have come from. They have several alligators, along with other exotic animals that aren't native to this area."

My eyes narrow. "Like what, exactly?"

"Well, they call themselves a sanctuary, but they offer what you would call a 'canned hunt'. They let you shoot exotic animals from all over the world, for a high price tag, of course. It's terrible. The animals never have a chance. Bruce always hated having that facility anywhere near his place or the National Forest. He was always concerned about what it would do to the business if any of those predators ever got loose and ate a camper," he finished bluntly.

"Oh my God! Do you think that's what happened?" Regina asks.

"It's the only explanation I have for what happened, for finding an alligator out here," Jason says, shrugging his shoulders.

"Well, how did it get out? Aren't they kept in cages?" Regina insists anxiously.

"They are supposed to be in cages, yes," Jason says. "I toured the sanctuary… or game ranch, as it should be called. It was very secure. The animals were kept in cages or fenced areas, and the perimeter fence was electrified. So even if the alligator got out of its enclosure, it would not be able to get out of the main compound. I just don't understand it. It doesn't make any sense. It would have to have gotten into this creek somehow. I think this is the one that flows through their property."

Regina opens her mouth to ask another question, but hesitates. "Would someone have let it loose on purpose?"

My arms are still crossed. I move them to my hips. My frown deepens as I take a step forward. I decide to cut off any response to Regina's question with something else. "Right now, I just want to know what other kinds of animals they have in there."

Jason, standing only a couple of feet away, looks down at the ground and swallows hard then shifts his gaze to me. "Big cats – tigers, lions, I don't know how many. But they had a lot of each when Bruce and I were there. They specialize in predator species and other animals that people might want a trophy of, like zebras and some fancy gazelles and antelope. They said they didn't have any endangered species; but they wouldn't take us everywhere, and they had huge buildings for the animals to stay protected during the winter months, so I never believed that myself."

"Big cats?! Great, just great," I growl, turning away from the others, shaking my head.

"What is it, Cole?" Regina asks. "Do you think somebody let some of those other animals loose, too? Why would somebody do that? Are they trying to get people killed?"

"Yes, that's exactly what I'm afraid of," I reply harshly, but look at Jason instead as I turn back toward our little group. "Something is out there. I've had the feeling we were being watched for a couple of days now. And a while ago, when I was up by the forest getting firewood, the hair on my neck was standing on its end. There was something in there, somewhere, I'm telling you. I wasn't imagining it."

The other three exchange looks.

"And there's no way it's those guys who were going to kill you back by Camp Correll, Alex." I shift my gaze momentarily to him in anticipation of what I think he might say next. "They're either dead or close enough to it that they couldn't come after us. But the animals, that makes more sense," I finish angrily.

"But how would they have gotten out?" Jason asks. "I told you, they were all in cages. And those cages were inside a big, electrified fence. There's no way they got out of there. The water supply to that place comes from one of the creeks around here; I'm pretty sure it's the one we found the alligator in. If he somehow got out of his cage, maybe he jumped into the creek and swam upstream or something, that's all it is. There's no way any of the others got out. The odds of one of those wild animals getting loose and coming right up here to where we are in order to hunt us have got to be astronomical."

"Really?" Regina speaks up. "You really think that? I'm sure Cole and Alex would both disagree with you after tangling with that alligator."

"Yeah," I respond, "if that thing got out, the others could have, too. What makes you conclude he's the only one?"

"Well, I don't know. I guess I was just trying to look on the bright side of things, that's all. It's more understandable that the alligator escaped, a lot less understandable that all of them did."

"Okay then, let me put it this way… what makes you think it's worth taking a chance on it? This is no time for optimism," I say.

Alex gets to his feet. "We need to keep watch – all night. Not you, Cole. You've been through enough today," he says quickly and points dismissively in my direction.

I look at him questioningly and open my mouth to protest.

"Jason and I will take turns," he says before I can get started. "We're the only ones who are armed."

Jason nods in agreement. "Alex is right, Cole. The only hope we have against a wild animal like a big cat is a gun. The fire might help keep them away, but we have to keep a close eye on all the kids. They'll be the primary targets. The cats will see them as easier prey; they're vulnerable. Hopefully, if you're right and those animals are out there somewhere, they will go for deer or something like that instead."

"We haven't seen any deer since we've been out here," Regina notes. "Maybe they know what's going on and they've all run away. They can move a lot faster than we can."

I don't know when I have ever felt this helpless. "Regina, why don't you come with me? I think it's time we settle those kids down for the night."

"Sure thing. We need to get them quiet so they don't attract the wrong kind of attention," she says. "And I'll let the other teachers know what's going on."

I stop and look back at the men. "You two are our best hope of defense. Whoever isn't on watch had better be sure to get some sleep when you get the chance so you aren't exhausted tomorrow. We need you to be on top of your game to protect those kids." I see them give each other a look of resignation.

Regina and I get the girls into their tents and sleeping bags and give them a few minutes to nod off. Then I call the other chaperones over so that Regina and I can let them in on our possible situation. It's going to be a long and probably sleepless night.

CHAPTER 20

The kids seem to have all awakened in a particularly chatty mood. They are rehashing the adventures of the day before with excitement that I just can't truly comprehend. For me, it had been a totally different experience. Except for Alex kissing me… that part was amazing. Even knowing there are new dangers we could be facing now, I can't stop thinking about it. I glance over his way while I'm wrapping up my sleeping bag and find him staring at me intently. I smile at him, and he returns it before resuming his breakfast preparations with Jason.

When we have eaten the last of the alligator, which has really become jerky at this point, thoroughly extinguished the remains of last night's campfire and finished our packing, it's time to get underway for the day's hike. This is going to be another day where I'm so very tired the whole time. I feel like I'm never going to get fully-rested as long as we're out here. I guess it's time for a self-pity party. Probably all the adults feel just as tired. My feet shuffle along in the dusty terrain. Occasionally, my spirits will lift as we pass a particularly pretty wildflower, but those are few and far between in this area. It's quite dry here. The course of the streambed has meandered off to the east and we decided against following it, giving up the possibility of fish for the certainty of no more alligator confrontations.

The sun is partway up in the sky, probably around nine in the morning, when everything changes. We've been hiking in the same formation as yesterday, so Jason and I are far ahead of the rest of the group. I spot something out of place in a patch of dirt, populated with a few isolated clumps of dying weeds, off to the side of where I have just placed my foot. I stop and squat down to examine it more closely. In an instant, I know what it is.

"Jason!" I call out sharply.

He stops so fast he almost stumbles. He jogs back to me. "What is it, Cole?"

"Look at this." I point to the ground in front of me. "It looks like a large paw print from a cat."

His expression becomes an intense, concerned scowl as he kneels beside me. "Oh my God… you're right, Cole. That footprint is from a big cat. And not a mountain lion, either. Tracks from a mountain lion are smaller and those animals generally stay away from people. The cats at the sanctuary were big… and they were accustomed to people and wouldn't be afraid of them." He hesitates. "They know that people bring them food."

"Which means, people are food," I surmise quickly.

"Yeah," he says, standing to scan the area thoroughly.

I do the same next to him. "Is there any way you can you tell how old it is?"

"No. Not exactly, anyway. It isn't all that old, because it's a clear impression. It doesn't look as if it has been worn away from the wind or rain at all; not that there's been any rain."

"Great," I say, exploring the area in my search for other tracks. I easily find quite a few. "I've got more tracks over here. They're about the same size and shape, so they're probably all from the same animal. They're pretty much in a line," I gaze toward another deep stand of forest and point. "It looks like it went in there."

Jason steps up beside me and peers into the distant forest, too. Neither of us makes a sound. It's easy to hear the kids approaching from behind us. Jason rests his hand on his gun in its holster; and we look back toward the kids, then at each other. He nods and I take several paces backward then turn as Elizabeth and the first members of the group come over to our location.

I watch until Alex, in his position of rear guard, comes into view then I hold up my hands to halt the group, just as Elizabeth reaches me. We've only been hiking for a little over an hour. I can see from Elizabeth's face that she knows something has changed, and probably not for the better.

"Kids, I want you to gather over here close to me," I call out to them. It's time they found out what we're up against. Now that we have been presented with proof, that is.

"Girls, I don't want to scare you; but there's something you need to know about." I glance over at Alex and see that he isn't listening to me. He must have read Jason's body language instantly because he has placed his hand onto the grip of his gun and is scanning the area behind us dutifully.

"There is an animal sanctuary near here. It looks like some of their animals have gotten out somehow. That's where we think the alligator came from. We believe the sanctuary also had some big cats…" I hesitate, but they have to know. "They had some tigers and lions. There is no way to know what they had in there at this time or how many there were. Jason visited there last year at this time; and that's what they had, but it could be different now."

The poor kids; their eyes are growing wider, and they aren't uttering a sound. They're starting to put two and two together as I speak. "We don't want you to be afraid, just careful; very careful. We just found some tracks in the dirt over here from one of the big cats. We don't know exactly what kind it is or how many of them there are, and there's no way for us to be able to tell. But it's vitally important now that you listen to all us adults and do everything we tell you. And I mean absolutely everything and without question. Do you understand?"

Their heads are nodding in unison. So far, so good.

"We're going to stay close together. No wandering off for anybody," Regina says.

She continues to talk to them as I walk around the group toward Alex. "Alex," I begin when I reach him.

"What happened?" he asks me without taking his eyes off of some nearby trees.

"I found some tracks from a big cat. Jason said mountain lions' paw prints aren't that large. The tracks lead into the woods over there, just past where Jason is standing."

"Okay, listen," Alex begins, "I'm going to go over and talk with Jason for a minute. I need to make sure he's not going to try to go off after it. He kind of looks to me like he might be thinking about it. I want you to stay put in this spot until I get back and keep watch back here, do you understand me?"

"Yeah, sure… of course," I say.

"Don't take your eyes off the area behind us, just to make sure. If you see anything at all, you yell for me, and I'll be right beside you before you can finish calling my name, okay?" He has his hand on my shoulder and is looking at me with a very stern demeanor.

"I understand. Don't worry. If I see anything, you'll know it," I face the trees he was watching and start scanning all around me as he jogs off. I'm nervous; but I'm trying hard not to show it, especially in front of the girls. Those kids need all of us adults to remain calm and confident. Some of us are doing a better job of it than others.

I take a chance on a quick glimpse toward the group, just for an instant. The adults at least seem to be trying to put on brave faces. The kids and adults are clustered together in a tight group, waiting and watching the two men ahead of them, who appear to be in a deep discussion.

Now I'm thankful that it has been so dry here. There's plenty of wood for fires. Fires will help us stay alive by keeping the predators away during the night. Hopefully, tomorrow we'll be able to reach some kind of excuse for civilization and get help. All we have to do is make it through the next twenty-four hours or so, provided that Jason's estimates are right, that is. He knows this area better than any of us, for sure.

Alex is back by my side quickly. "What's the plan?" I ask.

"We're going to keep moving, just like we have been for the past couple of days. You and Jason take the lead, and I'll bring up the rear. You keep a sharp-eye lookout for more tracks. Jason will stay a lot closer to you, and you'll stay closer to the group. We're tightening up the formation even more. There's a lot to be said for safety in numbers."

"That sounds good to me," I say and start off toward Jason, but Alex stops me short by grabbing my arm and pulling me close enough to give me a quick kiss.

"You make sure you stay safe," he says as he releases me.

"Don't worry, I will," I say. "You make sure you do the same."

He winks and faces away from me, his hand back on his gun.

I walk past the girls and catch Elise's eye. I give her a quick thumbs up as I pass by and have just enough time to see her return the gesture, albeit nervously. Retrieving my walking stick, I adjust the sheath with my knife in it so it is as close at hand as possible.

We all move out as one. I do not look back. I know the girls will do their best and the adults behind me will take good care of them. Each of us has a job now, and I must stay focused. Fortunately after a short while, we move farther away from trees altogether. That means more open land and fewer potential hiding places and thus less to worry about. It's then that I start having trouble. I wish my mind wouldn't start straying away periodically, while thinking of those kisses from both Jason and Alex… again. Damn it. I need to have my brain scanned when we get back home.

Lunch is a brief pit stop. We resume hiking right away and manage to get something close to four miles without another break.

I continue with my lookout duties, just behind Jason. So preoccupied am I with focusing on the ground around me for tracks that I walk right past Jason, who has halted at the top of the latest hill we have come to. I stop and glance over at him, puzzling at the expression on his face. What in the world? Then I follow his gaze and see why he looks the way he does. Spread out before us is more forestland, and it is fairly dense. My heart sinks.

"Jason, we're going to have to stop and make camp here for the night," I look into his eyes. "You know there's no way we can get through that before dark, and we certainly can't camp in there."

"You're right. We're safer out in the open. We can make a defensible position here at the top of this hill," he says as he studies the terrain.

"Defensible position?" I grin. "You sound like Alex."

"Do I? I'll take that as a compliment. He's a good guy. I like him, Cole. It's obvious to anyone who cares to open their eyes that he's crazy about you. I just don't want you to forget that I'm crazy about you, too, and…," he's taken ahold of my hand, but the close approach of the group cuts him off. "We'll talk later." He releases my hand quickly.

"I'll get everyone settled in." I watch as he takes a few steps away from me and stops, checking out the surroundings.

"Okay, everybody, we're going to make camp here. Start getting everything set up," I announce to the group.

"Jason, you, me, DeShondra, Caryn, Lisa, and Regina will go and gather what we can find to eat. But firewood is the most important thing of all; we can always eat off of the supplies we're carrying in our backpacks. I want the rest of you to set up camp and make it a nice, tight grouping, okay? We're all friends here, so there should be no problem sleeping close together. And while I'm gone, Alex and Elizabeth are in charge. We'll be back soon, and we're not going to be far away." I finish by looking at Elise and giving her a wink.

"Jason," Alex calls out, stopping our little foraging band for an instant. "You keep your eyes open and your gun drawn. Let the women do the gathering; you need to have their backs. Understood?"

"Yeah, I've got it," Jason answers with a deep voice and the weight of responsibility. "I'll take good care of them – don't worry."

"Let's go," I say. "The sooner we leave, the sooner we get back."

We walk down the hill toward the forest. It's certainly the best place for firewood and the most likely place for anything edible. It looks so dark and foreboding, though. The sun is getting lower in the sky, and we'll probably only get three or four trips inside and back up to camp before dark.

Wood for the fire is the unstated priority; besides, there is little food to gather where we are, where the tree cover is relatively sparse – and we are afraid to go any deeper just now. With only five of us to haul firewood, we are overloaded but manage to get through it, and by the third trip we have what we believe is enough to get us through the night.

On the fourth trip, we hope to bring back some food, too. "DeShondra, you are the youngest and strongest, so I'm going to need you to carry extra firewood for this last load. Regina and I will stuff our backpacks with edible plants and then I can carry a regular load of firewood along with that, too. Regina, you just carry food, both in the backpack and in your arms, provided that we can find that much. Does that sound like a good enough plan to everyone?"

"Yes, that'll be fine," DeShondra says and starts gathering the better pieces of wood she can find.

We make it back without encountering any dangerous animals, but dusk is leaving us. Alex, Elizabeth, and the kids have camp set up and have started two smaller fires, rather than a single large one. This idea affords our large group a little extra protection with a fire at each end of the campsite. It seems to brighten up the area better, too. We eat in relative silence then turn in early, adults along the outsides, kids in the middle. Alex sleeps on the side nearest the woods; and I sit near him, taking the first watch. Opposite us, Jason also has first watch. We will stay in position until midnight, when I am to switch off with Alex. Jason will stay on guard until around one o'clock in the morning, when Regina will take over, with our guide sleeping near her.

Alex is very quiet and not moving, so I assume he's asleep; he is facing away from me. I have no idea how he can sleep so soundly. I'm tired, but I don't know if I'll be able to sleep at all when my turn comes. My nerves are on edge. At least there will be a full moon tonight.

The ground here is hard, baked by the sun as it has been; it certainly isn't comfortable. My rear is getting numb from sitting on it. There probably hasn't been any rain for quite some time. I start to wonder about the potential threat, somewhere out there. What would a wild animal like a lion do? He probably lived his whole life in confinement, a prisoner, maybe under inhumane conditions – who knows? All the while he's waiting. Just waiting for an opportunity to be free, to run away, far away from the hunters who would claim his hide as a prize and mount his head on a wall.

Then one day, someone decides to let him go free. Now, why would someone do that? It could easily prove to be from an act of suicide, since people do stupid things like that while committing suicide sometimes. But what if there is an alternative scenario? What if, say, the power is turned off or goes out somehow; and he got free that way? Something is not quite right about that. Think, what is it? He wouldn't get free just because the power went out. Thunderstorms probably do that sometimes anyway. Or bad storms in the winter. They must have multiple generators there, to keep the power going, especially to run the interior facilities for the comfort and enjoyment of the guests. And for the winter housing of the animals. So what makes this time different? Did the generator not turn on? Why not? Why did the animals escape the entire compound this time? If someone did set them loose, why would they do that? Could it have something to do with the power?

The "sanctuary" must be like Camp Correll, with several employees to feed and care for the animals and the grounds and to escort the hunters around. There is supposed to be something like Camp Correll's cabins, too, only on a grander scale, way more luxurious. The customers there have money, and lots of it. They are used to being treated special. Jackasses.

And where are these employees? Now that there's a situation that requires their help, or anyone's help, for that matter. It just doesn't make any sense. None of it does.

Camp Correll is empty. The "sanctuary" is probably empty, too. And there have been no airplanes, no search parties for us. What in the world is going on here? What could have happened in the world beyond this place to cause everyone to disappear? No, that isn't right. Disappearing doesn't happen.

People leave, that's what happens. They deserted, or maybe evacuated. Just like at Camp Correll. They left. And the animals were starving, and some of them escaped. Or else they were set free by their captors. The animals were their bread and butter; why would they let them go?

Because they weren't planning on coming back, that's why. At least, not for a long time… or maybe ever. What could have possibly happened to make people believe the situation was that hopeless, if that's what happened? Could it have been the fires? No one is coming to fight them, so maybe the fires drove them away. That is a possibility, at least. It also happens to be the only one I can come up with. The puzzle I've been working on in my head has become much larger, and quite dire.

CHAPTER 21

The new day dawns bright and clear… this is rapidly becoming the norm out here, I think. We eat more breakfast than usual, because we are planning to walk straight through the forest to the community on the other side without stopping. We gather our belongings, making sure everything is secure so no one drops anything to require stopping to pick it up. Everyone who has a walking stick is prepared to use it, as Alex uses mine now to show the kids a few defensive moves they would be able to handle if necessary. Everyone also has a knife where they can get at it quickly.

I give one last bit of instruction to the kids. "If you see one of the big cats, or anything else, don't run. Do you understand me, kids? No matter what, you don't run. The cats will see you as prey and come after you. I'm not trying to scare you; I'm just trying to protect you. We can only keep you safe if you stay together and do everything exactly as we tell you. Alex and Jason won't let anything happen to any of us, okay?"

Alex and Jason nod and smile reassuringly at the kids; then with a quick nod to each other, their expressions become stern. The kids form a tight group as we head out, with Jason leading the way. Alex and I are bringing up the rear, as an attack from behind is much more likely, according to Jason. The rest of the adults space themselves out and walk along the sides of the group of kids. We are all on high alert and stay relatively quiet as we hike.

Every step I take seems like I'm moving deeper and deeper into a trap. From the demeanor on the faces around me, everyone must feel the same way. I haven't known the girls to be so hushed on the entire trip. Each crack of a branch under someone's foot causes a spasm to course through everyone else. Walking through a forest makes it extremely difficult to be quiet, not to mention how hard it is to stay in a tight grouping without tripping over one another.

At mid-afternoon, we emerge on the other side of the forest, at long last. There have been no incidents of any kind, and the relief is palpable. There, before us, is the small community we have been marching toward. We breathe a collective sigh of relief, and I see smiles on the girls' faces. Jason motions for us to be silent as we continue toward the house that is nearest us. There are about forty or so structures all together. Easily more than half of them are barns or storage buildings of some sort or another. One of the buildings in particular looks like it was made to serve the little village, perhaps as a store or some such purpose. That would be wonderful; maybe we could get supplies there, in addition to the use of a telephone. Off in the far distance, I can see another little cluster of buildings, likely a ranch house and barns. There is yet another grouping down a road off to our left, much farther away.

We stop at the front porch of the closest building, which is a large, two-story, weather-beaten white farmhouse. Its black shutters have been painted sometime within the past year, it appears. They have a little silhouette of a man on a tractor carved out of them. White-laced curtains hang in the closed windows, preventing us from seeing inside. Strange, I would have thought in a little community like this that the curtains would mostly be open and inviting. Maybe that's just me, though, recalling a stereotype.

Jason walks slowly up the steps to the front door, which has also recently been painted a shiny black, with a small glass panel near the top. We collectively hold our breath as he knocks. No one answers. He knocks again, louder this time.

While we wait, I look around us, as Alex is doing. I lean over to him and whisper, "Nobody's home. Anywhere. There aren't any cars, no tractors are moving, no people, no dogs or cats or any other animals."

Alex narrows his eyes and looks at me. "I know. This isn't looking good for us getting some help."

Jason tries the doorknob, which is locked. He goes around to the back door with the same results. Next, he tries the first-story windows. The wide one to the side of the front door lifts obligingly. It will make for an easy entry, being only about two feet above the level of the porch.

"Hello!" Jason calls out first, reaching in to slide back the curtains obscuring view of the interior. "Hello, is anyone home? We have a bunch of kids with us here, and we need help."

Again, we all wait hopefully; but there is no response. The house seems to be unoccupied.

Jason turns to the group. "I'm going inside to look around. The rest of you just wait out here." He climbs through the window, and we wait anxiously for him to return.

Within a few minutes, he opens the front door. "Come on in; there's no one here. It looks like they packed up and vacated this place in a hurry. But they left plenty of food behind."

At the magic word, food, the kids surge forward, nearly knocking Jason over. Alex holds my arm to stop me from going along and calls out, "Jason!"

Jason reappears in the doorway.

"I'm going to take Cole and scout some of the other buildings. We'll be back before dark. Keep an eye out, just in case the homeowners come back. We don't want any surprises."

"Okay, I will. You two be careful... and don't let anything happen to her, whatever you do," he orders pointedly at Alex then closes the door.

The kids are chattering away again, I can hear them through the open window. I turn back and run up on the porch. "Hey, Annie! Come close the window, please, honey."

She obliges. "Thanks!" I wave and rejoin Alex in the crunchy brown front yard.

We head down the long, dirt driveway, toward the building at the center of this community, which has the sign 'Anderson's General Store' posted on the front of it, about a quarter mile from the house. Little clouds of dust rise beneath our feet as we walk. Looking up, I see no clouds and still no contrails, not that I expected anything different.

The General Store is locked up tight; but Alex successfully picks the front door lock, and we enter the relative darkness, which becomes even darker when he closes the door after us. We open curtains at the dirty windows, which admit some scant light.

"Wow, look at all this food, Alex!" I marvel at the relative bounty on the shelves.

I hear a repeating click and look back at Alex. He's trying the light switches.

"No power," I say.

"No, it doesn't look like it," Alex says, scanning the large room.

I find a basket and begin filling it with canned goods.

Alex goes over to the refrigerated section against the back wall. "What of this do you think is drinkable with no power? Other than the milk, of course. I know that must be bad."

There is obviously no power there, either. I could tell when we walked in, since there were no lights showing through the glass and no sound of motors running to keep the products inside cold. "No orange juice or other fruit drinks, unfortunately. I don't know anything about beer, so you'll be taking your chances." I add that in, as he's obviously eyeing that part of the refrigerator.

"It might be worth it," he calls to me as he reaches for a case.

I just shake my head and sigh. "The waters will all be fine, and the power drinks. The sodas are okay, too. The kids will just have to drink them warm, which is no big deal, really."

Alex props one of the doors open. "You know, either we're going to have to make a ridiculous number of trips back and forth, or we're going to have to enlist more help to get this stuff over to the farmhouse."

"Hey, maybe there's a wheelbarrow somewhere," I suggest. "Most farms have at least one wheelbarrow. When we walk back over with an armload of drinks and food, we can check the old barn."

"Sounds like a plan, boss lady. And that way, we won't have so many people out in the open to watch over."

When I look at him, he is resting his arms on the end of a low shelf and smiling at me.

"What?" I ask.

"Nothing; I just like looking at you, that's all."

I can tell my cheeks are reddening. Now I'm glad it's so dark in here. "Okay..." I'm not feeling too swift on the comebacks at the moment.

"You're smart, too. You always seem to know just what to do; and even if it seems impossible, you find a way to make it work."

Now my cheeks are flaming. "Thanks, Alex. You do a really good job of that, too, you know." I get the funny feeling he's going to come over and kiss me. He's got this look on his face. I think fleetingly of Jason and suddenly I'm confused. I like Alex, but it has been so long since I've really had a relationship, it makes me nervous. Fight or flight.

I choose flight. "I'm going to take what I've got and go find a wheelbarrow or something we can use to haul this stuff in. I'll be back in fifteen minutes. Don't drink too much beer while I'm gone."

Alex looks back at the case of beer propping open the refrigerator door. "Hey, that's not a bad idea," he grins at me. "No, I'm just kidding, don't worry. Actually, you'll stay here while I go. You can't be out there walking around unprotected. Jason gave me a directive, remember?"

He walks past me without waiting for a response and picks up the one box I have ready by the front door. "Stay put." The door closes behind him.

I find myself wondering why he didn't kiss me on his way out. Now wait a minute. Only moments before, I wanted to get out of that situation. What in the world is the matter with me?

I place some of the food into boxes while I'm waiting for Alex, then start putting the bottles of water, soda, and power drinks near the front door so we can get them out quickly. After nearly a half hour, in my estimation, I begin to wonder where Alex could be. I walk behind the counter with its old cash register and peer through the dirty window. I can't see anything, so I spit on the window and wipe it with a tissue from the box by the register. It smears the dirt, but it's better than it was. There's no one outside, at least not from this vantage point. Where is he, for crying out loud?

A rattling of the back door scares me so badly that it's now easy for me to understand the saying about someone jumping out of their skin. I rush to the refrigerator and pick up one of the bottles of beer. Then I move down the short, narrow, dark hallway to the back door. I raise the bottle over my head just as the door opens to reveal Alex with a small tool in his hand. The same tool he had used to break into the front door of this building.

"Whoa, there, angel!" He ducks his head and lifts an arm in reflex then lowers it as I put my arm down in response. "Who in the world did you think it was? After all, we seem to be the only people out here."

"You're late! I was beginning to think maybe something happened to you," I reply with a touch of harshness in my voice, shifting the bottle to my left hand. "I was worried."

"You were?" he says in a soothing voice, stepping up into the entryway and closing the door behind him. I take a step back as he reaches out and takes my left hand, placing his other hand around my waist.

There isn't really enough time for me to get nervous. He pulls me close to him and kisses me, softly at first, then with an intensity that is growing by the second. I can feel it flowing through me. I run the fingers of my right hand through his hair and pull him deeper into the kiss. I don't think there has ever been anything remotely like this feeling in me for any other man, but then, it has been a long time. I know I don't want to let him go.

He pulls his face back from mine slightly, just enough to end the kiss, but not so far away that he can't do it again. "Wow… Cole, would you believe me if I told you…"

He is cut off by the sudden sound of barking, loud and not too far away. It's coming from multiple dogs, and they are frantic about something. Alex extends his arms while holding onto me, thus pushing me back. He puts a finger to his lips and draws his gun. He opens the back door in a quick motion, his eyes scanning for the dogs.

Meanwhile, I rush to the front door, thinking the dogs might be heading for the white house and the children. I open the door and see in the distance what looks to be several antelope or some such creatures, with long, twisted horns, running away along a hilltop at full speed. The dogs, three of them of various sizes, must have spotted the unusual animals while they were somewhere nearby; they are headed off away from us in pursuit now. It is possible that they are not chasing them for a kill, only out of curiosity. But then again, who knows how long they've gone without food. Several additional dogs are already close behind the wild animals.

I close the door and turn to find Alex bringing in a wheelbarrow, pausing only to close the door behind him. "Come on, let's hurry up. We might have enough time to get the drinks loaded and over to the house before those dogs lose interest in the sanctuary refugees and come over this way and find us. As soon as they see or smell us, the jig is up. We don't know if they're friendly or not, and I don't want to wait around to find out."

"Yeah, okay," I say, still a little dazed by everything that has happened over the past couple of minutes… first that incredible kiss, then a pack of dogs and the herd of antelope; now the rush to get back to the house safely before we might possibly be attacked by the dogs.

We get the wheelbarrow loaded quickly; and Alex opens the door and runs off down the handicapped ramp with it, not waiting for me. He knows I can handle myself, I guess. I close the door and sprint after him, carrying a box of canned meats and lots of beef jerky. I find it hard to keep up, even though the wheelbarrow is overloaded and is sure to be heavy.

As we approach the house, the front door swings open; and Jason bolts out, leaping the porch stairs in an impressive bound. He runs past Alex to me and takes the box from my arms without missing a beat, allowing me to dash for the porch. The other adults are there with bags and boxes to unload the drinks. They swarm the wheelbarrow; and we have it unloaded in less than a minute, tops. We leave the wheelbarrow and scramble for the safety of the house, slamming the door behind us and locking it.

My arms and legs are throbbing from the exertion, bringing back memories of running so frantically from the wildfire. I sit down on the sofa, and I'm soon joined by Alex. It takes a few minutes for us to get our breathing back to normal and we gratefully accept the water bottles offered to us by a couple of the kids. Jason and the other adults have vanished, but we can hear them in the kitchen. It sounds as if they are preparing a meal.

I take a long drink and then allow myself to relax, sinking back into the couch. Alex does the same, placing a hand on mine, and giving it a squeeze. I let my head lean over his way and rest it on his shoulder. We did it. Now we just need to figure out our next steps.

Our dinner that night tastes like it came from a fancy restaurant, even though it is cold and comes from cans. There is no electricity here, either. It is so wonderful to eat something besides jerky, fish, and greens. After we have all stuffed ourselves like it was Thanksgiving, Alex and Jason walk through the house and double check the doors and windows on the first floor, to be certain they are secured for the night. The adults divide up for the five bedrooms in the house, sharing the almost-forgotten luxury of soft beds with those kids who have the most bumps and bruises. The other kids sleep on the floors of various rooms, both upstairs and down. Alex and Jason sleep on the first floor, one on the sofa, the other in a recliner.

During the night, howling awakens me. I get up and move from room to room on the second floor, checking on the kids up here and peering through the open windows, looking toward the other buildings in the area, searching for lights or other signs of life. Everything is dark. I hear another howl, more distant this time, and return to my assigned spot to lie down. Sleep comes quickly in a soft bed, safe inside the house.

CHAPTER 22

The sun is well up above the horizon when I stir to consciousness. I have slept relatively late, at least for me on this trip. I get up and go downstairs to find Alex in the kitchen, pulling together a breakfast. He smiles as I approach. "You must have slept well. I haven't known you to sleep this long. You must have needed it pretty badly."

I rub his back affectionately when I reach him. "I did, you're right. I hope you slept well, too. You're fixing breakfast?"

He ceases his preparations momentarily and kisses me. The world stops for a brief moment, and we are the only ones in it. He pulls back and looks longingly into my eyes. "Yes, I am. I am a man of many talents," he says in a low voice, putting his lips by my ear. "One of these days I'll show you what I'm convinced is my best one. I think you'll like it."

"I'm sure I will," I say as I tighten my grip around his waist and he kisses me again, soft and lingering.

I let go of him reluctantly when I hear the sound of feet walking around upstairs and pitch in to help. We open cans of fruit and boxes of granola bars. Cereal is also available. I don't think anyone will mind eating it without milk. The girls come in small waves to collect food and go elsewhere to consume a fairly normal breakfast, for a change. Alex and I eat as we prepare food for the others. Periodically, I stop to look out the glass panes of the back door, checking for the dogs. I find it suspicious that they never returned. I wonder if they are friend or foe to us. If they are hungry, I would be happy to feed them. I saw dog food on a shelf in the General Store. Why would someone leave without their dogs? The memory of how Noel had reacted at the thought of having to leave her cat behind when we were children and preparing to escape that wildfire comes flooding back.

Maybe those dogs had also run off, and their owners had been unable to get them to return before they evacuated... maybe.

"Alex, I think we should go back to the General Store and see what else we can bring over. We need to finish checking the other buildings today, too; since we didn't do it yesterday," I say while looking out the back door again.

"Yes, you're right about that, angel. We'll need to get more supplies. We also need to be thinking about getting out of here and finding some help," Alex says as Jason enters the kitchen. "Jason, where is a decent-sized city around here?"

I turn from studying the farmland outside, interested in the answer to Alex's question.

Jason pulls up a chair at the table. "Well, that would be too far to take these kids, at least in my opinion. Besides, there are two more communities between here and there to check out."

"Really?" Alex asks. "Either of them bigger than this one?"

"Sure. One is almost twice this size and the other one beyond it has something like a few thousand people in it," he pauses, stretching his arms. "Look, this area doesn't have a lot of people. It's isolated. Some people like that kind of life, some don't. Most don't, I guess. Still, we've got a better shot at the second community down from here. The other one is a lot like this one; so we may not find any help there, either. It looks like everyone around here abandoned ship. Whatever happened, they decided to get out and quick."

"Yeah, about that," Alex begins. "Any ideas what might have happened? I already know what Cole thinks. And seeing this place empty makes me think she might be right." He watches for my reaction, but I just cross my arms and say nothing, leaning back against the counter.

"And what might that be?" Jason asks, looking at me.

"Terrorism," Alex answers simply.

"There haven't been any airplanes in the sky, and no one came to fight the wildfire," I say.

Jason thinks about that for a moment. "You're right about that; they should have come to fight the fire. It was plenty big enough, and especially as dry as it has been around here this spring. You think the government stopped all the air traffic, like after 9-11? I was just a baby then, but I read about it in school."

Wow, I keep forgetting how young he is. He's several years younger than I am. "Maybe."

Alex looks at me with a puzzled expression. "You also noted that no search and rescue parties have come to find the kids. You're all way overdue, after all."

"Yeah, that's true. I hadn't thought about that," Jason says.

Regina steps into the kitchen to join in on the conversation. "I've thought about that, too. So, how bad do you think it might be, Alex?"

"Me?" He seems surprised.

"Well, you're the secret agent from out of Washington, D.C., right?" she winks.

"Not quite, and I'm out of the San Francisco field office, most recently, anyway."

"Oh, that sounds lovely," she says, getting distracted.

Elizabeth and Caryn walk in to join us.

I laugh at Regina then get serious. "There is another possibility that I think we have to consider." I have their full attention now; and I look directly at Regina as I speak, since she is the science teacher. I take a deep breath before I begin, because even though everything fits my new theory better than an act of terrorism, the others will most certainly believe I'm reaching pretty far out with it. "And it's a lot worse. Regina, I'm sure you've heard of the Carrington Event of 1859. The sun is coming out of what's called solar minimum right now. The maximum is still a few years away, but these explosions can happen at any time. At the beginning of our trip, we saw a really large group of sunspots and that night we experienced a rather dramatic display of aurora."

"Yes, I remember that," Jason says. "But what does that have to do with any of this?"

"The sun is very powerful. It sometimes bombards the Earth with material ejected in explosive events," Regina explains. She's following my train of thought, just as I'd hoped she would.

"And the most powerful event is called a CME, a Coronal Mass Ejection. If that happened while the sun and the Earth were in just the right positions, the Earth would have been hit," I say quietly.

Regina's face becomes somber with the realization. "These things have hit our planet before with a glancing blow and taken out radio and satellite communications in Canada and other parts of the Earth. If we were hit by one a couple of weeks ago and it was big enough, it would knock out communications everywhere."

"And not just that," I pull out a chair and sit across from Jason. "It could have knocked out everything, not just communications. The theory is that it would overload power stations and substations everywhere, causing explosions, ruining the equipment and destroying the power grid all around the world."

"Wait," Alex inserts himself into the line of reasoning. "Wouldn't it just knock it out, and then we can turn it back on after, what... a few days? They can fix it... right?"

"No, this would essentially be permanent – for all of that equipment, anyway – especially if the event was powerful enough. It would have blown everything, overloaded it all. All of the computers, everything; they're all connected. There won't be power to run anything – electricity, water, sewer, anything, anywhere in the world. I have heard scientists warning that this needs to be taken as a serious threat to human civilization. That when, not if, it happened, it would set mankind back a hundred years or maybe even more. They even warned Congress. Congress chose to take no action." I look from face to face, seeing their astonishment.

Regina adds, "No electricity, no computers, no telephones… no cars, even, because there won't be any power to run the gas pumps. Nothing will work."

"There are projections that billions of people will die, whether it's from fighting over food or shelter or from diseases," I explain. It has to be said.

"There would be wars and chaos worldwide," Alex says slowly. "My God in Heaven."

"Exactly," I say. "We should all pray that isn't what happened. If it is, I don't know what we're going to do…"

"That isn't what happened," Jason stands, pushing back his chair. "It can't be. That's got to be so crazy impossible that we don't even need to be talking about it." He strides quickly from the room.

"Is it wrong to hope that it was terrorists instead?" Elizabeth whispers it so softly I almost don't hear it and follows Jason out.

I stare down at the table and don't seem to be able to move. It is out in the open now, my latest theory. I hope so desperately that I'm wrong. Alex touches my shoulder so I stand up and spin around to face him, throwing my arms around his neck and holding on tightly.

He takes me in his arms and puts his lips near my ear. "Don't worry, we'll be alright. I don't know how, but I know we'll be alright. Let's not worry about something we're not even sure of right now, okay?"

"Okay," I mumble as I push back from him and try to regain my composure. He's right, I know. "I don't want to worry the kids too much."

"Let's get that wheelbarrow and go get some more supplies. That will give us something productive to do. Let's take Jason along, too. Regina, please be sure to keep the kids inside while we're gone."

All she can manage is a nod of agreement. She settles heavily, almost unsteady, into Jason's chair at the table. Caryn pulls out the chair beside her and buries her face in her hands.

Alex heads off, I'm sure to fetch Jason's help. I stand in the kitchen with Regina and Caryn, staring out at the view from the back door. No dogs are in sight.

"Okay, let's go," Alex comes down the stairs and heads for the front door, Jason close behind. I fall in at the rear.

We cut across the huge yard today, saving a few minutes by avoiding the long, winding driveway. The General Store provides us with drinks and food for the day. It seems it could supply us for a week or more, but we will be long gone by then. There has to be help for us out there, somewhere.

I wait, standing guard near the front door while the men first load boxes and then place the boxes onto the wheelbarrow. Alex takes the wheelbarrow again, while Jason manages to carry boxes piled so high he can't even see where he's going. I only have two boxes, so I walk alongside him to guide where he places his feet. We scarcely talk. Our small group proceeds up the driveway, as it is smoother for traveling with our load.

After dropping off the supplies at the house, we leave the others to sort through them. The three of us head off to begin a search of every structure for anything we might be able to use. The second house has supplies, much like the first one did. We have enough, so we leave the belongings untouched. We move to the next structure, which is a huge, old Dutch-style barn with several boards missing and peeling red paint. We search the barn, looking for anything helpful.

I open a large tool cabinet and can hardly believe my eyes. "Oh my God!"

Both men rush over to my side. "What is it, Cole?" Alex asks first.

I remove a small, dark orange-and-black device from one of the cabinet shelves. "Do you guys know what this is?"

Jason's eyes widen. "It's a hand-cranked emergency radio! Cole, that's fantastic! Now we can find out what's going on."

He takes it from me, flips on the power switch and begins cranking the handle with practiced skill. Alex and I wait anxiously. When he has finished cranking, the light on top of the radio turns from red to green. Jason extends the antenna. His smile gradually erases itself as he turns the dial slowly, trying to find any station, or any human-made sound. There is nothing but static.

"What do you think that means?" he asks me.

"I don't know, Jason," I answer. "Maybe we're just out of range. We'll take it with us and keep trying it later, okay?"

"Sounds good," Jason says dejectedly over his shoulder as he walks away.

"Hey, don't worry about him, he'll be okay;" Alex watches him exit the barn, heading across the field toward the nearest structure, some sort of storage shed. "He's just a kid. He needs to come to grips with the possibility that his life could be taking a radical change."

I'm watching him walk away, too. "So do all of us," I nod affirmatively to Alex and follow in Jason's footsteps, carrying the radio, Alex close behind me. The dust stirred by my feet makes little billowy clouds that float up a few inches before settling back to the ground. I feel the weight of what might have happened on my shoulders. But I'm not going to allow Jason to treat me like it's my fault. I didn't make it happen; I merely put the pieces of the puzzle together and told everyone what I had figured out.

Besides, it's only a theory. There are other possibilities, including ones we haven't even thought of yet. And regardless, whatever has happened, it isn't the end of the world and doesn't have to be the end of civilization as we know it. It will just be a setback. And hopefully a learning experience for our descendants. Wow, I sure can't keep thinking like this. I need to focus so we can get out of here and find out for sure what has happened out there, somewhere. There is an answer; we just have to find it. Then we can figure out the future from there.

When we enter the dark, dusty shed, we find there is little that will help us. There are lots of tools of varying sizes and uses. We don't need tools, at least, not at the moment. We move on to the next, much larger, shed, which is used to store hay. Lots and lots of hay, which leads to quite a bit of sneezing on the part of Jason and me, impacting Alex to a lesser extent. We leave the premises and head for the next outpost, another farmhouse and set of barns and outbuildings. The results here are the same as the others, as are the next and the next. By late afternoon we have scoured everything in the area and found nothing of real use. We were hoping for a fleet of fully-fueled cars or trucks, but no such luck. The ones that had been left behind were either siphoned of their gasoline or non-functional rust heaps. There has been no sign of those dogs.

I am exhausted and turn in with just a half can of green beans. It is so wonderful to sleep in a soft bed for a second night. Part of me dreads the thought of leaving, of sleeping on the ground again; but it cannot be avoided.

The next morning, we eat a hearty breakfast, then pack up and move the group out, sticking to the dirt road as we travel. We remain rather tightly packed, but I walk ahead of the group this time, yet I'm not so far away that Jason can't reach me quickly in case of an emergency. There isn't much to scout, which is why the men have allowed me some measure of freedom in this regard. I like being alone with my thoughts again.

We continue on this way well into the afternoon, once we have finished our lunches. Peanut butter on crackers tastes delicious to everyone. We follow it up with packs of dehydrated fruit and trail mix that we made from the General Store's supplies.

As we walk, I notice the weeds are becoming ever-so-subtly greener. Farm fields lie along both sides of the road as far as the eye can see, but the young plants are dry and dead, unsalvageable by rain for the most part. Some of them show a bit of green, but not many; yet that increases as we progress down the road. Obviously, it has rained in the area at some point in the past couple of weeks here, or else they had irrigation. By the time we stop to camp for the night, the vegetation is no greener, as I had been hoping it would be, to eliminate the fire danger. There are no clouds in the sky, though. The air is dry, so the risk of wildfire is low at this point.

Camp is set up in record time; the kids haven't forgotten a thing in their two nights of comparative luxury of blankets, pillows and towels to cushion their bodies. We have set up in a farm field that got a bit of a head start over some of the others we passed earlier in the day. The young corn sprouts are dry and lifeless, but they make for a softer bed than the bare ground, which has been baked dry in the sun. I lie on my back in my sleeping bag, in a predetermined position on the perimeter of the kids, staring up at the stars. They are so beautiful, twinkling away out here, so far from civilization. Given that we had experienced easier walking conditions today, courtesy of the dirt road, nearly ten miles have been put between us and the small community that had given us temporary refuge. We will do the same tomorrow, hopefully arriving at the next outpost before dark. It is quiet and peaceful here, but I find myself restless, thinking about what we might find tomorrow. Eventually, I am able to fall asleep.

Much later during the night, I find myself sitting upright, wondering why. I think I sat up before fully awakening. I look around, but nothing seems out of place and everyone else appears to be sleeping soundly. After a couple of minutes, I lie back down and close my eyes, but I make sure to pull my knife from its sheath inside my sleeping bag and hold it firmly in my grasp. Something woke me, and I don't believe it was just a dream. I try to relax and go back to sleep. Within a few minutes, I have almost talked myself into it... that half-dream state, where everything is confusing. Then I hear, far off in the distance, what sounds like it could be the death shriek of an animal. It is scary and sickening. Everything remains still in the camp. It was very far away, so I take a deep breath and close my eyes again. I spring back up quickly upon hearing the distant roar of a large cat.

Looking around at my companions, I find them all asleep, except for Jason. He is likewise sitting up, illuminated in the light of the fire that is closest to him. He is staring into the darkness in the general vicinity of the roar. I get up and thread my way carefully amongst the sleeping campers to the second fire, which is nearest to me. I slowly add on more wood. There was not as much wood for our fires tonight, because there are more farm fields than trees in this area, but I can tell from the sky that dawn is approaching

160

anyway. Jason stands by the other fire, stoking it with the last of its woodpile. We wave an acknowledgment to each other then move back to where we were, but sit as guards, rather than trying to do anything futile, like sleeping.

I look over and see Alex propped up on an elbow. His gun is in his other hand. He looks to be completely focused, staring out into the darkness in the vicinity of the animal sounds.

As the sky brightens, I breathe a sigh of relief. At least now we'll be able to see better. There are no signs of any threat, so we eat our breakfast while packing and head out. We continue to follow the dirt road, which Jason has said leads to the next settlement, then not far beyond that is a paved two-lane state highway. In turn, that will lead to the community of a few thousand people. Surely, someone will be there. They have to be there.

CHAPTER 23

The best thing about the farm fields is that they provide a wide open vista on each side of our group. All the better to watch for predators approaching. We know they are out there, somewhere; but here they have no cover. So maybe instead of being near us, they have stayed behind, back at the other village. Hopefully they are pursuing the herd of antelope, rather than us. We adults allow ourselves to relax and just enjoy the peaceful surroundings as we start the day's hike in earnest. Jason is pretty far ahead of the rest of us, who have likewise spread out in a long configuration of randomness.

At the crest of the next hill, which is quite high, Jason slows, then turns and walks back to me. He takes my arm and pulls me forward and away from the kids, moving me into a faster walk. "It looks like we're going back into the woods, Cole, just up ahead." He is speaking in a hushed voice, trying not to alert anyone else just yet.

It has to be some sort of a cruel joke he is playing on me; it cannot be true. I had been walking along with my niece and her friends, talking. I had a smile on my face as I walked, and even as Jason approached me I smiled at him, just as he was doing to me then. He was faking it; and now this. I jog on ahead of him, lengthening my stride, not wanting to believe him. When I reach the top, the forest is spread out below us. I nearly drop to my knees. Jason is telling the truth. It is just as dense as any stand of trees we've passed through thus far, and stretches as far as the eye can see to the east and west. I swallow hard on the lump in my throat, but it doesn't want to go down. I stand there alone and immobile, trying to breathe, for what seems like an eternity.

Strong hands touch my shoulders then rub down my arms in a comforting gesture. I glance over my shoulder to see Alex.

"We'll be okay. We'll make it through this, boss lady. I promise... remember the kids," he whispers in my ear.

I straighten and find I can swallow that lump now. He's right. I have to be more positive about this. The kids will need all the adults to be confident, because they'll be afraid as soon as they see this sight for themselves. We all have to be ready before we go any farther down this road.

We turn to face the kids, with the first cluster of them nearly on us. I smile and hold up my hands for them to stop. I wait until the last of them reaches us. "Okay everybody, listen up. We're going to have to go through some more forest before we reach the next community. It's going to be just like before. We'll be traveling in a tight group, everybody on full alert. The adults will be on the outside. Jason will be in front and Alex will bring up the rear. If you have a walking stick, be ready, okay? Just in case. Everything will be fine; and we'll be to that little village in no time, definitely before it gets dark, right Jason?"

"Of course, no problem at all." He flashes his smile at the girls and winks. "We got this, right kids?"

They nod their heads affirmatively as he walks past, some smiling, some not. He nods to Alex and me, too, but doesn't stop. He is striding confidently ahead. The kids are following behind him without hesitation, like he's the Pied Piper or something. I fall in at my place on the right side; Alex trails a bit after the last of the kids goes by him.

The forest begins abruptly at the edge of the farm fields. We travel in silence, yet I can't help but notice that even silence is loud. The trees seem to almost magnify every sound, although I know it's just the result of my heightened awareness. Almost immediately, I sense it. That feeling we are being watched. I continue along without telling anyone else about my suspicions, because that is all I have. But I am keeping a very close watch on the trees. Something is in there, I know it. Dear God, please let it just be my paranoia.

We have been walking for nearly six hours when we decide we must stop for a break. Lunch is pulled hastily from backpacks, things that we can consume quickly. Jason and I volunteer to take the girls in small groups into the forest for a 'bathroom break'. We head toward a small clearing that we are able to see from the road. There appears to be enough sun shining through the smaller trees there that it will allow us to see for a short distance around us while we are inside.

It's hard on everyone to wait for these breaks, but especially the kids; and they have been waiting on this one far longer than usual. They haven't complained even once, though. I know I have had a difficult time with waiting myself; and now I really have to go quite badly. Jason scouts out the area first then gives us the all-clear sign, and I bring a pod of girls in. Regina watches us from the road carefully, until we reach the clearing and Jason. Then she turns back to the others, helping where she can with lunches while waiting for the next group to be allowed in. The teachers and Alex will be last of all.

I have just pulled up my pants when I swear I hear a low growl, but I can't tell where it came from. I turn to look behind me, into the trees. I don't see anything. I don't hear anything now, either. It must be my overactive imagination. I check the girls to be sure they're finished. It is bad enough they have to pee with a man standing close by, even though his back is turned; I don't want to interrupt them midstream, too. "Okay, girls. Let's head back so I can get the next group." I look over at Jason and nod, giving him a signal to watch behind me, even though I now neither see nor hear anything.

We proceed to the dirt road unmolested, as do each of the other groups as we walk back and forth. It is just as the last group of kids is finishing up that everything goes to hell in a handbasket, as my mother used to say when I was growing up.

I hear the first scream of pure terror split the air, and it comes from one of the adults. Elizabeth, it sounds like. The kids with me run instinctively toward Jason, who has drawn his gun and is sprinting toward the road at full speed. As he passes me, he yells at the kids, "Stay with Cole! Stay with Cole!"

The group at the road is losing their cohesion rapidly, scattering everywhere, just as we had told them not to do. I can barely see them in the distance through the trees. I'm trying hard to tell what's going on. There is screaming to curdle your blood, and a horrifying animal roar and yelling; and I can't tell what's going on. It looks like total chaos. Elise is with me here, but I am just as concerned for all the others back at the road. The girls are strung out ahead of me, except for Elise and Anastasia, who stay where they were, behind me. Then, before I know what's happened, my little group has turned tail and is rushing first toward me then around me, like water past a rock in a fast-moving stream. Why? What the hell?

Glancing toward the main group, I can see why my pod of girls has now bounded past me. A number of the girls from the road are running our way through the trees and fast, causing my group to take flight. Fear is a powerful force. I turn and yell after them. "Wait, girls, wait! Don't run! Come back! Stop!"

Everything I say is useless. They are absolutely terrified. The ones left behind here with me, those remaining at the road and the ones in the edge of the forest coming toward us, are all screaming and calling out to one another. I hear a gunshot, followed closely by another. I want to go to those being attacked at the road, but I can't. I have to get to the other kids and get them under control. Then convince them to come back with me. And if anything should go wrong while we are too far separated from the others, I have no weapons, save for my walking stick and knife.

I charge after the girls, still shouting for them to stop. They have a good head start on me, though. Suddenly, for no apparent reason, they split off, those in the rear turning back toward me, while the others scream and shift their course to the right. In moments, I am able to see what has changed.

A sizable pack of large dogs is barreling through the woods toward the handful of girls who are continuing to flee from me. I meet the girls coming back my way and gesture pointedly toward the road, "Run! Keep running! Get to Jason! Go!"

I pivot and follow the other group as fast as my feet will carry me. We are all racing into the dark shadows of the nearly impenetrable woods, jumping fallen trees and brush in our paths as we go. If one of the girls should fall, it will all be over. The dogs are more agile, more fleet of foot than we are. They are catching up to the girls and they don't look friendly. I shift course sharply to my right, intending to cut the dog pack off before they can get to the girls, who seem to be running in something of an arc, maybe curving back toward the road and the adults.

It works better than I had planned. In my desperate race, I am able to change direction from the right to my left at just the precise moment I needed to in order to cross between the girls and the dogs. The dogs shift their attention to me instead. That part worked great. The problem is that now they are right on my heels. I continue running; but a couple of them come along either side of me, barking and nipping at my feet and legs. I think they might be trying to clip my Achilles tendon. If they succeed, that will bring me down hard and fast, with no recovery. Maybe they are intending to cut me off. I can't let them stop me, whatever I do. Stopping is not an option. There is no help for me out here; I am too far from the road. I'll never make it back to the others in time. Besides, it sounded as though they have enough problems of their own to deal with.

The trees come to an abrupt end at a rocky clifftop, with a relatively narrow river roaring over the top of it. The two dogs alongside of me are unable to stop, so focused are they on catching me. They simply drop over the side, yelping loudly as their legs and bodies twist fruitlessly through the air.

"Whoa," I say aloud to myself. I stop fast, doubling over and waving my arms in large arcs in an attempt to prevent my momentum from taking me over the precipice as well. I look down and see that the river coursing past merely a single yard from my feet dives over the edge in a wide waterfall. After that, it proceeds to drop into a tumultuous pond, which I estimate is about forty feet below me. The water continues onward out of the pond in white, violent frothiness, tumbling over boulders in its path. Damn it. Now I am cut off, with no escape option. I have only my own wits to rely on; the others are too busy with whatever is happening back on that road. The most frustrating thing of all about my situation is knowing the others are in danger and that there isn't anything I can do now to help them.

Some of the dogs are snarling at me, others are barking. They definitely don't look friendly; but they don't seem sure of themselves, either. I am thinking they don't quite know what to do with what they've caught. Humans used to feed and care for them; but now they are abandoned and starving, or maybe they've always been wild like this. "Hey! No! Sit! What's the matter with you dumb mutts? Don't you listen to people anymore?!"

Several dogs take a step forward and I step back, but only once. Small rocks fall beneath my right heel, loosened enough that they are now free to tumble noisily down the side of the cliff. The only thing stopping the animals from attacking me is my walking stick, which I am holding out in front of me desperately, first jabbing it toward one dog, then the next. I know this won't work much longer. One or more of them will eventually breach my feeble defense.

I have no idea how deep the pond below is or what may be hidden beneath the surface, but from the looks of it, the boulders in there are enough to kill me if I don't hit the water just right. Then there is the white water beyond to deal with. I wish I was a better swimmer. All I know is that I have no choice. I give a guttural yell then throw my walking stick lengthwise at the group of mutts to push them back a bit. I spin on one heel and leap over the side, hoping for good aim and no surprise rocks waiting to greet me on impact. I scream as I plunge toward the water.

It is true, what they say, what you always hear about. Time slows to an inexorable crawl as you are dying, or at least if you're convinced you are dying. You see the people you've cared about, major events in your life; just quick flashes, not much sense to it all. Then the cool water engulfs me and my right shin strikes against a large rock under the surface. I use my arms to push up to the air and gulp it in as I bob to the surface briefly.

Next, the current grabs me, pulls me under and twists me around so I can't tell which way is up. There is a strong circular current coming out of the pool into the river; and it throws me against a boulder, nearly knocking me senseless. I manage to push off and away when I come to the next stone obstruction, and I'm forced into a small eddy. The reduced pull of the current here allows me to be able to swim over to the far bank and hoist myself up halfway, where I slip to the ground gratefully.

167

It is then I am able to hear a sound over the loud roar of the water. It's a whimpering, pathetic cry. I climb out of the water and creep carefully around the nearest boulder. On the other side of it, pawing against the water, is a German Shepard, one of the two dogs that went over the side of the cliff before I did. It is attempting to climb up the bank but is unable to gain a foothold on the sheer rock. The animal is whining loudly as it struggles. Stupid dog. You tried to kill me, so this is what you get.

The other dog is nowhere to be seen. I watch this one struggling for a minute, but then I can't take it anymore. I do love animals, especially dogs; this one, not so much, though. I drop back into the water alongside the dog. He snarls at me once, when I first touch him. He struggles against me and his back claws dig into my left shoulder. I cry out in pain, but he continues to fight me and pushes me under. I pop back up, spewing water. Finally, with enough of my pushing, he gets his front feet on a spot where he has traction and pulls himself up the rest of the way.

I get myself out at the same spot where the dog went up. I sit and cough, breathing heavily. I must be such a moron. I could have been killed trying to save that dumb, ungrateful dog.

When I am breathing something close to normal again, I look back up at the cliff over on the other side of the river, the side I had started out on before I jumped. I doubt there is any way for me to climb up it. The escarpment is steep and curves around the landscape as far as I can see in both directions. Those stupid dogs are looking down at me. After a minute, they appear to have given up, because they turn away and don't come back. I get to my feet and begin striding along the edge of the escarpment ahead, hoping to find a way up. My right leg hurts some, but I'm alive. I sure wish I had my walking stick, though.

CHAPTER 24

I think I have been going along for a good thirty minutes before I stop to take a break for my leg. It's throbbing, but the pain is easing a little as I walk out the kinks. I pull up my pant leg to examine my shin. It's red in one small spot, but there are no signs of major bruising yet. I am very fortunate, I know. But I am so concerned about the girls and those damned dogs. The dogs had given up on me, but did they then go back after the girls? Hopefully the girls were able to get back to the relative safety offered by the others in our group by the road. If that group is even safe itself, of course. They have to be okay; all of them. I can't get the sound of the screams and those gunshots out of my head. I clamp my hands over my ears momentarily at the memory. I'm sure they're fine; Alex and Jason are taking care of them. I lower my pant leg and resume my search for a way back to my group.

After about another thirty minutes, the ground I am walking on begins to rise in elevation, gradually, reaching toward the top of the escarpment in the distance. I break into a jog for a moment then have to slow down because my leg begins to object. I resume walking. I can't stop; I have to get back. This is taking way too much time.

Every few minutes or so, I look behind me and see that damned wet dog is following me, about ten yards back. If I stop, he stops. It is kind of unnerving, since he was in the group that was trying to bring me down not too long ago. I'm not sure if he's waiting for me to collapse so he can eat me or if it's maybe that he's grateful I got him out of that river. I never thought of dogs as thinking like that, but I suppose maybe they can. There's really no other reason for him to be accompanying me like this. Unless maybe he thinks I have some food and I'm going to give it to him. He doesn't look fierce or anything. Still, if he's going to come along, I wish he'd walk beside me, or even ahead. I'd sure feel more comfortable about him being around if I could keep a better eye on him, just to be on the safe side. I don't trust him. Of course, the only weapon I've still got on me is my knife. It's a good-sized one to be sure, but probably no match for an angry, or hungry, German Shepard. Why couldn't this dog have been a Chihuahua, or some kind of little ankle-biter dog like that? Just my luck. I roll my left shoulder around. It is sore, too, from the dog's claws. A couple of short streaks of blood show through tears in my shirt. It isn't too bad, though, I suppose… considering everything that has happened today.

Why is it taking so long to get to the end of this stupid cliff? Is there in actuality no end to it, is that why? Good grief! I think I've been very patient up until this point, personally. I can't stop worrying about everyone I have left behind. There has to be a leveling off of the ground somewhere up ahead and soon, so I can get up there and work my way back to the group. However long it takes me to get to the top, I can at least double that reversing course to go back in the other direction to where I came from, to where we took our bathroom break. That is assuming I can find a way across the river.

It will make more sense if I instead shift my path to where the road we were traveling on lies. That would have a bridge over the body of water. Then I can make my way back from there. But what will I find when I get back to that spot, the scene of the attack? I clamp my hands tightly over my ears again. I still can't get the sound of those screams out of my head.

My leg is continuing to be sore, but I break into a jog in spite of it. I have to find a way up and get back to the group. I glance back and see that the dog has quickened his pace, too, apparently so he can keep up with me. Maybe if I can find a place that is climbable I can get to the top sooner and have the added bonus of leaving this dog behind. That way I'll have one less thing to worry about.

Only minutes later, my wish comes true. The escarpment becomes dramatically lower and the top is only about ten feet above my head now. The bank here seems doable. I reach up and grab the woody branch of a shrub protruding from the soil. It holds firm. Using it, I am able to gain one foothold, then two. I pull myself up from there, using vegetation and careful placement of my feet into grooves caused by past torrential rainstorms. The dirt slides away from under my feet in some places and I slip a few times, but I manage to claw my way to the top. I look back down at the sound of a sharp bark. The dog is wagging his tail and looking up at me. I remember that earlier I had a big packet of jerky in my back pocket to eat for lunch as we walked on, after the bathroom break. I push my hand in the still-damp pocket and sure enough, it's in there. I take a big bite from one of the pieces then toss the rest of that one down to the animal, putting the remainder back into my pocket in case I need it later. "See ya, dog." I say as I wave goodbye.

He barks a few more times as I walk away. He sounds pitiful; so I cover my ears with my hands as I keep moving, until I can't hear him anymore. There is no time to worry about a blasted dog. I have to get back to those girls.

CHAPTER 25

I have been proceeding at a slow jog for nearly fifteen minutes, and I still haven't come to the river. I can't even hear it yet. I had to travel for well over an hour just to find a place where I could climb the escarpment, so it's reasonable that I haven't yet reached the river. It should still be a long ways off. I'm angling myself so I'll encounter the river maybe halfway up to the road. It's time to stop for a brief rest, but brief it is. After a couple of minutes, I start walking again. There will be time enough for resting tonight, once I have caught up to the group. The conflict on the road keeps playing in my mind, over and over. It is the only thing I can think of. My focus is lost; I manage somehow not to trip over rocks and other objects in my path, but that's about it. What has happened to everyone else? Are they okay?

It didn't really occur to me to wonder if I would be able to find them again. Due to debris and multiple fallen trees creating obstacles in my path, it is taking me much longer than I thought it would just to get back to the river. By the time I finally reach it, the sun is creeping lower in the sky. I still have a little bit of daylight left, but now I have to find a way around the river. It's impossible to cross in this area, as the water is moving too fast, not to mention all the slippery rocks around it.

My heart sinks. I would like to call out, to yell for the others; but if any of the predators are still around, it would bring them right to me. And my friends probably wouldn't hear me anyway. Enough time has passed that they would have surely given me up for dead and moved the kids on, hopefully toward civilization. But maybe they have decided instead to opt for some shelter, possibly back the way we had come this morning. It would certainly be more easily defensible; but they would end up hiking through part of the night or camping in this forest, neither of which is an acceptable option. If they have continued on along the original trajectory, as planned, they should still reach the next community before dark. Nightfall… it is coming, and I'm all alone and essentially defenseless. I have to find someplace where I can hole up until the morning comes.

A tree would work. I can climb a tree and that pack of dogs can't. But a big cat certainly would have no trouble climbing up after me. Then what would I do? I have to find a safe place. I can try to rejoin the others tomorrow. Walking along the river, I come upon a suitable candidate, a tree that twists out over the river. It would be hard to hear the approach of a big cat here next to the noise the water is making, but I probably wouldn't hear one coming anyway, as quiet as they are supposed to be. I decide to take my chances with this tree. If I have to and have sufficient time, I can drop into the river and float down it a while, either finding a way up the opposite bank somewhere, or taking the plunge over the cliff again. I think it might be a much preferable death to the one I would meet in the jaws of a big cat. At least I would be less likely to be eaten, anyway, I suppose.

It is settled. I climb the tree slowly, making sure I don't slip. There is a really good bend near the top, where two branches split off and a third makes for a good safety net should I be able to fall asleep. At least I think I'll be safe enough here. I settle in and am asleep before the sun goes down.

The sky is brightening with the coming dawn when I startle myself awake from a nightmare. It takes me a few moments looking around to realize where I am and remember what happened the day before. Unfortunately, now that I'm fully awake, I know it was all too real.

The first thing I do is make sure I'm alone. I see no signs of animals anywhere around. Wait a minute. What the hell? That German Shepard is back! He is curled up, asleep beside a rock at the base of my tree. I let out a loud sigh, a mixture of frustration and, curiously, relief. I guess I kind of like the idea of company. As long as the company doesn't try to eat me, that is. I won't be alone in my search for the others. It's an especially comforting thought, considering that I have a lot more forestland to traverse before I reach that next little community. Cautious over my lack of tree climbing expertise, I move slowly from one limb to the next then drop the last few feet to the ground. The dog has awakened and is wagging his tail. Okay, a good sign. Maybe he won't eat me after all.

I pat his head cautiously and scratch him behind his ears, "Good boy, that's a good dog." His eyes are half closed. "Hey, do you have a name?" I check for a collar, but find none.

"Figures. Whoever you belonged to didn't care enough about you to give you a collar. I hope they cared enough to give you your shots. I don't want you going all rabid on me or anything." His tail is wagging again. "I've got to get some water before we go, okay? Hey, how about if I call you Rin? I know there was a TV show about a German Shepard a long time ago, way before I was born. That dog was a hero. Maybe you'll be like that." His tail continues to wag.

At the river's edge, I sip water thirstily from my hand. It is untreated; but I have no supplies with me, so there's no option. My backpack was left by the roadside yesterday, along with my canteen belt. The dog laps at the water, too, following my lead, I guess. I chew on the remaining beef jerky strips in my pocket, sharing pieces with Rin. He wags his tail at each bite I offer him. Sometime today, I will either find the girls and their food supplies, or the little village we have all been hiking toward, which likely has food as the other community did, whether or not there are people still living there.

I keep to the river, both so there is water for me as I go along and in case of predator attack so I can jump into the water. The river is more calm here, enabling me to hear better. I try to keep an eye out all around, just in case. Having the dog around helps; surely he will detect a threat long before I do. Along the way, I pick up a long, sturdy branch. I also find a rock with a sharp edge to it. As I walk, I'm working the end of the branch with the rock, stripping away bark and sharpening the end further with my knife into a decent point. Now I have a spear, too.

Eventually, we should come to the bridge over the road. There may even be signs of the kids having passed that way yesterday afternoon. That's what I'm hoping for, anyway.

What I'm guessing is around an hour later, we do find our way to the road. It's been a long, convoluted path that river took from this point down to the cliff, adding a great deal of distance to my walk. Fortunately for me, the journey to get here has been uneventful; no predators have revealed themselves, and the dog has remained calm. I haven't had that strange sensation of being watched, either. It hasn't really helped my nerves any, though. I'm still jittery, jumping at every little sight or sound.

It's a simple matter of climbing up a small incline to reach the roadbed, which lies just above my eye level. When we get to the top, the first thing I notice is all the footprints in the dirt on this far side of the bridge... dozens of them. Thank God! They had made it through after all. It is impossible to tell if they are all present and accounted for, since there are so many tracks. I'll have to wait on that until I reunite with them again. I'm sure they all must have survived, though. They have to have made it. I refuse to allow any negative thoughts to play about in my head. They must have all gotten safely to the little village we were heading for yesterday. I am so happy I can scarcely contain myself. I want to yell out a whoop of joy to the world; but I know that would be unwise of me, given the precarious circumstances I'm still in, what with the wild animals on the loose and all.

Instead, I pat the dog, "Hey, they made it! We're going to find them soon. Those kids are going to love you. You're going to get lots of attention." Rin wags his tail happily. He doesn't know what I'm saying, but he'll find out soon enough. My niece has always wanted a dog, but her dad doesn't like animals. Noel and I had grown up with several dogs over the years, as well as plenty of cats back then. There were definitely lots of creatures on our farm, for sure.

As we walk along, I notice how dense the forest is through here, but we should come out of it in a few hours or so. That is, providing that Jason's calculations were right. I sure do miss Jason... and everyone else. I wonder what they are all thinking about me. Surely, they must think I'm dead. I would. Even Elise, the poor little thing. She must be really scared. I'm sure the others are taking good care of her, though. What about Alex? If they killed the big cat, I have to wonder if he went after me, where the kids told him they last saw me. I hope not... then he might have come across that pack of dogs. There's no time for these thoughts, and there's no time to waste. I press myself into a slow jog along the dirt road, keeping watch to my left and right. I feel on edge again, but focused. My right leg is much improved today. I scarcely notice any pain from it now. The most important thing to focus on is the trees… and all the dark shadows that lie in between.

The sun will be at its peak for the day in about an hour or less. That will help to light up the forest a little better. I reduce my speed to a walk; it is both slower and quieter. My nerves are beginning to bother me, overcoming my resolve. It is a difficult thing, walking through a scary, dark forest alone, knowing there may very well be predators in the vicinity. But then I remind myself that I'm not totally alone. I glance down at the dog. He's a pretty good dog, after all. Why would someone leave him behind… bad owners? I'm going to take him all the way back to Atlanta with me and the kids and then on to live with me in Raleigh. Maybe, anyway. I'm thinking now that it could be time to move back to Atlanta to be near Noel. I love Raleigh and my friends and even my job. So, we'll see. But I'm keeping this dog. That much, I know for certain.

Up a few feet ahead of me, something catches my eye on the ground to the left side of the road. Upon reaching the spot, I kneel to examine it more closely, though I'm pretty sure I already know what it is… multiple drops of blood. They have dried to brown, an indication of the time passage since they were left here. The scariest thing about it is that it lies in the clear impression of a paw print from a large cat. The same size and shape I remember from the day before yesterday. The difference in those prints and these is that now there is the addition of blood. There are several prints, leading from the forest to this spot, then back into the forest up ahead. The cat appears to be following the kids, because his prints are on top of theirs. My eyes trail along the direction of the tracks, to where they disappear into the tree line. Then my eyes move from that spot to the road, where the kids had gone. I swallow hard. I hope the kids made it to a house or some kind of shelter for last night and that the adults have them staying put for a while.

"Come on, Rin," I whisper. He's busily drinking in the cat's scent.

As we walk now, I make a choice to focus more on the terrain to my left than to my right. Most likely, the cat stayed on that side of the forest, rather than crossing the road, although I have no proof, except that I have seen no tracks going across. Birds are singing a lovely tune in the trees as we walk. If not for the situation, it would be a nice place for a walk, just me and my dog. The sun has passed its zenith, and the tree shadows are just beginning to lengthen across the road. The time is passing, and my mind is starting to wander. Not too far this time, though. I find myself thinking about yesterday and all the chaos that ensued, while I try to analyze the bigger-picture situation. Everything is so crazy now. What has happened to the world out there? I still haven't seen any contrails. How I would love to see one right now. How I would love to see another human being right now; especially if it was someone from my group. Actually, all of them; I'd like to see the entire group, to know they are all safe and sound. That's the only thing in all the world I really want right now.

When I look more closely at the trees, I can tell they are spaced a bit further apart now than they were an hour ago. The forest is thinning out. There is a wide, deep ditch alongside the road in this location, too. Off in the distance ahead, a thin column of smoke is rising. From here, it looks like it would be smoke generated by a chimney. It has to be the kids. I've almost reached them!

It's here that I notice two things about my immediate situation that have changed. For one thing, the birdsong has stopped. I don't see them flying around, either. In fact, there is no sound at all, except for my breathing. I don't even hear any noise coming from the dog, which then brings me to the second change. Rin isn't beside me anymore. Then I hear it. It's the only real sound around here just now.

A low growl, barely audible, reaches my ears. I look back to find Rin, who has stopped walking without my having noticed it. No… please, it can't be. He is staring into the forest, growling. The fur along the ridgeline of his back is standing straight up all the way to his tail. Now the hair on the back of my neck is standing up, too.

I look where Rin is staring so intently, amongst shadows cast by the trees. He is focusing somewhere deep inside, where I can't see. But I can hear. One thing that I know for sure is that we're not dealing with a pack of dogs; not this time. There are no other dogs growling. Think, I have to think, and fast.

What can I do? The only thing I can think of is to run. But, you aren't supposed to run… right? Or is that little rule applicable to some other kind of animal and not this one? I doubt it applies, because I know cats are very fast runners. Under normal circumstances, that is. This one is injured… at least I am assuming this is the one whose blood I found by the road. The question is, how badly?

I unclip the holster of my knife and then shift my spear so I am holding it at the ready, pointing into the darkness permeating the trees. The dog isn't moving, just growling, with his head down low. His muscles are tensed. My eyes still can't pierce the darkness; the trees and brush are just too thick in there. "Rin, let's go, boy," I say quietly and give my hip a little pat. I walk sideways, afraid to take my focus off of the forest. We are so close to the relative safety of the others, or at least the guns I know they carry with them. We can make it.

We keep moving along the road in this side-stepping manner, but it is incredibly unproductive in its relative lack of progress. After about a minute, we have only traveled some thirty feet. We have, however, reached the crest of the hill we were heading toward. I risk a glance away from the trees and look down the other side of the hill to see the little village community spread out before us. There are more structures here than the other one had, and they are grouped more closely together. Smoke is indeed coming from the chimney of the nearest house, less than the length of a couple of football fields away. All I have to do is beat the cat there. Or just beat it close to there, if Jason or Alex can be alerted to my presence and reach me in time. They will come out armed, so I won't actually need to make it all the way to the house. At least, I hope I'm right about that.

My options are extremely limited at this point. Taking a stand doesn't really seem like a wise course of action. My knife will be totally useless against such an adversary. If the animal is close enough that I need to use my knife for self-defense, I won't stand a chance against those teeth and claws, not to mention the animal's advantages of strength and speed. That leaves the spear in my hand. It won't be very effective against an angry big cat, either. It is time for fight or flight, and again I choose flight. I'm going to make a break for the community ahead. The farmhouse isn't that far away… at least I hope I am gauging the distance accurately enough.

Until I see more evidence of an immediate threat, though, I'm going to continue to walk in the hopes that whatever it is won't charge if I'm moving slowly. Maybe if I continue this way, I won't look so much like prey. I have no idea if that is true or not, but it's all I've got to go on. The dog seems reluctant to continue moving, but he follows me. He keeps growling, now showing his teeth. Even though he is about twenty feet away from me, I can clearly see that. His bearing indicates to me that he would prefer to stand his ground and fight. Not me.

I don't know how much time we're going to have left, but I doubt we'll have much of it before the wild animal attacks us. I get this inexplicable feeling that it's time to go. I can't justify it; it's just pure instinct, and it's completely overwhelming any sense of logic I have in me. We need to go…right now and very fast. Come on, dog. I try to mentally will him to pay attention to me. Regardless of whether the dog comes with me or not, this is it; my fear has built to a crescendo. My muscles stiffen, I take a deep breath and I count to myself: one… two… *three!*

"Rin!" I yell out as I sprint off my imaginary mark into the fastest pace I can manage. I can hear the dog barking behind me, which lets me know he is following close. My arms are pumping like crazy, but I make sure to keep ahold of the spear, just in case I need it. From inside the forest, I can hear branches as they snap, the sound coming from back behind me. Something large is plowing through the trees and underbrush, heading for the road.

I know I shouldn't do it, but I can't help myself. I chance a look behind me, only to see a huge tiger leap from the forest over the ditch and onto the dusty dirt road, losing his footing a bit at first. That skid slows him down. The dog and I, on the other hand, are already moving at full speed. Seeing the frightening animal at last, however, does a remarkable job of providing me with an extra burst of energy.

Still, I fully expect him to chase us down. When I glance back a second time, I see the tiger is moving with a definite limp. Otherwise, he would have been on us by now. Maybe we do have a chance after all.

The dog has caught up to me and is matching my strides, even though I'm sure he could leave me in his wake if he wanted to. The tiger is racing along much more slowly than it otherwise would be, but in spite of his injury he's getting closer with each stride. That's the last time I'll look back. I'm determined to force my attention instead on running. I can't afford to fall. It would all be over with then. Rin continues to bark as he runs, which is good. It will help alert Alex and Jason. It's all I can do to focus on my escape. Yelling out for help isn't an option for my lungs at this point. I know anyone looking up the hill from the house below can easily see us.

At least our flight is taking us downhill. That's an advantage to all three of us; but I don't think I, at least, would be able to scamper uphill fast enough to have much of a chance. The farmhouse is very close now. Run, keep running, I tell myself. You can do it, you're almost there. But the tiger is closer, and gaining. I can hear him behind me now and I know he's only maybe twenty feet in back of us, but probably a lot less. I expect that within a few seconds I'll be hit from behind by the large animal, and he'll topple me to the ground.

I see the front door of the farmhouse fly open, nearly springing free from its hinges with a loud cracking sound as Jason emerges from within, already moving at his top speed. In less than two strides he reaches the railing on the side of the large, rambling porch. He takes a massive vault over it, hitting the ground running. He has a rifle in his hand.

Jason is covering the ground between us faster than I am. All of a sudden, he comes to a stop and raises the rifle up to his shoulder. I know he can't shoot because I'm in the line of fire.

"Cole, get down!" he yells.

Since I'm running so fast, there's nothing I can do except fall down. I put my best effort into a move I've only ever seen on television, a tuck and roll, aiming to my right so I'm farther out of Jason's way, giving him a better shot at the tiger. The ground rises up to meet me faster than I thought it would. It's also a much harder impact than I thought. The blow shocks me with the amount of pain involved from hitting the firm surface at this rate of speed. I seem to be rolling for far too long, using up my momentum less quickly than I would have liked. I can hear a gunshot being fired. When my body finally comes to a stop, I look up through the dust cloud around me to see what has happened.

The tiger has ceased its pursuit of me and is turning on Jason. Jason is standing his ground and firing a second time. The tiger is nearly on him. No, this can't happen. *"Jason!"* I call out, grabbing my makeshift spear and sprint forward toward him, clutching my meager weapon at my side.

Rin reaches the tiger before it can reach Jason, however, colliding with the animal hard enough to throw off the injured beast's balance and knock it to the ground. The large animal is unable to scramble up as fast as the dog, and Rin leaps at him, latching his teeth tightly around the tiger's throat. That position leaves him vulnerable to the cat's front paws, though. The tiger gets a grip on Rin with his claws and viciously slashes him to the ground, pinning him. The dog lets loose a horrible, pathetic yelp of pain as the tiger's claws tear into him. Rin is trying desperately to bite the tiger's legs now, in a vain attempt to get him to release his grip. I run up to them just as Jason steps forward, aims quickly and gets off another round, directly into the tiger's skull. The tiger's body jerks awkwardly then the animal collapses in a heap, dead. The dog wriggles free and lays there near the tiger, whining and bloodied.

I turn my attention momentarily from the dog to Jason. With an expression that plainly shows his relief, he drops the rifle and lifts me up into his arms then spins me around a couple of times before putting me down. He looks into my eyes for just an instant before leaning in to kiss me. I'm so happy to see him and to be safe and alive. I kiss him back enthusiastically. When I drop my chin to break free from his lips, he settles for kissing my forehead then holds me close and tight. I couldn't get loose from him right now if I wanted to. I hold onto Jason, hugging him back with no desire to let go, not yet. For now, it's all I can do not to cry.

Young voices are growing louder, invading my reverie. I loosen my grip on Jason enough look past his shoulder. There, I can see several girls on the porch of the farmhouse. They look unsure about the situation. I think they want to come over to us, but they are clearly terrified of the tiger. Regina is running toward us, tightly clutching a handgun. She stops about ten feet away. "Is it dead now?"

Jason looks back at her, still keeping his hands on my waist and smiles, "Yes, Regina. It's okay, he's dead."

"Oh, thank God. And Cole, you're alive!" She walks up and pushes past Jason to give me a bear hug, which I do my best to return. She is a little bigger and a lot stronger than I am.

"Yeah, I'm okay. I'm just glad y'all are all safe and sound," I say and notice a dark cloud come over her face with my words.

My smile is slowly fading as I watch her. Just as I open my mouth to ask a question, Regina notices Rin.

"Oh my goodness! The poor dog. What happened to it? Is it okay?" She says with her concern now focusing on the injured canine.

I had momentarily forgotten Rin. "Rin, are you okay, boy?" I kneel next to him. His body starts to quiver, I'm guessing with shock. "Regina, can you get me a blanket so we can carry him into the house?"

"Yes, of course. I'll be right back, just hang on." She hurries back to the house, shouting ahead. "One of you girls run and fetch me a blanket now, quick!"

"It'll be okay, boy. It'll be okay." I try to be soothing, but my voice breaks. This dog saved Jason, just as readily as he would have saved me. He isn't bleeding too badly, but he isn't moving around much, either. Damned tiger. Damned power outage.

I look up suddenly. "Jason, what happened?" I look back toward the girls at the house. There is only Jason out here. Someone who should have come running to help is not present. "Where's Alex?" I am so afraid to hear the answer.

Jason averts his eyes and begins rubbing the dog's hindquarters, where Rin appears to be uninjured. He clears his throat then looks me square in the eyes. "I don't know, Cole. I really don't. The tiger pounced at one of the girls; and Elizabeth blocked him, so he turned on her. After the tiger grabbed Elizabeth, Alex shot it as soon as he got a clear view so he wouldn't hit Elizabeth or anyone else in the way; the kids were all over the place. That was right before I got there. It dropped Elizabeth and ran back into the woods as I came up. It took us a while, but we got all the girls back together. DeShondra and Alex patched up Elizabeth as good as they could. We were sure hoping to find a doctor here to take care of her. The last of the girls I rounded up were crying and hard to understand. Regina got one of them settled enough to tell us what happened to you with that pack of dogs. And you hadn't come back."

He glances at the dog then back at me. "Alex helped us make a litter for carrying Elizabeth. Then he gave his gun to Regina and told us to get the girls out of there, to get them to the village. He said we shouldn't wait for the two of you. He took Elise by the shoulders because she was crying so hard. He promised her he was going to find you and bring you back to her. That made her stop crying. He shook my hand and told me I was in charge now… that it was up to me to keep everyone safe. Then he ran off into the woods. He hasn't come back."

"Oh my God," I swallow hard and gaze down at the dog as I stroke the canine's head. "Jason…"

He reaches out and takes my hand, holding it tightly. "That's not all, Cole."

I look up quickly, searching his eyes. There's more he's reluctant to tell me. The front porch draws my attention, as one of the girls emerges with a blanket, which she hands off to Regina. I suddenly feel sick to my stomach. I think I might actually pass out for a moment. "Elise. Where is Elise?" In spite of the perceived danger, she would have come running to me by now.

Jason's forehead wrinkles. He looks like he's aged ten years over the past week. "She… I don't know how it happened. Cole, I'm so sorry…"

"Sorry for what?! What happened to her? Tell me!" My stress and fears are boiling over.

"We were leading the girls down the road. We were so busy concentrating on the woods, watching for the God-damned tiger… I don't know when it happened, but somewhere along the way we lost Elise… and Anastasia. We figure they both ran off, looking for you. No one noticed when or where. By the time we realized they were gone, we were going into the farmhouse over there, and it was almost dark. We couldn't leave all the rest of these girls to go after the other two. I started to go after them as soon as we found out, but everyone else was afraid and insisted I stay. The tiger was still out there, and they were scared. It wouldn't have been right to leave them like this. Caryn and Regina were talking about going back themselves this morning; but we knew we all had to stay with the rest of the group, so maybe we could get those girls home safely," he paused for a breath. "Cole, I'm sorry."

It takes me a moment to absorb what he has told me. I can't believe it. My niece... gone; and her best friend. I had been upset about Alex, until Jason told me about Elise. Now I feel panicked. This is a nightmare. A horrible, horrible nightmare. What will I ever tell her mother? I sit down in the dirt. I am so stunned, I can't even think straight. She's such a good, sweet, smart girl. She has always been so good with computers. It was almost like she could communicate with the darned things on a level no one else could. She had a gift; that much was certain. Elise never had loads of friends, just several special girls from school or the neighborhood who were close to her, Anastasia being the primary one. Anastasia was always there, at Elise's side, even when it meant getting into trouble on occasion.

The tears are streaming down my face now. I close my eyes and cover them with my hands. Jason leans over and rubs my shoulder. "It's not hopeless, you know. Alex is out there, somewhere, looking for you. Maybe he'll find them... maybe they'll find each other."

Opening my eyes, I angrily wipe away my tears. How dare I give up on her! Elise hadn't given up on me. She had gone off with Anastasia to find me.

Regina arrives with the blanket and hands it to me. I spread it over Rin then the three of us roll the dog over. He whines, but doesn't otherwise object.

"We need to get him inside, carefully," I say.

Regina and I use the blanket to lift him up into Jason's arms. He carries the dog gently into the farmhouse and lays him on a first floor bed. I notice my pack from Camp Correll on the floor against the wall nearest the bed and retrieve it.

"Regina, I need for you to take care of this dog for me. His name is Rin, like Rin Tin Tin," I whisper in her ear.

"What? Where are you going?" She doesn't bother to whisper back when she sees the backpack I've strapped on. "Oh, no… you're not going after your niece all alone, are you?"

"I am," I say, taking a deep breath. "I have to."

Jason steps around Regina. "No, I won't let you go."

"Jason," Regina interrupts him for something more important, "maybe you can try your cellphone again."

"Cellphone?" I ask. With the lack of technology permitted on this trip, I had forgotten Jason carried a cellphone.

"Yeah," he answers. "The next town has a cell tower. Normally, when the weather is just right, you can get a signal from here."

"And?" I prompt him impatiently.

"And nothing. The weather conditions are great. I tried it and there was nothing. My phone didn't even pick up one bar." His face clearly shows his frustration. "I've tried several times since. It's like there's nothing out there for my phone to latch onto. And the emergency radio hasn't picked up anything, either."

Giving Jason a slight smile, I hug him goodbye tightly. "Then there's no other alternative. There's no one else who can help us. You can't stop me, Jason. And you can't come with me, so don't bother asking. I need you to stay here and protect these girls. If I don't make it back, you have to take care of them, just like Alex said. Do you understand?"

"Of course I do," he says softly. He rubs my hair between his fingers, as he had done what seems like a month or two before, but in reality was just a few days ago, after our group had successfully survived separation during the wildfire and had found our way back together again.

I see Regina behind Jason, excusing herself from both the room and the situation promptly. "I'll go get bandages, towels, and some water for the dog."

"Thank you, Regina," I say after her.

"I don't want anything to happen to you, that's all." Jason leans in and kisses me tenderly, one arm wrapping around my waist. He stops kissing me but doesn't let go, rubbing his cheek against mine affectionately.

"Nothing is going to happen to me," I whisper. "I'm going to find the others and bring them back. Then we'll all go to the next town together," I pull away from his grasp. "I'll be back before you have a chance to miss me," I say, walking out of the room.

"Too late for that," I hear him say behind me.

CHAPTER 26

"Cole, wait a second, please," Jason says.

I hang my head for a moment then turn to face him. "Don't ask me not to go, Jason; it won't work."

He has a serious expression. "Don't worry, I know that. What I was going to say is that we found a rifle in this house, and ammunition. It's what I used to shoot the tiger. I want you to take it with you for protection."

"Jason, I don't really even remember how to use a gun. I only saw my dad using one when I was a little kid."

"That's okay. I can teach you in just a few minutes," he pauses, watching me. "You can spare a few minutes to learn how to use it. It could save your life… or someone else's."

I narrow my eyes at him and hesitate. "Okay, but you'll have to make it quick. I want to make some good progress getting back down that road before the sun sets."

We head out back, to an old barn that looks like a stiff wind would blow it to the ground. We go inside and Jason puts the weapon in my hands and points to an old bale of hay by the opposite wall.

"Okay, hold it up like you're going to shoot at something besides a hay bale," he tells me.

I do as he instructs, but it doesn't feel right in my hands. "I don't like this, Jason. I know you're right and I fully intend to take it with me, but I don't like it at all."

"Just watch," he says, taking the rifle from me.

He holds it as I saw him grip it when he shot the tiger. I cover my ears as he squeezes the trigger and fires it off into the hay bale. "Now it's your turn. Just treat it gently."

I take the weapon back and lift it up as Jason had just done. He then moves to stand close behind me. He slips his arms around my shoulders, one hand over the top of the rifle, the other on one of my hands. "Look along the barrel, right here," he motions.

He is whispering his words into my ear, his lips brushing my skin. That really doesn't help my aim at all. I squeeze the trigger and miraculously it hits the hay bale, but just barely. It skims the edge and lodges in the wall. I lower the weapon and turn to him, giving him a look of stern reproach.

"What?" he asks innocently. I can tell he's trying hard to suppress a laugh.

"If you would be serious for a minute, I can learn what I need to do and get going," I say. "This is no time to play around." I put the weapon back into position against my shoulder.

"I wasn't playing," he says.

I lower the rifle and face him again. "Then what do you call it?"

He puts his hands on my hips. "I call it letting you know I've never felt like this about anyone before in my life."

He did *not* just say that. "Jason! Come on, you can't do this to me." Oh, my God, this can't be happening... not now. He's so young.

"Do what, tell you how I feel about you? You can't control my emotions, Cole. I can't help how I'm feeling."

"Jason, I'm leaving to go find the girls... and Alex," I add.

"I know that. And I can tell how he feels about you. I just don't want you to forget he isn't the only one. And I don't want you going out there alone, Cole. I'm afraid I'll never see you again," he pulls me close and leans in, kissing me, deeper and deeper. One of his hands begins to slide slowly down along my hip and pull my lower body in up against his, suggestively.

At first, I give in to the desire he is causing to rise in me. Yet then I think of Alex running off after me with no weapons, and I move my face away from Jason. In reality, I am having difficulty with Jason's affection toward me. I can't seem to sort it out with the attraction I have for Alex. This is all so confusing, and I don't know what to do. Is it possible? Can I really be attracted to both of these men at the same time? Am I just a bad person; is that what it is?

"We don't have time for this, Jason. Not now, okay? I need you to show me how to do this right, just one more time; then I'm leaving," I turn back toward the target, but I take an instant to look over my shoulder. "And you will see me again… I'll be back."

"Okay… try it again," he says softly, his eyes searching mine.

I aim at the hay bale; and he helps me get it right this time, or at least close enough to hit a large animal. If that animal is standing still, that is… or maybe dead already. Yeah, that would make my shot way more accurate. I'm not going to say that out loud, not to Jason, though. All I need to do is find Alex, who I'm sure must have stumbled upon the girls already by now, and give the rifle to him. That way, we'll all make it back safe and sound. As long as I'm not the one in charge of the stupid gun, that is.

Jason puts his arms around me from behind. "That wasn't bad. You just make sure you come back in one piece. I intend to give Alex some serious competition for your affections." He nuzzles against my cheek then kisses it just once, but very slow and tender.

"I've got to get going now," I say and pull away from him. He needs to leave me alone. I carefully place the fully-loaded rifle in my backpack and put the pack on, along with my canteen belt. I only get one step toward the open barn door.

Jason quickly moves to block my path, slips his hands under the shoulder straps of my backpack and pulls me in to him. He kisses me, long and slow, his lips almost hypnotizing me. I think a part of me is afraid I won't see him again, or any of the others, after all. And if I'm honest with myself, I have to admit my heart is fluttering. He is a really good kisser. I find I am struggling for a moment to remember what it felt like to kiss Alex. In spite of his persistence and undeniable animal magnetism, Jason can't erase Alex from my mind. I need to find Alex… he is the man filling my thoughts now, even with Jason standing right here in front of me.

Jason releases the straps then takes my hand and escorts me to the front of the house. "Please make sure you come back, no matter what happens or how you feel," he whispers and lets me go.

I nod, but I don't know what to say; I believe it's better to put some distance between us instead of talking. That's the easier choice for me, anyway. Stick my head in the sand. Ignore the problem and hope it goes away on its own. My emotions are the problem. I have feelings for two wonderful, attractive men, who seem to have feelings for me, too. But I'm still reluctant to trust any man with my heart; or with my body. Well, maybe my body… I can't stop thinking about those kisses. I shake my head, trying to clear it as I turn away and jog up the hill, past the dead tiger, pausing just long enough to retrieve my spear. The more weapons, the better, I figure. I have to get a move on; there's no time to waste.

I had made it to the farmhouse in this little village; why hadn't Alex and the girls? Of course, my journey here had been in a relatively straight line. They were likely all over the place, searching for me or signs of me, not knowing where I was. I realize my chances of finding them aren't good, unless I come upon them while they are traveling on this road. If they aren't on it when I am, I'm liable to miss them altogether; timing is everything, they say. I keep jogging until I reach the top of the hill. There, I stop and look back. I can barely make out who is who from here. It appears as if they are waving. I can tell Jason is in front, standing apart from the rest. I give them an exaggerated wave in return then continue on my way.

Even though the tiger that tried to attack the girls is now deceased, there is no way to know if there are more of the animals around here or not. According to Jason, the sanctuary was a large facility; and the hunters they served particularly relished the opportunity to kill big cats. There is no telling what animals are out there now, creatures that don't belong here. There is only the hope that none of the other animals got loose… but if they did, that they went someplace else to search for a meal.

I kind of wish I hadn't thought of that. Now I'm feeling really alone and more paranoid than I think I've been on this trip, if that's possible. The lump is in my throat again. Water doesn't do anything to help relieve the sensation, so I replace the canteen onto my belt. Everyone missing had their own canteens and backpacks with food. They should be fine in that respect. And if they're near the river, they can drink that water safely enough. So far so good for me, anyway; no symptoms have shown up yet from consuming bad water. But then, they'll have their filters, too, as I now have.

Occasionally, as I travel along, I stop and call out to all three of them, one by one, then wait impatiently for a response that does not come. The forest is becoming so dense I don't know how I'll ever find them. My eyes cannot pierce the depths. My plan is to follow the road until I reach the spot where our group was ambushed by the tiger. If I haven't found them by that time, I'll go back to the waterfall and follow the river upstream to the road, just like I did before, except from the opposite side. Probably not a very well-thought-out plan, I suppose. I wish Rin was with me. I could use those dog senses on this search.

This becomes especially true when my eyes meet a disturbing sight by the side of the road. I walk over to examine the two carcasses after first scanning the area to be sure I'm alone. It seems that way, but it's hard to tell what might be concealed in the shadows. I have come upon the remains of what I believe to be two small dogs, killed and ripped apart. Maybe they were from the group that chased me over the cliff, but there's no way to tell. What little is left behind stinks a little, but not too badly yet; and they are covered in flies. They don't appear to have been here too long. My first thought is the tiger. Surely, it must have been the tiger. I decide I'm going to go with that; it makes me feel a bit more secure. Yet, I have to keep my guard up. And keep moving.

Still, I find that I have to fight continually with my mind to keep it focused. I shouldn't have this much trouble. For someone who has been so firm in her assertions that she isn't interested in a relationship with any men at this point in her life, I find myself unable to stop thinking about two of them. Both are appealing in their own ways. But why are they focusing on me, though? I'm nothing special; and there are other adult females of varying ages in our party besides me, and four of them are single. Elizabeth is the only one who is married. The women are all wonderful company and are all attractive; I think all of them more so than I am. So again, why me?

It is nearly nightfall when I decide I have to give up my search for today and find a safe enough place to stop and rest. I haven't really made that much progress, just a few hours' worth. I discover a suitable tree near the road and climb up to try and sleep. This tree isn't as conducive to a decent rest as the one I had been in last night, the one that hung over the river. But that tree is too far away and on a different path from mine, at least for now.

Sleep only comes to me in brief increments and is disturbed by either bad dreams or a noise somewhere around, usually an owl's call. When dawn makes its initial appearance, I'm already awake, staring at the sky, lost in thought. As soon as it's light enough to see by, I make my way carefully down the tree. My body is stiff and sore. I don't know what has had the worst impact – the events from yesterday or the contortions I had to make in my body last night in that tree, in order to not fall out.

I stretch before I head out and pull a package of granola bars from my backpack to munch on for breakfast. Once I've strapped on my gear, it's time to get moving. My mouth lets loose a massive yawn. I sure hope I can find the others today and get back so we can all sleep in real beds tonight or at least inside the house so we don't have to be constantly on alert.

CHAPTER 27

When I reach the spot along the road where the rest of our group was ambushed, I'm about to call out to our three missing members, but a sound stops me short. It's unmistakable… the snort of a grazing horse. My eyes are wide as I check around me. It doesn't take too much looking to spot them, though. Not horses, but rather a small group of zebras grazing in what was our bathroom break area two days ago. Yuk. I guess hunger can overcome the nostrils sometimes. I can easily see their stripes through the trees. They occasionally stomp their hooves and switch their tails at the flies that must be biting them.

Wow, this is so eerie, standing here watching a herd of zebras. This is so not Africa, nor is it a zoo. A couple of them stop grazing to stare at me for a moment before returning to their meal. They don't seem to be spooked by people. Of course, I know they are used to people, having lived probably their entire lives at that sanctuary. They are very calm… can I surmise from their demeanor that there are no predators in the area? I decide I am going to take it as a good sign. I don't have much choice in the matter, so I might as well be positive about the situation.

The area where they are grazing is where I need to go; so I enter the clearing, moving slowly and trying to avoid any unnecessary noises. The herd is watching my approach with definite interest now. I remember bringing groups of the girls through this way, seeing Jason ahead of us, standing guard to make sure everything was safe for us. Now I am remembering how Jason kissed me yesterday. I shouldn't have let him kiss me, but when he did I wanted more. Now all I want is to find Alex… and the girls. I know when I find them, Alex will be happy to see me; and there's no doubt in my mind that he'll kiss me. I can hardly wait for that. I miss him a lot more than I thought I would… and I think he means more to me than I thought he did.

Oh, for crying out loud. Come on, snap out of it already! What is my problem? I smack myself on the side of the head to try and make myself focus. Stupid men... no, not them, if anyone is stupid here, it's me. I can't afford to stop concentrating on everything around me. I can't be complacent. I have to pay attention and find Alex and the girls; that's all that matters.

Some of the zebras are a little skittish when I move past them, but mostly they are just curious. A couple of them sniff at me as I move by. "Hey there, guys, don't mind me, I'm just passing through; no kicking or biting, okay? That's a good boy... or girl, whichever you are. Pretty little beasties."

It doesn't take long to wind my way through the herd and step back into the coolness of the forest. I can hear the occasional snorts from the zebra herd for a while after I've left them. A few minutes later, it finally dawns on me that one or more big cats could be close by, following the zebras, stalking them. I don't want to get in between them, that's for sure. And I'd better start using more caution while I'm walking. I need to be stealthy, not crashing through the underbrush like an elephant or something. Wow, I wonder if they had elephants at the sanctuary, too? That was something I hadn't thought of before.

As it turns out, it didn't take me as long as I had thought it would to get here. I'm standing at the edge of the waterfall, leaning out carefully to look over the side. Deja-vu. Been there, done this before already. I certainly don't care for a repeat of yesterday's terrifying events. It's time to start moving upriver, in the direction of the road. Hopefully I can find them somewhere along the way.

I sure do feel like I'm missing something, though... but I can't figure out what it is. I look all around me at the ground surrounding where I had been standing briefly the day before yesterday, before I jumped... my walking stick is gone. That's what I had forgotten about. Someone must have taken it, and it had to have been Alex. That thought lifts my spirits momentarily. My next step is to track his footprints. Mine were limited; I went over the cliff pretty quickly. His should be the only other ones around, yet I can't find more than a few. I'm suddenly hit with the sinking feeling that I'm not going to find them, not here, not with my original plan. I was supposed to reverse course from here and start heading back along the river to the road. But that's the safe route to take.

What would Alex have thought, discovering that my walking stick laying here and yet I was nowhere to be found? What would I think if situations were reversed? I play it through in my head, the cliff, the walking stick, maybe even spotting all the dogs' prints in the dirt, knowing what the girls must have told our group. I inhale deeply and release the breath slowly. I step cautiously back over to the edge of the cliff. I think I know now what Alex must have surmised. He must have guessed correctly that I had no choice but to leap from the cliff into the water below. And not being able to see me from this vantage point, he probably assumed I was swept away downriver. That's where I have to look. That's where I'll find him. I have to get back down the escarpment. But this time I will climb down; no more cliff-diving for me.

As I walk along the edge of the cliff, searching for a relatively safe route down, I can't help thinking about the girls. Would they have come to the same conclusion? Would they have gone downriver, too? Has Alex already found them, or vice versa? If I am wrong about any of this, at least there is the chance some or all of them would have given up without ever having gone down the escarpment. They would have taken the road to the little village. They could be safely reunited with the group by now. But if that were true, I would have seen them, most likely, anyway.

The girls would probably have been somewhere on the other side of the river. They certainly didn't leave the group until sometime after Alex had left. I may even have been close to them physically but we never saw or heard each other... unless they also went searching for me down the escarpment. This is so frustrating. I'd like to call out their names, but I'm afraid to now. I could end up inadvertently calling a predator to me, or alternatively to them if they call out in response to me and a predator happens to be near them. I can't take that chance, especially with those girls. They have no defense. Elise, what were you thinking, going after me like that?

After what seems like hours, but in actuality is probably less than even one, I spot what looks to be a promising path, at least the first half of it is, anyway. I run my tongue across my lips and take a deep breath before starting my descent. Then I take that first step and begin to very gingerly make my way down. It is slow going since the would-be path is steep. Soil slides loose under my feet with nearly every step, and I slide a little with it. It's unnerving that every placement of a foot feels like it could end with me getting down to the bottom a lot faster than I had originally intended to.

When I reach the halfway point, I discover that the remainder of the escarpment is at a much sharper incline than I had thought from my perspective at the top. Most likely at the time, I was just overeager to reach the bottom. My spear is quite useful as a brace and helps prevent that rapid descent I am so concerned about; I'm quite glad I decided to bring it along. It takes me about twice as long to get down the second half of the escarpment as it did the first. Yet, I make it without breaking my neck... or anything else.

At the bottom, I pause to look back up. I guess it's really not that far down, it's just that it's so very steep. I have to sit and remove my boots and socks so I can shake out the ample amounts of soil in each of them. My feet are not their natural color. The only way to get the dirt stains off is with a bath in the river, and there's no time for that. As I replace my socks and shoes, I peer into the distance. I still don't see anyone, so I get back onto my feet and strike out toward the river in the hopes of finding my lost companions.

CHAPTER 28

When I finally make my way back to the river, I decide to stop briefly to rest and eat lunch; my stomach is growling enough to distract me. I won't help anyone if I pass out from hunger; I need my senses sharp. I'm alongside the river, by an elongated, low-slung rock outcrop. It stretches for about fifty feet on this side of the river, longer on the opposite side. It casts only a short shadow; but if you sit in that shadow, the rocks it falls across are cooler than any other available surface, although not by much. Once I finish my food, I stare at the churning water. It's splashing over the rocks periodically and a little of the spray splashes into my face. The water in the river has the illusion of being refreshingly chilled, but in actuality it is only a couple of degrees cooler than the air. I imagine that might change as the sun continues to bake the water and its surroundings through the afternoon. I go over to the edge of the river and splash the water onto my exposed skin and thoroughly douse my hair. That should help keep me cool for at least an hour from evaporation.

When I put on my pack and stand up to start hiking again, my worries come flooding back. Not like they had really stopped or anything, I guess. I feel so alone in the world. As I walk along in the vicinity of the river, I wonder where Alex and the girls could be. There's so much land ahead of me still to search. A lot of hope remains alive in me, but the weight of the reality of my predicament is beginning to encroach. I can't give up on my niece. I would rather never return myself than to go back without her and Anastasia. If I can find Alex somewhere along the way, too, that would make the picture in my head complete.

"Cole!"

I jump reflexively. The sharp call of my name startles me out of my self-absorbed contemplation. I search the area for Alex, but it doesn't take long to find him. He isn't far... at least, not as the crow flies, that is. He's standing on the other side of the river. Just behind him are Elise and Anastasia. My knees have become incredibly weak. I can hardly believe it. I put a hand up to my mouth… I don't think I've ever smiled so broadly in my entire life. I've never been this relieved, that much is certain.

Strange, but there is a good-sized addition to their little crew; just beyond the girls is what remains of that pack of dogs that chased me. Alex and the girls must have befriended them somehow; probably with food. They don't look too happy, though. They are staring at me… now they are barking at me. Stupid dogs; they must remember me from having nearly killed me at the cliff. They must hate me for some reason.

"Cole, listen to me," Alex is shouting tersely through cupped hands. "I want you to stay calm, alright, angel? Just listen to me and do everything exactly as I tell you."

What? Why is he talking to me like that? Stay calm? And did he just call me angel? My smile is slowly fading, replaced by a frown as my head tilts to one side like a dog listening for a particular sound. Then the realization hits me. Oh, no… they are fine, but I'm not. Something is terribly wrong, and I'm in danger. Slowly, my eyes begin scanning my surroundings much more closely. Where? Where is it… and what is it?

Farther down along the river in the direction I was just headed, nestled into the high grasses between the water and me, I spot my latest foe. Wait a minute; I'd better make that foes, plural. A lioness lies there, almost perfectly camouflaged. She is maybe thirty or forty feet farther down along the river than I am. Not too far for a lion to travel at their top rate of speed, no doubt, whatever that may be. I have every confidence that whatever her top speed is, it's way faster than mine. About twenty feet beyond her is a second one, also close to the river. Both of them are staring at me unconcernedly, panting in the midday heat, shaking their heads at the occasional fly buzzing around them.

What does that mean? Are they trying to lull me into a false sense of security or something? Are they just pretending they don't care so that I will go on about my business and then when I'm not paying attention they will attack me? Is that what they're waiting for? How do lions go about hunting, anyway? Damn it, I should have paid more attention to all those nature shows on television when Noel and I were growing up. First a tiger, now lions. More importantly, I should have allowed more time for Jason to teach me how to shoot the rifle. The stupid rifle that's securely tucked away in the pack strapped on my back right now, out of reach; maybe, maybe not.

The closest lioness will be on me before I can do anything. Or will she? On closer inspection, I see that she now doesn't seem to be all that interested in me. Her panting head has turned momentarily and is looking to the other side of the river, toward the girls… or the barking dogs with them, I can't be sure which. My left hand, holding the spear as a walking stick, remains steady. Very slowly, I lift my right arm, intending to try to pull the rifle from my backpack… if I can even manage to do that. It had not occurred to me before now to see if it was physically possible for me to work it free from the pack from such as angle as this.

On the other side of the river, Alex has begun waving his arms furiously. "Cole, look out! Behind you!"

Slowly, I turn my head. Just about fifty feet away from me, behind and off to my right, well apart from the others, is a third lioness. Unlike the other two, she is on her feet, moving slowly toward me. Until I look at her, that is. Now she has stopped and is just standing there, staring. It doesn't take much guesswork to figure out who's on the lunch menu. I swallow hard and try to clear my head and think, quickly. I don't know what to do. I am convinced there's no way I can get the rifle out of my pack in time, and even if I could, I certainly can't manage to shoot all three of them before they're on me. Perhaps, though, I can shoot the closer lions, each with a shot that is good enough to slow them down. Then I'll just have to get into the river before the third one reaches me. If there's enough time. The risk of drowning in the turbulent water is a far more preferable option. It outweighs the certainty of being ripped to bits by a lion. Of course, I am guessing that part would come after she has killed me… hopefully.

Then again, I'm not a very good marksman. I've already proven that in the barn with Jason. Maybe just the discharging of the weapon will be enough to scare them off if I happen to miss my targets. That is the only plan I can come up with at the moment. And, as it turns out, a moment is about all the time I have remaining.

As I angle my head back toward the river, so that the other two lions will be in my field of view, my right hand reaches slowly up and over my shoulder, closing around the barrel of the rifle. It is then that my eyes fall upon three additional lionesses and a huge male walking toward the river.

My heart leaps into my throat in sheer terror. These four lions are all on the far side of the river, emerging from the heavily forested tree line into the tall grasses. They are heading directly toward Alex and the girls, who clearly have no idea what's taking place behind them. The pride will be on them in less than a minute, but much sooner if the animals decide to charge. My God.

I take the chance of calling out and possibly startling the lions on my side of the river into motion in an attack on me; I have to. "Alex! Behind you!"

Alex turns and must immediately take in their predicament. I can see him motioning quickly to the girls, for them to get behind him. The only weapons he has are my walking stick and his knife. Now he has the girls backing toward the river. The river that is rocky and consumed by turbulent whitewater rapids.

Tears are coming to my eyes, and I feel sick to my stomach. They are going to be killed right in front of me, all three of them. And then I will die, attacked from the side or behind, whichever of the animals on my side of the river reaches me first. Not that I would care anymore. This can't be happening. There has to be something I can do. I have got do something to try and save them, but what? I won't accept their deaths; I can't.

My brain is starting to work again, finally overcoming the grip of my fears, converting them into determination and a sharply-focused rage. I'm the only one who has a gun; it's entirely up to me now. I can't save both them and myself. But that doesn't matter; there is no choice to make there. My heart is on the other side of the river. I clench my teeth and stride forward with as strong a purpose as I've ever felt in my life. In one decisive motion, I successfully yank the rifle free from its resting place in my backpack and allow the spear fall to the ground as I break into an all-out run.

Just as my feet encounter the rocky shoreline with the roaring water just below me, I stop short and without missing a beat, cock the weapon and raise it to my shoulder, as I had seen Jason do. I quickly aim and fire, my target being the lioness closest to Alex. Thankfully, beginner's luck seems to be firmly on my side. I don't divert my attention from the animals as the bullet flies, but I'm sure the sound must startle Alex and the girls as much as it apparently startles the pride. The bullet impacts the body of the lead lioness; and she jumps backward and up, snarling in surprise and pain. The second lioness is very near her; and she halts suddenly, unsure of what has happened. They all seem confused now. The first lioness has dropped into the grass, initially in a sitting position but then allowing her body to flop over onto its side. She is wounded, but I have no idea how badly. I turn my attention to the second lioness and fire, missing this time, but the sound of the bullet striking a tree not far behind the pride confuses the animals further.

The dogs have now shifted their undivided attention to the more immediate matter of self-preservation. They are barking furiously at the members of the pride that are now threatening their own lives, although those lions have now ceased their forward progress. They seem to know what the sound of a gunshot means. And with all their years of living in the sanctuary they must have seen plenty of deaths this way. These hunters have now become the prey... *my* prey. And I fully intend to claim as many of them as I can before I die.

I fire the rifle a third time, striking the second lioness around the withers. She, too, jumps back; but I don't think she's badly hurt. I aim for her again, widening the stance of my feet in the hopes of improving my aim. I see the two standing females and the male lion reverse course and begin to retreat back toward the trees at a jog. My finger squeezes the trigger, and the second lioness jumps away as she is hit with another glancing bullet. That's all I'm able to see in the brief flash of time I have before being hurtled forward as a lioness on my side of the river charges with a painful crash into my back at what must surely be full speed. The tips of a couple of her claws find my shoulders and dig in briefly as we fall together into the water. It's all so surreal; one instant I'm firing the rifle, the next I am completely submerged in the turbulent river.

The churning water threatens to drown me, preventing me from surfacing. I can swim, but I've never been good at holding my breath underwater for very long… or even above the water, for that matter. The desire I feel to take a deep breath is overwhelming. Then all of a sudden, from no particular effort on my part, my head pops up to the surface; and I'm able to inhale a gulp of precious air before my ribcage collides with a boulder, spewing the oxygen and spinning me around. There I find I'm not alone in the water… the lioness who charged me is frighteningly near, attempting to swim and grab onto anything she can find for potential support. And she's far too close to me for comfort. A massive paw reaches out for my head.

Quickly, I suck in as much air as my lungs can hold and dive beneath the surface. The treacherous flow of the water pulls me deeper under than I had planned on going. It rotates me and causes a disorienting side effect. I'm being moved around so violently that I'm unable to discern whether I'm being pushed up or down. I feel my right hand emerge from the watery grave to touch the atmosphere above; then my face clears the water and I greedily inhale the life-giving air. I have no idea where the lioness is.

I fight harder to keep my head above the water this time, flailing my arms, struggling to counterbalance against the bulk of my backpack. It's pulling me down and making my struggle more difficult, but at the same time the pack is absorbing many of the blows from the boulders and assorted debris in the river. My head is struck twice in rapid succession against boulders, and it gives me the sensation of nightfall approaching. I find I can't remember much of what has happened up to this point. I imagine for a moment I am floating weightless into sleep. It's such a calm and peaceful sensation.

Yet I know I can't give in; I must fight back. Coughing up water brings me back to reality. I begin to struggle against the current, but it seems to be cooperating with me. The flow is slowing as the river widens. Just ahead of me, I see the body of the drowned lioness floating farther downriver. I pull myself together and try to ignore the pain. With a concerted effort, I'm able to work with the current to move myself into a shallower zone, until I am able to touch the bottom with my feet. It isn't easy; but I'm able to combat this reduced pull from the currents and haul myself out onto the gently sloping, rock-strewn bank. I crawl forward a few feet before collapsing, my feet still in the water. I lie there for several minutes, coughing up more water and letting my breathing return to normal.

When I have recovered sufficiently, I prop myself up to look at my surroundings. It takes some work, but I manage to disengage myself from my backpack. My shoulders sear with pain, either from strain, pummeling by boulders, or the claws of the lion; I can't tell which. I imagine I have traveled a substantial distance downriver from where I started. Perhaps the worst part about it is when I realize that I am still on the same side of the river I started on, opposite from Alex and the girls. Great, just wonderful. I sink back to the ground. The small, rounded stones on the riverbank have been comfortingly warmed from the sun. I will need to rest before trying to cross the river. I'm far too worn out to make it right now…

CHAPTER 29

First, I become aware of the sensation of extra weight dropping across my back. What happened? Where am I? My body jerks very slightly as I remember the pride of lions. Next, I feel fingers pressing against the side of my neck.

"She's got a pulse, Elise; she's alive," I recognize Alex's voice, relief overwhelming me even in my disoriented state. The weight on my back lifts.

I open my eyes and roll over, with Alex's assistance. Rolling over is easier than attempting to stand or even sit. Sharp pain runs through my head. Maybe the easiest choice isn't always the best, as my father used to say. I feel the two girls bending my legs at the knees to remove my feet from the water. I find myself looking up into three smiling faces. Oh, how I've dreamed of this moment! As Elise drops onto me in another delighted hug, some of the events of the day come swirling back into my head, although everything is still a jumbled mix. With effort, I raise a worn-out arm and let it fall onto her back. I look up at Alex. "Thank you."

"Hey, these girls happen to be really good company," he says, acknowledging each in turn before looking at me again. "And you're welcome." Now his demeanor becomes serious. "Okay, Elise, let her have some space for a minute."

Elise sits up but clearly has no plans to leave her place by my side.

"Do you think anything is broken, Cole?" he asks me.

"No," my voice comes out in a raspy whisper.

"Can you try to sit up?" he asks next.

"I don't know... I think so," I answer, but I'm sure I am projecting little confidence behind my words.

"Okay then, let's try it; nice and slow. If you feel at all woozy, just say so," he says as he gingerly slips a hand beneath my neck. The contact between his hand and my neck hurts, but it's far from unbearable.

Slowly, he helps me sit up. The world tips a bit, and I close my eyes. I open them to discover everything has righted itself. The next task is to try moving my arms. In spite of a little pain, they seem to be working. Next I try out my legs. Everything seems to be functioning. "I think I can stand up."

"I don't know about that; I think you should sit here for a few minutes first," Alex declares with authority.

"Anastasia, please get me Cole's canteen belt," he speaks gently to the girl, nodding his head toward my feet.

I must have removed that without realizing it. I sort of remember peeling off the backpack; at least, I think so. I do remember the pain in my head, which is still with me. Where is the rifle? I must have lost it in the river somewhere. Now what are we going to do? The memory of the lions returns to me again. There are still some of them out there, right?

Alex passes me the opened canteen. "Here, try to drink some water."

When I reach for the canteen, the pain shooting down my arm from my shoulder makes me wince and recoil. I guess my shoulders are worse than I thought.

Alex's expression is one of deep concern. "Take it easy; let me hold it for you."

He is very careful just to give me small sips. It still makes me cough a few times. I nod my head to indicate I've had enough. Even nodding my head hurts. Then I remember striking it against those boulders.

I look at Alex and see he is examining me with a critical eye. "What?" I ask.

"You've got some colorful bruises coming up on your forehead. And your shoulders are a little messed up. How bad is the pain?"

"My head hurts pretty bad, but I'll be okay. Why?"

"There are some blood stains on your shirt, but not bad. I just want to make sure there's no serious muscle damage," he leans around to check my back.

"What is it? Is it from the river?" I ask.

"No, it's from the lion. She got her claws into your shoulders, but I can't tell how bad it is. I'm going to have to get your shirt off to take care of this. She grabbed ahold of you when she jumped on you from behind and knocked the both of you into the river. You didn't know she cut into you?"

"I knew, but I didn't think it was too bad," I say. It certainly explains the pain, although I think the boulders hurt me a lot worse than the lion.

"We're all very lucky you were as close to the river as you were. There's no doubt she would have killed you about a second later if she had been able to get a better grip. Falling into the river prevented that."

Anastasia turns over my backpack. There, the material is shredded in long claw marks. I seem to have lost some of the pack's contents in the river through those gaping holes. The pack took almost the entirety of the lion's claws.

Alex motions to Anastasia. "Open my backpack, Anastasia, and put everything from Cole's inside. I'll carry it. We'll leave her pack here, it's no good anymore."

He examines my wounds again. "The cuts don't seem to be bleeding anymore and they're only superficial. I think your time in the water helped, too. You were very fortunate, Cole. I'm going to bandage you up as best I can. Then we'll get going if you can manage it. We'll be really careful on the way back to watch out for those other lions, but I'm hoping we can find your rifle. We just might end up needing it, and I know it'll make me feel better having it."

Alex and Elise help me remove my shirt. It adheres to the scratches in a few spots, but for the most part it comes off easily enough with their gentle help. My camisole is in better shape than my shirt. My shoulders don't hurt too badly while removing it. Anastasia passes a first-aid kit to Alex. Both girls take turns assisting him as he dresses my wounds and wraps them as well as he can in bandages that are still wet from being in the river. All in all, I guess they do a pretty good job of patching me up. And the Tylenol doesn't hurt, either.

"There." Alex sits back. "How does that feel?"

"It's good; y'all did a good job on me," I look at the girls and smile, flashing them a thumbs up.

"Are you sure?" Alex prods. "It's not too tight or too loose?"

I rest a hand on his. "It's fine, really. I'd let you know if it wasn't."

He smiles with visible relief and takes my hand in his. "This day has been unreal. I can't believe I found you, lost you, and then found you again, all in the span of less than an hour." He bends over and kisses my hand.

The hard shaking of a couple of wet dogs draws our attention from the rising emotions of the intense moment. The girls laugh with sheer joy, holding out their arms and turning their heads aside as the dogs shake themselves further, showering us all with stinky dog water. Come to think of it, I don't believe I've heard any of the girls laughing for a long time now. Or maybe it just feels that way. It seems as though a lot of time has passed since we got on the plane that brought us out here. Months, maybe even a year. All our lives have changed a lot more than we had imagined they would when we began this adventure.

The two late entries join the remainder of the dog pack, who must have swum over to this side of the river unnoticed, while the girls and Alex were tending to my injuries. They are quite the assortment; different sizes and colors. The majority of them appear to be mutts and roughly knee high. Rin is bigger than these and the only one that is readily identifiable breed-wise. As Noel and I were growing up, our family always chose to adopt mixed-breed dogs instead of purebreds. My parents always said it was better to rescue a dog whenever possible, that they needed homes, too. I remember one in particular, who apparently had a little German Shepard in her. Now I have Rin – as soon as we get back to the farmhouse, anyway. And provided he survived the tiger attack.

That, in turn, makes me think of Elizabeth. I never even took the time to go see for myself how she was doing. I hope she's going to be alright. It sounded as though she had been very brave and selfless.

It's comforting to have these dogs with us. They will hopefully help to ward off predators, or at least give us an early warning if any threats are around. Provided they can raise their awareness level more, that is. They haven't been all that impressive thus far, really. They had missed the lions behind them earlier today when they were too focused on the ones in front of them, the ones that weren't really a threat to anyone but me. Regardless, we have a larger group now for mutual protection as we travel. We'll need it, because I'm certain we won't be able to make it to the village before dark.

"Cole, do you think you can stand up now?" Alex asks.

"Yeah, I think so," I say.

"Okay, let's get your shirts back on you first. Girls, do you want to help me with this, too?" he turns to where they sit, near my feet.

"Sure," Elise replies; and they both run up to either side of me and very delicately assist me in getting my camisole and shirt back on. They even button my shirt for me.

I smile at them gratefully, "Thanks, girls. I sure do appreciate your help."

"You're welcome," they chime together as one. Then they burst out in a fit of laughter, for no apparent reason.

"Alright, you two. Get your backpacks on and let's get ready to go," Alex informs them gently, putting his own onto his broad shoulders.

"And you," he turns his attention back to me. "I'm going to help you get to your feet. If you feel even remotely like you can't walk or there's too much pain or if you feel like you might lose consciousness, you tell me right away, Cole; I mean it."

"I know you do and I will. I don't want to pass out, especially in front of the girls. They've had enough things to worry about lately."

"Okay then, ready?" he asks.

I simply nod my head affirmatively. He does most of the work, practically lifting me to my feet. He lets me lean against him, holding onto me protectively. At first, I think I'll be okay, but it only takes a few seconds for the world to start spinning; and I latch onto Alex instinctively for support. He immediately scoops me up into his arms.

"Let's go, girls. Keep your eyes open behind us, alright? That's your job. And keep a close watch on those dogs. They can sense a lot more than we can. If they start acting differently from the way they are now, you let me know," Alex orders, entrusting the girls with responsibility and giving them something else to focus on besides me.

I see Elise has my walking stick. She isn't using it for support as she walks, but rather holds it in a defensive position. That brings a smile to my lips. I'm so proud of her. I allow my head to rest against Alex's shoulder.

We proceed this way for nearly an hour. I realize we are probably getting close to the scene of the attack. The two lions on this side of the river could be anywhere. I really do feel much better, and I know Alex needs to be unencumbered by me so he can be ready to help defend us if necessary.

"Alex, I want to try standing on my own again. I'm sure I'm good to walk now," I say.

"Nope; not yet, I'm afraid, boss lady. You need to stay still for a little while longer."

"No, I don't. I need to try it again. I certainly can't help anybody in this position. And you have to be ready to protect us, and you can't do that while you're holding me."

"Sure I can. I'll just have to drop you if something happens, that's all," he glances at me momentarily, his eyes twinkling with mischief.

"You'd better not!" I respond.

"You'll be okay; it won't hurt that much. It shouldn't dent that cute little rear end of yours any," he says, giving me that crooked smile of his.

"Alright, that's enough, put me down." No luck, he keeps walking. I figured he would. "I'm serious, Alex. Put me down, right now."

"You're not heavy. I can carry you all day, sweet angel, no problem."

There he goes again, calling me angel. I think I like it. No, I know I like it. Still… "No problem? Really? Well, you're going to have a problem if you don't put me down right now, Mister."

He chuckles heartily, ignoring me.

"It's not funny, Alex. Put me down… now. I mean it."

At that, he stops and looks at me. "Okay. But if I think you look unstable, I'm picking you right back up again. And no arguments from you about it."

"Okay, no arguments." I'm sure he knows by now that isn't anywhere near the truth with me.

Still, he very gently lowers me until my feet are resting firmly on the ground. Before he can say anything, Anastasia is in front of me, offering me more water. I take it from her with a smile.

"Thank you, sweetie." I drink what's left in the canteen, which wasn't much. Anastasia hurries off to the edge of the river with it for a refill. "Be careful, honey, don't get too close to the deep water."

"Aunt Cole, here's your old walking stick, if you want it. It might help you," Elise says, handing it to me.

"Thanks, honey. That's exactly what I need."

Alex puts a hand on her shoulder. "Good thinking there, Elise."

After a few minutes, Anastasia runs back up with the water and straps the canteen belt around my waist for me. "Thank you, Anastasia."

"You know, you girls have been a really big help today," Alex says proudly. "You should have seen them, Cole. They tamed this pack of dogs like they speak the same language or something."

This whole time, I have been feeling a wave of dizziness coming over me; but I refuse to allow Alex to know anything about it. I'm just hoping as it builds in intensity that it will hurry up and reach its peak and pass soon. Then no one needs to know anything ever happened. I'll be fine and we can move on.

"Are you okay, Cole?" Alex is asking, I think for the second time, or maybe it's the third.

It almost sounds like he's in a fog. I hadn't realized he was watching me because I'm trying to focus both on not passing out and on the girls. I have been keeping my face angled away from Alex as much as I can so he would be unable to read my expression. I have a white-knuckled grip on my walking stick.

"Yeah, I'm fine." I make sure I don't turn his way.

He takes ahold of my arm and moves in front of me, forcing me to look at him. He narrows his eyes. "You look really pale all of a sudden. Do you need to sit down for a minute or do you want me to carry you again?"

He is plainly serious and not fooled at all. I sigh. "I'll sit down for a minute. I just need some more water, that's all."

He helps me sit down and hands me his canteen. "Thanks," I say. The girls plop down on either side of me and help themselves to water as well. Half of the dog pack is sniffing the area around us curiously; the other half sits down in the grass all around us.

"No problem." His disposition is quite stern as he stands in front of me.

I can see I've pressed my luck with him as much as I'll be able to get away with. My steadiness improves immediately. "I think I just need to sit for a minute. Then I'll be fine. As a matter of fact, I already feel better."

"Sure you do." His response is terse. His concerned demeanor speaks volumes by itself.

I drink a few more sips of the water. "I really am fine, Alex. My head isn't hurting or anything. And your water is gone, by the way."

He takes the canteen from my outstretched hand. "Okay. Anastasia, why don't we make sure all the water containers are full. We're getting closer to dinnertime. If we have all the water we need then the only thing we'll have to focus on is eating and finding a good, safe place to sleep for the night."

Anastasia gathers up Elise's canteen and the water bottles both girls carry. Alex takes his own. I can't hear what they're saying, but it seems that they are having an engaging conversation on their way to the river.

"So, Alex has been taking good care of you girls for me?" I ask.

"Yeah," Elise answers. "Pretty much all he talked about the whole time is you, though."

"Really?" She has my undivided attention now. "What did he say?"

"Oh, I don't know. I don't really remember all of it. He said you were pretty and nice; and he told us all about how brave you were, saving his life and all that. He said he'd never forget what you did... oh, and he asked if you were dating anybody or if you had a boyfriend or anything like that." Elise smiles. "He really likes you, Aunt Cole; a lot."

I'm sure I must be blushing. I really wish I could find a way to control that. I look out at the pair by the river. "Do you really think so?" Wow, I must sound like a teenaged girl. Exactly like most of the girls on this trip, I suppose.

"Yeah, I think so... do you like him back?"

I give a short, embarrassed laugh. "Yeah, I believe I do; a lot."

"Cool," she responds. "He's going to make a really awesome uncle."

"Whoa! Uncle? Who said anything about uncle?" I react more strongly than I meant to.

"It's okay, Aunt Cole. The other guy you were with was a real jerk. I know because that's what Mom and Dad always say. I know they'll like Alex. Anastasia and I like him. He's a really nice guy. And he knows all kinds of cool stuff. He knows survival stuff; he taught us some things about that, too. And he was telling us some old history stuff. And he taught us some self-defense stuff, too. He's cool. Anastasia and I really like him a lot."

I laugh again and shake my head. "Okay, you've convinced me. He's cool." Kids!

Elise smiles at her achievement then gets a serious look on her face. "Aunt Cole, do you think we're ever going to be able to get back home again?"

Yikes. I would prefer she keep talking about Alex. Or almost anything else instead of that. My smile drops. Honesty is the best policy, my dad always told my sister and me. "I'm going to do my best, honey. I hope so. I'm not going to lie to you, though. I don't think it's going to be easy. And it might be dangerous. I don't know what's going on out there."

"I know. We all know, all us kids. Ms. Regina told us everything you said. We all believe you're right, too. I told the other girls that you would take good care of us, though. Whatever happens," Elise says, her face showing a confidence I wish I felt.

"Thanks, honey. I appreciate the support." I decide to try a different tack. "I guess I'm going to try sitting up on my knees now. That might make it easier when I stand up."

"Okay, but you probably shouldn't stand up until Alex is beside you. He won't let you fall down," she asserts with utter certainty.

"I know, I won't," I grunt as I get myself into position. I can see Alex watching me closely as he and Anastasia continue their conversation on their way back to us.

"How does that feel, Aunt Cole?" Elise asks. She is holding my walking stick for me until I'm ready to try to stand.

"So far, so good."

I smile as Alex approaches with another unrelentingly stern look on his face. "It's okay, Alex, I think I'm fine now." I extend my hand so he can help me up.

He hesitates, just for a moment. I think he wants to make sure I know he isn't pleased. Like I couldn't see that easily enough. He takes my hand and puts an arm around my waist, helping me to stand.

"Just be still for a minute, please Cole," he requests with a frustrated tone.

"Don't worry, I will," I respond, trying to keep smiling. I bend at the waist and rest my hands on my knees before standing all the way upright, very slowly.

"Are you sure?" is the retort.

I raise an eyebrow quizzically and smile as I gaze up at him. "Yes. And I really do feel better now."

"Okay then," he looks all around and freezes. Without looking at me, he asks, "Do you feel like you're well enough to run?"

The smile drains from my face as I see his expression and his words register in my head. "Please, no. They're not still here, are they? They can't be. This isn't fair."

"I know," he whispers steadily. "Life isn't fair. Especially for us out here." He shifts his weight back and away from me. "Get behind me, Cole. Get the walking stick from Elise and give it to me. Then slowly move the girls toward the river."

This can't be happening again. Will it ever be over? I don't know how much more I can take. Without trying to see the lions that I know must be there, I take slow steps around Alex as he instructed. Elise is aware of what's going on and without a sound she hands me the walking stick, which I then pass to Alex. The dogs are standing there, sniffing the wind and staring at the lions. A couple of the dogs have begun growling.

"Go, now," he orders us.

The thing is… where are we going to go? There's nowhere safe for us. We can't run away – the lions will definitely charge us. The river is a better option, but its rapids will still likely bring death for these girls and for me, in my still somewhat-weakened state. And a walking stick won't help Alex against these two lions. There has to be another solution. I scan the area. Just ahead is where I plunged into the river with the lion on my back.

"Girls, get ready… I want you to do what I do. You have to be brave, okay?"

"Okay," they answer softly, in unison.

"Look around you and find some rocks the size of your fists. Two rocks each. Hurry," I instruct them.

"Alex, give me back my walking stick," I tell him firmly.

"What?" he responds with surprise from over his shoulder.

"You heard me… just do it. It's not a request."

He turns sideways so he can still see the lions out of the corner of his eye as he looks at me. "What are you trying to do? I told you to get out of here and take the girls with you."

"I know what you said, and it's a fallacy. It'll never work, and you know it. We can't outrun them and we probably won't survive the river. That leaves only one option. Now give me the walking stick. I have an idea, but you have to trust me," I say, my voice steady and firm as I refuse to deviate from staring at the lions.

"Cole, whatever you've got going on in your head…," Alex begins.

"No. It's our only chance. Listen to me, if my rifle didn't go into the water with me, it'll be on the rocks of the bank just up ahead where the lion knocked me into the river. You have to get to it. You have my ammo in your backpack; I saw Anastasia put it in there."

He hesitates a moment before answering. "Okay, I think I see where you're going with this. I'll go for the rifle, but you still have to get these kids out of here."

"No. We're not going anywhere. We're all in this together. There's no other way out. You go for the rifle," I say as I reach in front of him and take back my walking stick. "We've got you covered."

"What are you talking about?"

"You heard me. Now get going. Those lions are thinking while they watch us, and they won't keep doing that all day. It's time for a little confusion," I say.

Alex glances at me then over his shoulder; where he sees the girls with their rocks. "Okay. I don't know exactly what you've got in mind, Cole, but okay. Be careful. All of you be careful. Cole, I..."

I don't take my eyes off the lions. "We'll have plenty enough time for all that later, Alex. Get going. Ready, girls?"

We watch as Alex moves at an angle away from us, toward the river, yet closer to the lions. One of the lionesses takes a few steps in Alex's direction as he draws nearer to the riverbank.

"I'm sick and tired of being hunted, damn it. Let's go, girls; just stay behind me and don't show any fear. It's our turn to scare *them* now," I say in a growl, my jaw firmly set in anger as the lions watch Alex with too much interest for my tastes.

I let out the most threatening yell I can muster from somewhere deep down inside me. That is the unspoken signal to the girls, who begin banging their rocks together as hard as they can and yelling at the top of their lungs. The lions show obvious confusion, looking all around them uncertainly. The pack of dogs decides to join in, too, as I take several long steps toward the lions, continuing to yell and wave my walking stick high in the air. The dogs surge ahead of me, barking furiously. It's payback time.

One lioness, still confused about what's happening, makes a quick movement toward Alex, who is frantically scouring the river's edge. That's about all I can take. Or maybe I've finally just snapped, I don't know. I scream and yell, now running toward the damned lions, the dogs all around me. I can hear the girls yelling, too. One of their rocks hurtles past me and lands near the lioness that had moved on Alex, followed by a handful of pebbles, which hit their mark quite well. Then another large rock strikes the ground near the beasts, rolling just past one lion's feet.

The confused lions apparently decide all this noise and the unexpected attack on them is too much to take. They change course and break for the cover of the forest nearby. We cease our advance but continue yelling as the dogs keep barking ahead of us.

By this time, Alex has retrieved the rifle. I've been so focused on the lions I didn't even notice. Thus, when two shots fire in rapid succession it startles me. One of the lionesses falls dead on the spot. The other makes it into the cover of the forest, running fast.

I can't believe it. Yet again, we have managed to somehow cheat death. I turn to the girls and give them both a high five. "Good job, girls! That was outstanding!" My smile knows no bounds.

Alex jogs over to us. I meet him, dropping my walking stick to the ground. I throw my arms around his neck and pull him down for a nice, long kiss. I am vaguely aware of the girls behind me, clapping.

I look back at them without releasing my grip on Alex. "You like that, huh?"

"Yeah!" both girls answer with huge grins on their faces.

I return my attention to Alex. My heart is hopelessly lost in him; and I've never been so happy in my entire life, even in such desperate times as these.

CHAPTER 30

Even the dogs are tired in this heat. Don't get me wrong, I very much prefer being hot to being cold. But it is a bit much, especially in the late morning hours, when there is no shade along this dusty dirt road. Plus we are all so worn out; I don't think any of us got much sleep last night, even with the dogs around for protection. The only thing that makes it better is that we are nearly to the farmhouse. The settlement is just on the other side of the hill we are walking up.

Hopefully Jason has removed the body of that tiger by now. They don't need to be worrying about scavengers coming by for a feast or all the extra flies the rotting corpse would attract or even the stench, especially as hot as it is getting to be today.

None of the dogs seem overly concerned by anything around them. To me, that means we are safe; but you never know. Every day that passes makes it increasingly clear to me that you cannot rely on being safe out here. And it's obvious we are the only humans for miles around; we are alone in this. No authorities of any kind are going to show up here to help us. I have serious doubts that we will ever encounter that kind of aid again, except maybe in a big city. But I'm not sure it's worth the risk to try.

As we reach the top of the hill, I see the village spread out before us, just as I had seen it a couple of days ago, when Rin and I had been pursued by the tiger. Ah, at least that particular object is one thing that's missing. The tiger's body has been removed or buried. Thank goodness.

The closer we get to the farmhouse, however, the more my concern grows. No one is coming out to welcome us. I glance over at Alex when we are a scant twenty yards from the farmhouse.

"I thought you said they would be watching for us," Alex says.

"I did… but there's no welcoming committee," I reply warily.

There's no place to hide, and no cover of any kind between the top of the hill and this first house. This is the same house where I had last seen the group when I left to go in search of Alex and the girls. We have no choice but to continue on. I can see no faces at any of the windows, no signs of movement at all. I have a terrible sense of foreboding. Maybe it's just as simple as that they have moved into one of the other houses. Maybe they even decided not to wait any longer for us to get back and moved on without us; I mean, for all they knew we might well never have come back, any of us.

Upon reaching the house, Alex motions for the girls and me to stay outside with the dogs. Holding the rifle at his side, he enters through the unlocked front door. I don't like this, not one bit. I look around us nervously, waiting for who-knows-what to come and get us next, a firm grip on my walking stick. I'm even beginning to wonder about Jason's ghost stories. If we survive this experience, I'm definitely never going camping again… ever. In fact, when I get back to Raleigh, I may never leave my apartment again, except to go to work and back. And get groceries… well… then there's church, at least once in a while. And I like going to the library sometimes, when I have time to read. Gee whiz, Cole… *focus* for crying out loud.

There are no unusual noises that I can hear; and the dogs are acting normal, walking around and sniffing of everything, wagging their tails at us. According to them, all is well with the world. If that's true, then where is everyone else? Come on, Alex, where are you? I know it's a big house, but still…

Right on cue, I hear Alex emerge from the back door. I lead the kids around to the rear of the house to meet him.

"No one's inside. But they were in there. It looks like they just dropped whatever it was they were doing and left, Alex says. "But I did find this…" he opens the back door and there stands Rin, heavily bandaged, but alive.

"Rin!" I run up the steps to the porch stoop and scratch him behind the ears. He wags his tail and follows me slowly. The girls are all over him.

"It doesn't make any sense," I say, looking around again.

"What does?" Alex comments, mostly to himself I think. He's certainly right about that.

A movement of something brightly-colored catches my eye, far off in the distance. Squinting my eyes against the sun, I put up a hand to shade them. Sure enough, beyond the most distant house in the village, amidst a grove composed primarily of spindly little trees, I can see clothes and hair blowing in the gentle gusts of wind.

"There. There they are!" I say excitedly as I point and start walking. A lot of people are out there. In fact, I think it's the entire group. I am a little taken aback as I narrow my eyes. It looks like there are more people than just ours. A lot more.

"Thank God we found them," I hear Alex behind me. "Now let's go find out what's going on."

We proceed along a dirt path to meet up with the others, the dogs lagging behind. But the closer we get, the more confused I become. At first, I thought my eyes were playing tricks on me, but now I can see I am right... the numbers of people in our group have substantially increased since I left the day before yesterday.

"Cole," Alex begins.

"I know, I see them," I respond.

"Should we have the girls go back and wait at the house?" he asks.

"No, the other girls are out there, too. Besides, the house wouldn't provide any protection... if they needed any. Let's just all go together," I whisper warily.

I notice Alex get a firmer grip on the rifle, just as I am doing with my walking stick. The girls are looking past us with curiosity as we walk. The dogs seem calm enough.

The people in the grove of trees have noticed us now and are watching as we approach. When we are about twenty feet away, the group breaks ranks and swarms us with welcoming hugs and smiles. At least, the members of our original group do. Jason steps up through the sea of girls to hug the four of us, one by one.

When he gets to me, he gives me a quick peck on the lips and a long hug. One of his arms lingers around my waist. My peripheral vision lets me see that Alex doesn't appear to like it one bit, either.

"Jason, what happened? Who are all these people?" I ask. There are probably close to one hundred or more additional people, various ages of men, women and children, standing by and watching us newcomers closely… more than that, almost with fear, as if they think we might suddenly try to cause them harm.

"They showed up a few hours after you left, just before sunset. Some of them are from this village and some are family members or friends from the neighboring town we were supposed to hike to next. They were really surprised to see us here. Just as much as we were to see them, I suppose," Jason relates the story to us briefly.

"What are all of you doing out here?" I ask.

Jason's face sags, and he glances behind him, stepping aside so I can see for myself. Alex and I follow his gaze. There is freshly-turned earth, mounded and covered with stones and marked at its end with a crude cross. My eyes widen.

"It's Elizabeth's grave. She didn't make it. There wasn't anything we could do," Jason relays the information softly.

"Oh my God!" I say.

"She saved those kids," Alex states somberly. "If I had been closer to her, maybe…"

I place a hand on his arm. "You can't blame yourself, Alex." I wipe at the tears falling down my cheeks. I can't believe this has happened.

"Cole's right. You did the best you could. It wasn't anyone's fault; it just happened. It's a miracle more of us haven't died out here," Jason says. "The newcomers helped us dig through this hardpan soil. We just finished the service."

Looking over at the newcomers, I see they aren't paying us much attention anyway. They are busy talking to Elise and Anastasia, who are explaining to the entire bunch about their latest adventures. And the addition of the pack of dogs, of course.

Jason continues, "They initially abandoned this village when the power didn't come back on after a few days. And there was no telephone or radio reception, either. They went to the town, hoping to find out what was going on. Turns out you were right, Cole. Everything you said. The Earth was hit with a solar storm, I can't remember the technical term you used for it..."

"A CME... a Coronal Mass Ejection; it doesn't matter... what you just said is good enough... a solar storm," I say slowly. I had been hoping against hope I would be proven wrong.

"Okay, so why did those people come back here? Was it because there was the same problem in the town, or was it something else?" Alex asks with an unmistakable hint of foreboding in his tone.

Jason lowers his voice. "That's what they said... there's no power anywhere, no telephones, no refrigeration, no gas stations, nothing is working. And that seems to be the case *everywhere*. The only way to get around is by horse, bicycle, or on foot. Several groups of people came to the town from other cities. They all had the same story... at least, according to these folks, anyway. Everybody's out looking for food and shelter, and they're going for whatever they can find... or forcibly take. They need help. Crime is out of control in the cities; looting, robbery, murder, and lots of it. The police and the authorities are being completely overrun. Civil unrest is everywhere. They say there's no government, not anymore..."

"Oh my God," is all I can think of to say. Even though I knew what the possibilities were, I'm still shocked to hear it's happening for real.

The approach of two of the strangers catches my eye. "Hello, I'm Cole," I extend my hand to each of them in turn. I'm trying not to stare. The older couple looks almost identical to the famous painting of the old farmer with a pitchfork standing next to his wife. It's really uncanny. I don't want to say anything about it, as I'm sure they must get that all the time. Their hands are heavily-calloused from decades of manual labor.

They shake my hand with warm enthusiasm. "So you're the one we've been hearing about?"

My eyebrows arch with surprise. "I'm sorry?"

"You said your name is Cole, right?" the wife asks.

"Yes ma'am."

"Excellent!" a young girl says, peering around the elderly woman's skirt and giving a little fist pump in the air.

Simultaneously, Alex and I turn expectantly to Jason.

Jason scratches his head. "Well, I told everyone our story. So... it seems you came out as something of a legend in your own time, Cole," he smiles sheepishly. Several people in the crowd apparently overheard the exchange and are whispering to each other while they look at me, pointing and smiling.

"Congratulations," Regina leans in to whisper.

"Hey, if you think everything she's done before was something special, just wait until you hear what happened yesterday," Alex begins.

"What in the world did you tell them?" I ask Jason, cutting Alex off.

"He spoke nothing but the truth, honey. Honestly," Regina says in defense of Jason. "We just knew you'd make it back with those three in tow. The newcomers have been waiting to meet you. You're back in charge. It's just that there are twice as many of us now."

CHAPTER 31

In the beginning, the earth was without form. For me, that time is now. My world feels as though it is without form. Nothing makes sense anymore; everything has changed. And all I can do is push forward, hoping to alter the chaos of what the world has become into something that is logical and familiar again. It feels possible to me for just a moment, as I stand looking out over the low hills, scattered with bits of open spaces amongst the trees. Birds have begun to flitter about in the first light of this warm spring morning, selecting partners for the season and establishing territories. Colorful butterflies dance amongst the occasional bumble bee, awaiting their turn at those few wildflowers that are presenting their faces this early in the day. It's a tranquil scene, nature here uncaring and untouched by what has happened to humankind.

At least the humankind I am aware of. I gradually come to realize I'm leaning so heavily against my walking stick that the fingers of my right hand are beginning to complain. It has probably left a mark on the side of my face as well. I straighten my back and focus my thoughts toward those who are now depending on me. Almost overnight, it seems, I have become the leader of well over four hundred people, as refugees have been arriving throughout the past couple of days. How I've come about being chosen as their leader I'm still not quite sure. I'm no leader... not like this, anyway. I guess an apocalypse can change a person's circumstances pretty dramatically... and swiftly.

Alex beckons to me from the back door of the farmhouse. I guess it's time. I head back slowly, stalling, wanting to put off what I know must come for as long as possible. As if postponing the inevitable will transform our circumstances somehow.

As Alex and I walk through the large living room, I can see through the windows that all of the people are gathered and waiting, including our original group of campers. The girls are seated in front of all the others, on the ground around the porch. Everyone is busily talking amongst themselves in small groups. Jason grins, giving me a wink and a thumbs up from his position on the porch, where he leans casually against a column.

"Let's go, Cole. They're waiting for us. Or rather, they're waiting for you," Alex says to me, holding the front door open. He gives my shoulder a quick pat of encouragement as I move past him.

I know they're waiting for me, seeking guidance, leadership… but this isn't something I'm looking forward to. My jaw stiffens. I close my eyes and take a deep breath before stepping out onto the expansive porch.

"Well, what do you think we're going to do now?" Regina asks from where she stands, near the bottom of the porch stairs, her back turned to me.

"I don't know," DeShondra responds to her mother then looks up at me with hope on her face. "Cole?"

Looking around, I can't help but notice that everyone is staring at me expectantly. Jason and Alex are standing just in back of me on either side for moral support. How has this happened? Not the whole civilization as we know it falling apart at the seams thing, but the whole me being the leader of this part of what is left of civilization thing. I don't know any more than anyone else does, yet they are looking to me for a final call, to guide them down a path I'm not completely sure of myself.

Do I take our original group of campers and teachers and try to make our way through the extreme lawlessness and danger that our nation has apparently fallen into, on a journey back to whatever remains of the city of Atlanta? That would entail leaving the rest of these people to fend for themselves out here. Or do I turn around and take the entire group standing before me back to live out the foreseeable future at Camp Correll? The possibility remains that we will encounter the big cats again, even though we have greater numbers and are better armed than before. The whole of that option concerns me deeply. Do I deprive these children of the chance, however remote, of ever seeing their families again? But, on the other hand, is it really worth risking their lives on that obscure possibility?

Risking all our lives on it? The responsibility feels like an elephant is sitting on my chest.

As I stand in front of the crowd, I look back over my shoulder past the columns of the long, wide porch, toward the southeast. Along that path is the general direction of Atlanta, although that city is hundreds and hundreds of miles away... no, even farther than that. Sunrise is just beginning to illuminate multiple columns of smoke, large and small, from fires sporadically dotting the distant horizon. I can just make out another sizeable group of refugees trudging along toward us. I moisten my lips with my tongue. I shift my gaze back to address the crowd, watching in particular the faces of the young campers in front of me. It is time to let the group know where I have decided our futures lie.

THE END

ABOUT THE AUTHOR

 A.L. Nelson has a lifelong passion for all things science and yet she finds herself becoming inexorably drawn to politics and a search for justice. Tales for her do not hold interest unless they land in the suspense/thriller category, usually with a female central character that is preferably southern. Her stories must entertain and might teach, but not always must the "damsel" be rescued. She lives with her husband, children, and a dog in North Carolina.

Made in the USA
Middletown, DE
04 August 2018